Salvage the Bones

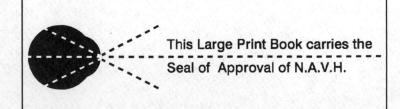

This Large Print Book carries the
Seal of Approval of N.A.V.H.

LIBRARY OF CONGRESS CATALOGING-IN-PUBLICATION DATA

Ward, Jesmyn.
  Salvage the bones / by Jesmyn Ward.
    pages ; cm-(Wheeler publishing large print hardcover)
  ISBN-13: 978-1-4104-4711-1 (hardcover)
  ISBN-10: 1-4104-4711-1 (hardcover)
  1. African American children—Fiction. 2. African American teenage
girls—Fiction. 3. Brothers and sisters—Fiction. 4. Motherless
families—Fiction. 5. African American families—Mississippi—Fiction. 6.
Rural poor—Mississippi—Fiction. 7. Hurricane Katrina, 2005—Fiction. 8.
Gulf Coast (Miss.)—Fiction. 9. Large type books. I. Title.
PS3623.A7323S36 2012
813'.6—dc23   2011050972

Published in 2012 by arrangement with Bloomsbury Publishing, Inc.

Printed in the United States of America
1 2 3 4 5 6 7 16 15 14 13 12

SALVAGE THE BONES

JESMYN WARD

WHEELER PUBLISHING
A part of Gale, Cengage Learning

Detroit • New York • San Francisco • New Haven, Conn • Waterville, Maine • London

For my brother, Joshua Adam Dedeaux,
who leads while I follow.

See now that I, even I am he, and there
is no god with me;
I kill and I make alive, I wound and I
heal, neither is there any can deliver out
of my hand.
— DEUTERONOMY 32:39

For though I'm small, I know many
things,
And my body is an endless eye
Through which, unfortunately, I see
everything.
— GLORIA FUERTES, "NOW"

We on our backs staring at the stars
above,
Talking about what we going to be
when we grow up,
I said what you wanna be? She said,
"Alive."
— OUTKAST, "DA ART OF STORYTELLIN'
(PART I)," AQUEMINI

The First Day: Birth in a Bare-Bulb Place

China's turned on herself. If I didn't know, I would think she was trying to eat her paws. I would think that she was crazy. Which she is, in a way. Won't let nobody touch her but Skeet. When she was a big-headed pit bull puppy, she stole all the shoes in the house, all our black tennis shoes Mama bought because they hide dirt and hold up until they're beaten soft. Only Mama's forgotten sandals, thin-heeled and tinted pink with so much red mud seeped into them, looked different. China hid them all under furniture, behind the toilet, stacked them in piles and slept on them. When the dog was old enough to run and trip down the steps on her own, she took the shoes outside, put them in shallow ditches under the house. She'd stand rigid as a pine when we tried to take them away from her. Now China is giving like she once took away, bestowing

where she once stole. She is birthing puppies.

What China is doing is nothing like what
Mama did when she had my youngest
brother, Junior. Mama gave birth in the
house she bore all of us in, here in this gap
in the woods her father cleared and built on
that we now call the Pit. Me, the only girl
and the youngest at eight, was of no help,
although Daddy said she told him she didn't
need any help. Daddy said that Randall and
Skeetah and me came fast, that Mama had
all of us in her bed, under her own bare
burning bulb, so when it was time for
Junior, she thought she could do the same.
It didn't work that way. Mama squatted,
screamed toward the end. Junior came out
purple and blue as a hydrangea: Mama's
last flower. She touched Junior just like that
when Daddy held him over her: lightly with
her fingertips, like she was afraid she'd
knock the pollen from him, spoil the bloom.
She said she didn't want to go to the
hospital. Daddy dragged her from the bed
to his truck, trailing her blood, and we never
saw her again.

What China is doing is fighting, like she
was born to do. Fight our shoes, fight other
dogs, fight these puppies that are reaching
for the outside, blind and wet. China's

sweating and the boys are gleaming, and I can see Daddy through the window of the shed, his face shining like the flash of a fish under the water when the sun hit. It's quiet. Heavy. Feels like it should be raining, but it isn't. There are no stars, and the bare bulbs of the Pit burn.

"Get out the doorway. You making her nervous." Skeetah is Daddy's copy: dark, short, and lean. His body knotted with ropy muscles. He is the second child, sixteen, but he is the first for China. She only has eyes for him.

"She ain't studying us," Randall says. He is the oldest, seventeen. Taller than Daddy, but just as dark. He has narrow shoulders and eyes that look like they want to jump out of his head. People at school think he's a nerd, but when he's on the basketball court, he moves like a rabbit, all quick grace and long haunches. When Daddy is hunting, I always cheer for the rabbit.

"She need room to breathe." Skeetah's hands slide over her fur, and he leans in to listen to her belly. "She gotta relax."

"Ain't nothing about her relaxed." Randall is standing at the side of the open doorway, holding the sheet that Skeetah has nailed up for a door. For the past week, Skeetah has been sleeping in the shed, waiting for the birth. Every night, I waited until he cut the light off, until I knew he was asleep, and I walked out of the back door to the shed, stood where I am standing now, to check on him. Every time, I found him asleep, his chest to her back. He curled around China like a fingernail around flesh.

"I want to see." Junior is hugging Randall's legs, leaning in to see but without the courage to stick in more than his nose. China usually ignores the rest of us, and Junior usually ignores her. But he is seven, and he is curious. When the boy from Germaine bought his male pit bull to the Pit to mate with China three months ago, Junior squatted on an oil drum above the makeshift kennel, an old disconnected truck bed dug in the earth with chicken wire stretched over it, and watched. When the dogs got stuck, he circled his face with his arms, but still refused to move when I yelled at him to go in the house. He sucked on his arm and played with the dangling skin of his ear, like he does when he watches television, or before he falls to sleep. I asked him once why he does it, and all he would say is that it sounds like water.

Skeetah ignores Junior because he is focused on China like a man focuses on a woman when he feels that she is his, which

China is. Randall doesn't say anything but stretches his hand across the door to block Junior from entering.

"No, Junior." I put out my leg to complete the gate barring Junior from the dog, from the yellow string of mucus pooling to a puddle on the floor under China's rear.

"Let him see," Daddy says. "He old enough to know about that." His is a voice in the darkness, orbiting the shed. He has a hammer in one hand, a clutch of nails in another. China hates him. I relax, but Randall doesn't move and neither does Junior. Daddy spins away from us like a comet into the darkness. There is the sound of hammer hitting metal.

"He makes her tense," Skeetah says.

"Maybe you need to help her push," I say. Sometime I think that is what killed Mama. I can see her, chin to chest, straining to push Junior out, and Junior snagging on her insides, grabbing hold of what he caught on to try to stay inside her, but instead he pulled it out with him when he was born.

"She don't need no help pushing."

And China doesn't. Her sides ripple. She snarls, her mouth a black line. Her eyes are red; the mucus runs pink. Everything about China tenses and there are a million marbles under her skin, and then she seems to be

13

turning herself inside out. At her opening, I see a purplish red bulb. China is blooming.

If one of Daddy's drinking buddies had asked what he's doing tonight, he would've told them he's fixing up for the hurricane. It's summer, and when it's summer, there's always a hurricane coming or leaving here. Each pushes its way through the flat Gulf to the twenty-six-mile manmade Mississippi beach, where they knock against the old summer mansions with their slave galleys turned guesthouses before running over the bayou, through the pines, to lose wind, drip rain, and die in the north. Most don't even hit us head-on anymore; most turn right to Florida or take a left for Texas, brush past and glance off us like a shirtsleeve. We ain't had one come straight for us in years, time enough to forget how many jugs of water we need to fill, how many cans of sardines and potted meat we should stock, how many tubs of water we need. But on the radio that Daddy keeps playing in his parked truck, I heard them talking about it earlier today. How the forecasters said the tenth tropical depression had just dissipated in the Gulf but another one seems to be forming around Puerto Rico.

So today Daddy woke me up by hitting

the wall outside me and Junior's room.

"Wake up! We got work to do."

Junior rolled over in his bed and curled into the wall. I sat up long enough to make Daddy think I was going to get up, and then I lay back down and drifted off. When I woke up two hours later, Daddy's radio was running in his truck. Junior's bed was empty, his blanket on the floor.

"Junior, get the rest of them shine jugs."

"Daddy, ain't none under the house."

Outside the window, Daddy jabbed at the belly of the house with his can of beer. Junior tugged his shorts. Daddy gestured again, and Junior squatted and slithered under the house. The underside of the house didn't scare him like it had always scared me when I was little. Junior disappeared between the cinder blocks holding up the house for afternoons, and would only come out when Skeetah threatened to send China under there after him. I asked Junior one time what he did under there, and all he would say is that he played. I imagined him digging sleeping holes like a dog would, laying on his back in the sandy red dirt and listening to our feet slide and push across floorboards.

Junior had a good arm, and bottles and cans rolled out from under the house like

15

pool balls. They stopped when they hit the rusted-over cow bath Daddy had salvaged from the junkyard where he scraps metal. He'd brought it home for Junior's birthday last year and told him to use it as a swimming pool.

"Shoot," Randall said. He was sitting on a chair under his homemade basketball goal, a rim he'd stolen from the county park and screwed into the trunk of a dead pine tree.

"Ain't nothing hit us in years. They don't come this way no more. When I was little, they was always hitting us." It was Manny. I stood at the edge of the bedroom window, not wanting him to see me. Manny threw a basketball from hand to hand. Seeing him broke the cocoon of my rib cage, and my heart unfurled to fly.

"You act like you ancient — you only two years older than me. Like I don't remember how they used to be," Randall said as he caught the rebound and passed it back to Manny.

"If anything hit us this summer, it's going to blow down a few branches. News don't know what they talking about." Manny had black curly hair, black eyes, and white teeth, and his skin was the color of fresh-cut wood at the heart of a pine tree. "Everytime somebody in Bois Sauvage get arrested, they

16

always get the story wrong."

"That's journalists. Weatherman's a *scientist,*" Randall said.

"He ain't shit." From where I was, Manny looked like he was blushing, but I knew his face had broken out, tinged him red, and that the rest of it was the scar on his face.

"Oh, one's coming all right." Daddy wiped his hand along the side of his truck.

Manny rolled his eyes and jerked his thumb at Daddy. He shot. Randall caught the ball and held it.

"There ain't even a tropical depression yet," Randall said to Daddy, "and you got Junior bowling with shine bottles."

Randall was right. Daddy usually filled a few jugs of water. Canned goods was the only kind of groceries Daddy knew how to make, so we were never short on Vienna sausages and potted meat. We ate Top Ramen every day: soupy, added hot dogs, drained the juice so it was spicy pasta; dry, it tasted like crackers. The last time we'd had a bad storm hit head-on, Mama was alive; after the storm, she'd barbecued all the meat left in the silent freezer so it wouldn't spoil, and Skeetah ate so many hot sausage links he got sick. Randall and I had fought over the last pork chop, and Mama had pulled us apart while Daddy

17

laughed about it, saying: *She can hold her own. Told you she was going to be a little scrappy scrawny thing — built just like you.*

"This year's different," Daddy said as he sat on the back of his trunk. For a moment he looked not-drunk. "News is right: every week it's a new storm. Ain't never been this bad." Manny shot again, and Randall chased the ball.

"Makes my bones hurt," Daddy said. "I can feel them coming."

I pulled my hair back in a ponytail. It was my one good thing, my odd thing, like a Doberman come out white: corkscrew curls, black, limp when wet but full as fistfuls of frayed rope when dry. Mama used to let me run around with it down, said it was some throwback trait, and since I got it, I might as well enjoy it. But I looked in the mirror and knew the rest of me wasn't so remarkable: wide nose, dark skin, Mama's slim, short frame with all the curves folded in so that I looked square. I changed my shirt and listened to them talking outside. The walls, thin and uninsulated, peeling from each other at the seams, made me feel like Manny could see me before I even stepped outside. Our high school English teacher, Ms. Dedeaux, gives us reading every summer. After my ninth-grade year, we read *As*

18

I Lay Dying, and I made an A because I answered the hardest question right: *Why does the young boy think his mother is a fish?* This summer, after tenth grade, we are reading Edith Hamilton's *Mythology.* The chapter I finished reading day before yesterday is called "Eight Brief Tales of Lovers," and it leads into the story of Jason and the Argonauts. I wondered if Medea felt this way before she walked out to meet Jason for the first time, like a hard wind come through her and set her to shaking. The insects singing as they ring the red dirt yard, the bouncing ball, Daddy's blues coming from his truck radio, they all called me out the door.

China buries her face between her paws with her tail end in the air before the last push for the first puppy. She looks like she wants to flip over into a headstand, and I want to laugh, but I don't. Blood oozes from her, and Skeetah crouches even closer to help her. China yanks her head up, and her eyes snap open along with her teeth.

"Careful!" Randall says. Skeetah has startled her. He lays his hands on her and she rises. I went to my daddy's Methodist church one time with my mama, even though she raised us Catholic, and this is what China moves like; like she has caught the ghost, like the holiest voice moves through her instead of Skeetah's. I wonder if her body feels like it is in the grip of one giant hand that wrings her empty.

"I see it!" Junior squeals.

The first puppy is big. It opens her and slides out in a stream of pink slime. Skeetah catches it, places it to the side on a pile of thin, ripped towels he has prepared. He wipes it.

"Orange, like his daddy," Skeetah says. "This one's going to be a killer."

The puppy is almost orange. He is really the color of the red earth after someone has dug in it to plant a field or pull up stones or put in a body. It is Mississippi red. The daddy was that color: he was short and looked like a big red muscle. He had chunks of skin and flesh crusted over to scabby sores from fighting. When he and China had sex, there was blood on their jaws, on her coat, and instead of loving, it looked like they were fighting. China's skin is rippling like wind over water. The second puppy slides halfway out feet-first and hangs there.

"Skeet," Junior squeaks. He has one eye and his nose pressed against Randall's leg, which he is hugging. He seems very dark and very small, and in the night gloom, I cannot see the color of his clothes.

Skeetah grabs the puppy's rear, and his hand covers the entire torso. He pulls. China growls, and the puppy slides clear. He is pink. When Skeetah lays him on the mat and wipes him off, he is white with tiny black spots like watermelon seeds spit across his fur. His tongue protrudes through the tiny slit that is his mouth, and he looks like a flat cartoon dog. He is dead. Skeetah lets go of the towel and the puppy rolls, stiff as a bowling pin, across the padding to rest lightly against the red puppy, which is moving its legs in small fits, like blinks.

"Shit, China." Skeetah breathes. Another puppy is coming. This one slowly slides out headfirst; a lonely, hesitant diver. Big Henry, one of Randall's friends, dives into the water at the river like that every time we go swimming: heavy and carefully, as if he is afraid his big body, with its whorls of muscle and fat, will hurt the water. And every time Big Henry does so, the other boys laugh at him. Manny is always the loudest of them all: his teeth white knives, his face golden red. The puppy lands in the cup of Skeetah's palms. She is a patchwork of white and brown. She is moving, her head bobbing in imitation of her mother's. Skeetah cleans the puppy. He kneels behind China, who growls. Yelps. Splits.

21

Even though Daddy's truck was parked right beyond the front door and Junior hit me in my calf with a shine bottle, I looked at Manny first. He was holding the ball like an egg, with his fingertips, the way Randall says a good ball handler does. Manny could dribble on rocks. I had seen him in the rocky sand at the corner of the basketball court down at the park, him and Randall, dribbling and defending, dribbling and defending. The rocks made the ball ricochet between their legs like a rubber paddleball, unpredictable and wild, but they were so good they caught to dribble again nearly every time. They'd fall before they'd let the ball escape, dive to be cut by shells and small gray stones. Manny was holding the ball as tenderly as he would a pit puppy with pedigree papers. I wanted him to touch me that way.

"Hey, Manny." It was an asthma squeak. My neck felt hot, hotter than the day. Manny nodded at me, spun the ball on his pointer finger.

"What's up?"

" 'Bout time," Daddy said. "Help your brother with them bottles."

"I can't fit under the house." I swallowed the words.

"I don't want you to get them. I want you to rinse them." He pulled a saw, brown with disuse, from his truck bed. "I know we got some plywood somewhere around here."

I grabbed two of the nearest jugs and brought them to the faucet. I turned the knob and the water that burst out of the spigot was hot as boiling water. One of the jugs was caked with mud on the inside, so I let the water run through the top. When the water bubbled up at the rim, I shook the jugs to clear them. Manny and Randall whistled to each other, played ball, and others arrived: Big Henry and Marquise. I was surprised that they all came from other places, that one or two of them hadn't emerged from the shed with Skeetah, or out of the patchy remains of Mother Lizbeth's rotting house, which is the only other house in the clearing and which was originally my mama's mother's property. The boys always found places to sleep when they were too drunk or high or lazy to go home. The backseats of junk cars, the old RV Daddy bought for cheap from some man at a gas station in Germaine that only ran until he got it into the driveway, the front porch that Mama had made Daddy screen in when we were little. Daddy didn't care, and after a while the Pit felt strange when they weren't there, as empty as the fish tank, dry of water and fish, but filled with rocks and fake coral like I saw in Big Henry's living room once.

"What's up, cousin?" Marquise asked.

"I was wondering where y'all was. The Pit was feeling empty," Randall said.

The water in the bottle I held was turning pink. I rocked on my feet with the sloshing, tried not to glance at Manny but did. He wasn't looking at me; he was shaking Marquise's hand, his wide, blunt fingers swallowing Marquise's skinny brown hand almost to nothing. I set the bottle down clean, picked up the next, began again. My hair laid on my neck like the blankets my mother used to crochet, the ones we still piled on in the winter to keep warm and woke up under in the morning, sweating. A bottle of dishwashing liquid landed at my feet, slapping mud on my calves.

"All the way clean," Daddy said as he stalked off with a hammer in one hand. The soap made my hands slippery. Suds blanketed the mud. Junior quit searching for bottles and sat next to me, playing with bubbles.

"Only reason Manny was up here so early was because he was trying to get away from

Shaliyah." Marquise stole the ball. Although he was smaller than Skeetah, he was almost as quick, and he dribbled to the raggedy hoop. Big Henry winked at Manny and laughed. Manny's face was smooth and only his body spoke: his muscles jabbered like chickens. He spread himself over Marquise, guarding him from the goal, and Randall clapped his hands at the edge of the beaten dirt court, waiting for Manny to steal and pass the ball. Big Henry shouldered against him, guarding. He was almost as tall as Randall but much wider, graceful and light as a spinning top. It was a real game now.

The crack of the bottle I was shaking sounded like change clattering in a loose fist. The bottle shattered, and the glass fragmented, slid along my palms. I dropped what I held.

"Move, Junior!" I said. My hands, which moments before had been pink, were red. Especially the left. "I'm bleeding!" I said under my breath. I didn't yell; I wanted Manny to see me, but not as a weak, sorry girl. Not something to be pitied because I couldn't take pain like a boy. Randall caught Manny's rebound and walked over to me as I kneeled, my left hand under the faucet, a ribbon of red making for the mud at my feet. He threw the ball backward. The cut was the size of a quarter, bleeding steadily.

"Let me see." He pushed around the wound, and it pulsed blood. I felt sick to my stomach. "You got to push on it until it stops bleeding." He put my thumb, which had been stopping the head of the bottle, over the cut. "You push," he said. "My hands are too dirty. Until it stops hurting." It was always what Mama told us to do when we went running to her with a cut or a scrape. She would push and blow at the wound after putting alcohol on it, and when she'd stopped blowing, it wouldn't hurt anymore. *There. See? Like it never happened.*

Manny was throwing the ball back and forth with Marquise so quickly it sounded like the fast beat of a drum. He glanced over at Randall kneeling over me; his face was even redder than it usually is, but then he hissed like he always does when he's playing basketball, and I knew he was excited, not concerned. *You got to push . . . until it stops hurting.* My stomach tilted. Randall squeezed once more and stood, and the glimpse I saw of Mama in his mouth when he'd told me to push was gone. Manny looked away.

China's next puppy is black-and-white. The

white circles his neck before curling away from his head and across his shoulder. The rest of him is black. He jerks and mewls as Skeetah lays him on the blanket, clean. His mewl is loud, makes itself heard among the crickets; and he is the loudest Mardi Gras dancing Indian, wearing a white headdress, shouting and dancing through the pitted streets of the sunken city. I want him because he comes out of China chanting and singing like the New Orleans Indians, like the Indians that gave me my hair, but I don't think Skeetah will give him to me. He is worth too much money. His bloodline is good. China is known among the pit bulls in Bois Sauvage for locking on to dogs and making them cur. She pulls tendons from necks. The daddy dog from Germaine, a few towns over, is equally fierce. Rico, his owner and Manny's cousin, makes so much money fighting him he only has a part-time job as a mechanic at an oil change shop, and he spends the rest of his time driving his dog in his pickup truck to illegal dogfights set back in the woods.

"I wish he was all black," Skeetah says.

"I don't care," I say in return to Skeetah, to everyone, to the dogs multiplying in the shed, but no one hears me over China. She yelps. She sounds like I do when I let go of

27

the swinging rope that hangs from the tall tree over Wolf River: terrified and elated. Her clipped ears curl forward. The puppy slides from her. It looks yellow, streaked with black, but when Skeetah wipes it off, the black vanishes.

"Blood look black at night," Randall says.

The puppy is pure white. She is her mother in miniature. But while her mother moans, she is silent. Skeetah bends over her. The other puppies are opening their jaws, twitching legs. We're all sweating so badly we look like we just ran into the shed from a hard, heavy summer rain. But Skeet is shaking his head, and I don't know if it's all sweat or if he's crying. He blinks. He scrapes his pointer over the pure white skull, down the puppy's chest and her belly. Her mouth opens and her belly inflates. She is her mother's daughter. She is a fighter. She breathes.

I tied the strip of an old rag around my hand and kept washing until I had all the glass bottles lined up on the wall inside the kitchen. Junior had run off into the woods surrounding the house after declaring that he was going to hunt armadillos. The boys had finished playing basketball; Big Henry pulled the old Caprice his mama had bought him for his sixteenth birthday into the yard next to the house after drinking from the faucet, wetting his head, and shaking it like a wet dog to make me laugh. Randall and Manny were arguing about the game. Marquise was lying on the hood in the shade of the oak trees, smoking a cigar. Big Henry only has two six-by-nine speakers that work because he blew his amp and his bass, so their talk was louder than the music. I picked up the jug I broke and put the shards in an old half of a garbage can lid. I knelt and stared for glass, wondered if I could find the piece that had cut me. When I finished, I walked toward the back of the property, the woods. My eyes wanted to search for Manny so badly the want felt like an itch on my temple, but I kept walking.

My mama's mother, Mother Lizbeth, and her daddy, Papa Joseph, originally owned all this land: around fifteen acres in all. It was Papa Joseph nicknamed it all the Pit, Papa Joseph who let the white men he work with dig for clay that they used to lay the foundation for houses, let them excavate the side of a hill in a clearing near the back of the property where he used to plant corn for feed. Papa Joseph let them take all the dirt they wanted until their digging had created a cliff over a dry lake in the backyard, and the small stream that had run around and down the hill had diverted and pooled into the dry lake, making it into a pond, and then Papa Joseph thought the earth would give under the water, that the pond would spread and gobble up the property and make it a swamp, so he stopped selling earth for money. He died soon after from mouth cancer, or at least that's what Mother Lizbeth used to tell us when we were little. She always talked to us like grown-ups, cussed us like grown-ups. She died in her sleep after praying the rosary, when she was in her seventies, and two years later, Mama, the only baby still living out of the eight that Mother Lizbeth had borne, died when having Junior. Since it's just us and Daddy here now with China, the chickens, and a pig when Daddy can afford one, the fields Papa Joseph used to plant around the Pit are overgrown with shrubs, with saw palmetto, with pine trees reaching up like the bristles on a brush.

We dump our garbage in a shallow ditch next to the pit, and we burn it. When the pine needles from the surrounding trees fall in and catch fire, it smells okay. Otherwise it smells like burnt plastic. I dumped the glass into the ditch, where it sparkled on top of the black remains like stars. The water in the pit was low; we hadn't had a good rain in weeks. The shower we needed was out in the Gulf, held like a tired, hungry child by the storm forming there. When there's good rain in the summer, the pit fills to the brim and we swim in it. The water, which was normally pink, had turned a thick, brownish red. The color of a scab. I turned around to leave and saw gold. Manny.

"Been too dry," he said. He stopped beside me, an arm's length away. I might have been able to scrape him with my fingernails. "Ain't no good to swim in right now."

I nodded. Now that he was speaking to me, I didn't know what to say.

"If your daddy's right, we'll get it soon, though," he said.

I beat the side of my leg with the garbage lid, forgetting the dirt caked to the side. It drifted and fell like powder. I wanted to shut up, but it was my only thought, so I spoke.

"Why you ain't out front?"

I looked at his feet. His once white Jordans were the color of orange sherbet.

"With them?"

"Yeah." I glanced at his face, the sweat like glaze. My lips were open. Another me would've licked it off, and it would've tasted

31

like salt. But this girl wouldn't lean forward, wouldn't smile as she mouthed his neck. This girl waited because she wasn't like the women in the mythology book, the women who kept me turning the pages: the trickster nymphs, the ruthless goddesses, the world-uprooting mothers. Io, who made a god's heart hot with love; Artemis, who turned a man into a deer and had her dogs tear him cartilage from bone; Demeter, who made time stop when her daughter was stolen.

" 'Cause I don't smoke weed," Manny said, and his shoe slid next to mine. "You know I don't do that no more." His feet were in front of me, and suddenly, tall as he was, he was blocking the sun. "You know what I do." He was really looking at me, bold, for the first time all day. He smiled. His face, marked with red sunburn and dimples and pockmarks and the glittering of scars from a car accident when he was seventeen and drunk and high in a car with his cousins upcountry at midnight, and they swerved to hit a deer; when he came out the window and hit the pebbly asphalt and glass, he scraped, and the road marked him with its own burn, broke him in places. He was the sun.

Manny touched me first where he always touched me: my ass. He grabbed and pulled, and my shorts slid down. His fingers tugged my panties, his forearms rubbed my waist, and the brush of his skin burned like a tongue. He had never kissed me except like this, with his body, never his mouth. My underwear slid down my legs. He was peeling away my clothes like orange rind; he wanted the other me. The pulpy ripe heart. The sticky heart the boys saw through my boyish frame, my dark skin, my plain face. The girly heart that, before Manny, I'd let boys have because they wanted it, and not because I wanted to give it. I'd let boys have it because for a moment, I was Psyche or Eurydice or Daphne. I was beloved. But with Manny, it was different; he was so beautiful, and still he chose me, again and again. He wanted my girl heart; I gave him both of them. The pines seemed to circle like a ring-a-rosy, and I fell. *It will be quick,* I thought. *He will bury his face in my hair. He will growl when he comes.* I dug my heels into the backs of his thighs. Even though I knew all the other boys, I knew him and his body best: I loved him best. I showed him with my hips. My hair my pillow in the red dirt. My breasts hurt. I wanted him to lean down, to touch me everywhere. He wouldn't, but his hips would. China barked, knife sharp. I was bold as a Greek; I was

33

making him hot with love, and Manny was loving me.

China is licking the puppies. I've never seen her so gentle. I don't know what I thought she would do once she had them: sit on them and smother them maybe. Bite them. Turn their skulls to bits of bone and blood. But she doesn't do any of that. Instead she stands over them, her on one side and Skeetah on the other like a pair of proud parents, and she licks.

"She ain't done yet," Daddy says from the bed of his truck. "The afterbirth." He disappears again off into the darkness with the sound of the bottles I cleaned rolling after him through the dirt.

It is as if China has heard Daddy. She backs into a corner, wedges herself between a stack of cinder blocks and what I think is most of a car motor. She makes no noise, just bares her teeth. Grimaces. Skeetah makes no move toward her. She does not want to share this; he will not make her. Her muzzle glistens pink and yellow with what she has licked from her puppies. There is a wet sound behind her, and she turns quickly, still leaking a thin line of mucus, to eat what has fallen. I squat and peer through Skeet's legs. It looks dark purple, almost

34

black, in the corner, and with a shake of her head, the glistening mess is gone. It had looked like the inside of the last pig that Daddy had, that he slaughtered and emptied into a tub before making us clean the intestines for chitterlings: it stank so bad Randall threw up.

"I heard they always eat the afterbirth," Randall says. China walks past Skeetah, licks his pinkie. It is a kiss, a peck. She stands over the dirty towel that holds her puppies.

"Look," I say.

There is something moving where she dropped, where she ate. Skeetah crawls over on his hands and knees, and picks it up.

"A runt," he says. He carries it into the light.

It is brindle. Stripes of black and brown ride its ribs like a zebra's. It is half the size of its brothers and sisters. Skeetah closes his fist, and it vanishes. "It's alive," he says. There is delight on his face. He is happy to have another puppy; if it lives, he can get maybe $200 for it, even if it is a runt. He opens his hand, and the puppy appears like the heart of a bloom. It is as still as a flower's stigma. Skeetah's mouth falls straight, his eyebrows flatten. He lays it down. "Probably going to die anyway."

China does not lay down like a new mother. She does not suckle. She licks the big red puppy and then forgets him. She is looking past Skeetah to us. She bristles at us standing at the door. Skeetah grabs her neck collar, tries to calm her, but she is rigid. Junior pulls his way up Randall's back. I think about hugging Skeetah before I go, but China is glowering, so I just smile at him. I don't know if he sees me in the dark. He has done a good job. Only one puppy is dead, even though it is China's first time birthing. China scratches at the earth floor of the shed as if she would dig a hole and bury the puppies from sight. In the ruins of the refuse-laden yard, Daddy is hitting something metal. We leave. Skeetah refastens the curtain behind us, pulling it tight against the still clear night. The shed falls dark.

I tell Junior to take a bath once we enter the house, but he ignores me, and it is not until Randall turns on the water and carries him to the bathtub that he washes off. Randall stands in the doorway watching Junior because he is convinced that when Junior closes the door to wash, he only sits on the edge of the bathtub and kicks his feet in the water. Junior hates bathing. I am the last to take a shower, and the water, even

36

though I have only the cold spigot on, is lukewarm. August is always the month of the deepest heat, the heat that reaches so far in the earth it boils the water in the wells. When I go to bed, Junior is already asleep. The box fan in the window hums. I lie on my back and feel dizzy, light-headed, nauseous. I only ate once today. I see Manny above me, his face licking mine, the heat of his sweat, our waists meeting. How he sees me with his body. How he loves me like Jason. Junior snorts a baby snore, and I drift off with Manny's breathing in my brain.

THE SECOND DAY:
HIDDEN EGGS

Mornings after birth should be quiet; the air should muffle sounds. But quiet comes and goes here on the Pit like the pack of stray dogs that Daddy used to run off with his gun before Skeetah brought China here to stay. When Daddy kept hogs, in the morning the sows squealed at their sticky piglets. The chickens hatched the chicks from their hidden eggs, and they woke us with flapping and clucking. China's pups' first day in the world was no different. I woke up to hammering.

Outside, Skeetah looks clean. He's wearing a different shirt at least, and his face is shining like he's just scrubbed it. He is hammering a nail into a two-by-four, attaching that two-by-four to another. I am still in my night T-shirt, and it is so early that the morning could be called cool.

"What you doing?"

"Building a kennel." Skeetah smacks in a

nail. "They're going to need it in six weeks."

"Ain't it a little early for that? A kennel?" I rub my eyes. I'm hungry, and I know I won't be able to go back to sleep. I should've yelled out the window and told him to stop hammering, and then pulled the sheet over my head.

"They're going to live, and they're going to be big. I can't have them running free all the time. They might get hit." He tilts the upside-down bucket he's sitting on forward, and he slips the hammer into his pants leg. "Want to see them?"

I nod.

In the shed, the slick squirming balls are gone. In their places are new fluffy, downy balls. They almost look like chicks. Their eyes are still sealed shut, still thin black lines that look like closed mouths. But their mouths are open. They are wheezing and huffing and mewling in squeaks that would be barks. They are rolling against each other, tumbling one over the other to land against China's side. She watches me. Skeetah closes the curtain.

"I never thought I'd get five, Esch. With it being her first, I thought I'd get two, maybe. I figured she trample them or that they'd just come out dead. But I never thought she'd let me save so many."

Skeetah is standing so close we touch shoulders for a minute. He won't look at me when he tells me this; he will study the ground. These are the things he says to no one, not even China. Sometimes he confesses to me; I always listen.

"You know how you hear daddies on TV talking about seeing birth being a miracle? For all them pigs and mutts and rabbits I seen give birth, I ain't never felt nothing like that. Them puppies is *real*," he says.

"You want something to eat?" I can't talk past my stomach.

China grumble-barks, and Skeetah looks at me as if I haven't said anything.

"No." He grips the hammer. "I want to finish the frame, and then I got to make sure she nursing." He scratches his forehead, shrugs. "Breeder stuff." His glance is a comma, and then he begins to bang again. I go look for breakfast.

Mama taught me how to find eggs; I followed her around the yard. It was never clean. Even when she was alive, it was full of empty cars with their hoods open, the engines stripped, and the bodies sitting there like picked-over animal bones. We only had around ten hens then. Now we have around twenty-five or thirty because we can't find all the eggs; the hens hide them well. I can't remember exactly how I followed Mama because her skin was dark as the reaching oak trees, and she never wore bright colors: no fingernail pink, no forsythia blue, no banana yellow. Maybe she bought her shirts and pants bright and they faded with wear so that it seemed she always wore olive and black and nut brown, so that when she bent to pry an egg from a hidden nest, I could hardly see her, and she moved and it looked like the woods moved, like a wind was running past the trees. So I followed behind her by touch, not by sight, my hand tugging at her pants, her skirt, and that's how we walked in the room made by the oaks, looking for eggs. I like looking for eggs. I can wander off by myself, move as slow as I want, stare at nothing. Ignore Daddy and Junior. Feel like the quiet and the wind. I imagine Mama walking in front of me, turning to smile or whistle at me to get me to walk faster, her teeth white in the gloom. But still, it is work, and I have to pull myself back and concentrate to find anything to eat.

The only thing that's ever been easy for me to do, like swimming through water, was sex when I started having it. I was twelve. The first time was laying down on the front seat of Daddy's dump truck. It was with Marquise, who was only a year older than me. Skeetah's closest friend, he was so close to the both of us that he basically lived at our house during the summers. The three of us would run out back and get lost in Daddy's woods, would spend days floating in the water in the Pit on our backs. We spent the summer dusted an orange color, and when we woke up every day of our months-long sleepover, the sheets would feel powdery like dry red clay. We were in the dump truck hiding from Skeetah, waiting for him to find us, and Marquise asked if he could touch my titty. They were growing then, but still small as the peaks of cream on lemon meringue pie with hard knots at the middle. I let him, and then he asked me to show him my private because he was scared he was going to never see one when he got older. I did. And then he started touching me, and it felt good, and then it didn't, but then it did again. And it was easier to let him keep on touching me than ask him to stop, easier to let him inside than push him away, easier than hearing him ask me, *Why not?* It was easier to keep quiet and take it than to give him an answer. Skeetah found us after. I was sweating so badly my eyes were stinging, and some of it was Marquise's sweat, who was half smiling and then not, his eyes big at what we'd done. *What was y'all doing?* Skeetah asked, and I said, *Nothing.* It smelled like boiled milk in the truck. I was afraid that Skeetah could smell it, could smell Marquise and me, the way we slid together, all elbows and knees, bones and skin, Marquise's face shocked and grinning and dirty, so I slid out of the cab first, and I left them looking around for a grill they could drag into the woods to cook Spam that Marquise had stolen from his house; we were supposed to camp out that night.

In the bathroom, I looked at myself in the mirror. Undressed and rinsed. Dressed again. My clothes fit the same. My stomach, my hips, my arms all fell in the same straight lines; there was nothing fine or curvy about me. I was still short and skinny, my hair big and curly and black, my lips thin. I didn't look any different. Daddy taught every one of us to swim by picking us up when we was little, around six or so, and flinging us in the water. I'd taken to it fast, hadn't coughed up the muddy pit water, hadn't cried or flailed; I'd bobbed back up and cut the surface of the water and splashed my way back to where Daddy was standing in the shallows. I'd pulled the water with my hands, kicked it with my feet, let it push me forward. That was sex.

The chicken eggs in my shirt are warm as stones, but light, too light to be the color of rocks. I expect them to be heavy as the clay pebbles that share their color, to pull me down in the front. They don't. I've seen frog eggs that turn into tadpoles; in the springtime the ditches around the property are alive with them. When me and Skeet were little we'd lay on our stomachs over the ditches and reach into them and pull up some of the eggs, hold them close so we could see if the little wormy frogs in them had begun to shake, to squirm, to turn long and pointed to spear their way out. When they look like hundreds of little shut eyeballs still, they are lighter than light, cool as a breeze. I wonder if inside eggs, the kind that need the shelter of a body — horse eggs, pig eggs, human eggs — are so light. Would they look clear as jelly with firefly hearts, or would they look as solid and silent as stone? Would they show their mystery, or would they cover it like a secret? Would a human egg let itself be seen?

Junior is pouting because he doesn't want scrambled eggs again. He is sitting on the floor in front of the TV that works, which is

44

on top of a big old wooden TV that doesn't work, and he is ignoring the plate of eggs I set in front of him because he won't eat at the table unless Daddy whips him to it or Randall talks him into it.

"They taste like rubber bands!" he mutters.

I remember the taste of rubber bands. Sharp, like metal. Bitter. For something so soft and forgiving, its taste is awful and not right; the tongue jerks back like an earthworm from a child's hand. And I know these eggs taste nothing like that.

"Junior, stop being orner." It's what Mama used to say to us when we were little, and I say it to Junior out of habit. Daddy used to say it sometimes, too, until he said it to Randall one day and Randall started giggling, and then Daddy figured out Randall was laughing because it sounded like *horny*. About a year ago I figured out what it was supposed to be after coming across its parent on the vocabulary list for my English class with Miss Dedeaux: *ornery.* It made me wonder if there were other words Mama mashed like that. They used to pop up in my head sometime when I was doing the stupidest things: *tetrified* when I was sweeping the kitchen and Daddy came in dripping beer and kicking chairs. *Belove*

45

when Manny was curling pleasure from me with his fingers in mid-swim in the pit. *Freegid* when I was laying in bed in November, curled to the wall like I was going to burrow into another cover or I was making room for a body to lay behind me to make me warm. Junior doesn't giggle. "Somebody has to eat the eggs, Junior. You can't waste food. They got kids in Africa that's starving."

"Give them to China," Junior mumbles. He is rubbing his ear. "I'm going to eat some noodles."

"I ain't cooking you no noodles, Junior. I already cooked you some eggs."

"You don't have to cook them." He stares at the television. There's a commercial for toys on. He will eat them dry, and he will stick something sharp that he will sneak from the kitchen into the flavor packet to make a small hole. He will suck the spice from that damn flavor packet all day. I grab his plate, and the eggs jiggle like rubber.

Skeetah walks me in the shed after I interrupt his hammering by nudging his leg and pointing at the plate of eggs. I don't feel like yelling. Feels too embarrassing, too big, too showy, even when it's only me and Skeet around. Inside, China is laying on her side, and the puppies are squirming in a pile

46

against her, sucking. She looks up, bares her teeth. Sees Skeetah and lets her lips fall a little bit, but still shows fangs. I want to pick one of the puppies up and hold it like Skeet did when China gave birth, let the puppy shove its wet nose into my shirt. Instead I stand at the door and watch Skeet set the plate in front of her on the ground.

"The white one is almost as big as the red one."

China decides to ignore me and shoves her nose into the plate, licks up some egg. She leaves a slimy web of spit.

"Want to see?" Skeetah says. He bends and picks the red puppy away from China's tit, and milk dribbles down her belly. All eight of her titties are so swollen with milk they look like human breasts. I breathe in air and swallow past the rock in my throat. The rock melts and burns. I run outside and crouch down and brace myself on my knees and throw up all over the red dirt, my hair falling forward like a black cloud. I can feel Skeetah watching me. When he touches my back with the puppy-free hand, I know this is how he touches China.

Daddy is grinning a beer out of Big Henry, who can buy beer at the gas station on the interstate because he's so tall and solid, his face so square and serious, that he looks like he's over twenty-one. He never gets carded, even though he's only eighteen.

"Big boy like you, I know you know all about that."

Daddy is leaning into Big Henry's bulk so that he is cloaked in his shadow, and Daddy looks like he doesn't know whether he wants to poke or punch.

"Them women like to have something to hold on to."

Daddy elbows him in the ribs; he has his head down and he's grinning. This is the way he tells a joke.

"Cost me some women back in the day, not having nothing to me."

Daddy rubs his hand over his stomach, which I know is flat under his shirt, lean and dark with a thin layer of skin and fat that hangs over his muscle like a light T-shirt. With all that beer, you'd think he'd have a bowling-ball gut, but he doesn't.

"Used to tell me, 'Claude, I need a little more man than you. Need something warm. Don't want no bony hard legs up on me at night.' "

Big Henry nods like he's agreeing. Opens his eyes like Daddy's interesting.

"Used to say, 'You know how them big men is.' "

Big Henry hands Daddy the beer he'd been sipping on and slumps over the top of Daddy's truck. The last of the jugs from under the house catches the light; the soap and water look like diamonds inside.

"What y'all did to get ready for them hurricanes today, Mr. Claude?" Big Henry asks. He scans the yard for Randall, for Skeetah, and when he doesn't see them, snags on me and, resigned, shrugs.

When we were little, Big Henry used to let me ride on his back in the deep part of the pit, the part that was lined with oyster shells. He used to carry me so my feet wouldn't get cut, even though his feet were bare as mine. They never bled. He hasn't touched me since then. I thought that one day we would have sex, but he never came for me that way; since the boys always came for me, I never tried to have sex with him. He's always around, moving in that big careful way of his. He bounces when he walks, sways side to side on his tiptoes. He swings his arms like he's wading through water. He holds his beer bottles with three fingers.

"I'm going for dog food. Want to come?"

Skeetah asks me this as he rounds the side of the house; Big Henry looks relieved. Skeetah hits the shed, makes China yell.

The jugs sit still in the dirt, but the water won't stop shimmering and swishing inside. Big Henry cranks his car, and we ride.

Most times when we go to the grocery store in St. Catherine, cars fill half the parking lot. Now the whole lot is full, and we have to ride around for ten minutes waiting on a spot. The heat beats at the car like Mardi Gras parade-goers looking for a ride. It slinks in the seams of the windows like beads. Big Henry's air-conditioning brushes across my face and chest, light as cotton candy, and melts like the heat is a tongue. The walk across the parking lot is slow and long, even though we have a decent spot that's almost in the middle; Skeetah walks so quickly, he leaves me dragging through the heat, but Big Henry lingers, looking at me out of the corner of his eye.

Inside, I follow Big Henry, who follows Skeetah, who bumps past carts pushed by ladies with feathery-light hair and freckled forearms pulling tall men wearing wrap-around sunglasses. The rich ones wear khakis and yacht club shirts, the others wear camouflage and deer prints.

"We need water and batteries and . . . ," one woman lists as she swerves her buggy away down an aisle, a teenage boy with a mop of big curls loping along in her wake. He is not listening; he looks over Skeetah and Big Henry, and away.

Skeetah ignores everyone like they're pits of inferior breeding. Big Henry dances past, mumbles "Sorry" and " 'Scuse me." I am small, dark: invisible. I could be Eurydice walking through the underworld to dissolve, unseen.

There are only a dozen or so different kinds of dog food, and I know that Skeetah already knows what kind he wants. He always gets the same kind: the most expensive. Daddy once bought Skeet a big fifty-pound bag of generic dog food at the feed store. Skeetah fed China the food and she ate it in gulps, swallowed it down like it was water, and shat it out in runny lumps, like sunny-side-up eggs, all over the Pit. After that, she ate table scraps Skeet sneaked out the house for a month. He spent that month in the shed, banging at one of Daddy's junk lawn mowers until one day he started it screaming to life, and then he went down to the Catholic church and convinced them to pay him to cut the grass and pull weeds at the graveyard. Mostly because they knew about Mama, I think, they let him do it. He mows three times a week during the summer, and in the winter, he weeds. That's how he gets his dog food money. On a few of Daddy's drunk nights when he's down at the Oaks nodding off to the blues, I've seen Skeet walking out of Daddy's room with his hands balled into stealing fists in his pockets. I keep expecting Daddy to wake up one morning to find some of his money missing. He'd be out in the hallway, yelling for Skeetah, throwing off anger and alcohol like steam, but we've been lucky. That hasn't happened yet.

"My dog do good on that one." When I walk up, Big Henry is pointing to a big green bag; it's not the cheapest dog food, but it's not the most expensive either. Skeetah ignores him; he's already pulling at a fifty-pound sack.

"China like what she like." He mumbles this. The bag hangs like a limp child over his shoulder, and it crunches.

"Next thing you know, you going to be buying her allergy medicine. Marquise said there's a white girl at y'all school that got a dog that's allergic to grass. *Grass,*" Big Henry whispers.

"That's 'cause some people understand that between man and dog is a relationship." Skeet jumps and shifts the bag. It hangs even, covers half his chest. "Equal."

"My dog would just be sneezing." Big

Henry says. He shrugs and laughs. He has eyes the color of bleached-out asphalt, and when he smiles, they shrink to fingernails in his face.

"Your dog wouldn't be able to breathe. And he'd hate you," Skeet says.

All the checkout lines are long. All the steel baskets are full. Skeetah rocks from side to side on his feet, and me and Big Henry bump into each other and don't know what to do. He ricochets back and rocks the candy and magazine rack, and I cross my arms and pinch my elbows. I feel like I should have a basket, wonder if when these people look at us, they wonder where our supplies are. The cabinets at home have enough food to get us through a few days until the stores are back up and running, and if the cabinets don't, Daddy will make sure to stock them if a storm hits. But the way the cashier's apron hangs off one shoulder, like she hasn't had the time to pull it up with all the groceries she's been scanning, makes me nervous. She's made up of all the reds: red hair in a ponytail, red cheeks, red hands. I put my hands in my pockets, and the pregnancy test I ripped out of the box and tucked into the waistband of my shorts when I wandered away from Skeetah on a trip to the bathroom scratches my side.

Maybe it's China that made me get it. I know something's wrong; for weeks I've been throwing up every other day, always walking around feeling like someone's massaging my stomach, trying to push the food up and out of me. Some months when I eat a little less because I'm tired of ramen or potatoes, I'm irregular. But the sickness and the vomiting make me think I should get a test, that and me being two months irregular, and the way I wake up every morning with my abdomen feeling full, fleshy and achy and wet, like the blood's going to come running down any minute — only it doesn't. I think back to all the times I've had sex, and it seems like every memory has gold and silver condom wrappers, like chocolates covered in golden foil to look like coins, that the boys leave behind once they get up, once we pull apart. This is what I'm thinking when I see the woman laying half in the road, half in the grass.

"That's a woman," I say.

"That's a car," Skeetah says. And there, caught in the pines like a cat ascending a trunk, is a car. It looks as if it jumped there, as if it wanted to see what bark felt like, and flipped over to grip the tree.

"Didn't they know to slow down coming through here?" Skeetah asks. "Got signs everywhere."

"Maybe they not from here," I say, because there is a man pacing in the ditch, and he is holding his head. Blood slides in a curve down the side of his face, between his fingers and down his forearms. He could not have known the road would curl like his streaming blood in this, the trickiest part of the bayou to drive. He could not have known that the road clung to whatever dry land it could find, and that it was no place to drive over the speed limit. Daddy had wrecked his truck here once, when he was drunk. When he came home after the police let him out, he cursed for a good two hours about Dead Man's Curve.

"Y'all need help?" Big Henry asks out the window as we slow to a stop. Skeetah looks straight ahead, ignores the scene out his window, the pacing man.

The man looks up, climbs from the ditch. It is as if he doesn't see the woman as he steps so close to her, he could kick her. He has a cell phone in one hand, smashed up against his ear, his thin brown hair in his other. He is wearing a white shirt with white buttons, and the blood has made a beauty contestant sash across his chest.

"Can you tell me where I'm at?" he says. His voice is loud, as if he is shouting at an old person who is hard of hearing. "I'm on the phone with 911, and they need to know where I'm at."

"Tell them you in between Bois Sauvage and St. Catherine's, on the bayou. Tell them the closest road is Pelage, and you right before the Dedeaux Bridge."

The man nods, opens his mouth to speak. "I'm . . ." He closes it. "Can you? I'm . . ." He reaches into the passenger-side window, holds the phone in a red grip in front of Skeetah's face. Skeetah doesn't shrink away, doesn't move. Instead, he stares through the man's hand. Big Henry, in his way, takes the phone with just two of his fingers. It is polka-dotted with blood.

"Yeah, it's been an accident. Two people, and they car flipped over in a tree." Big Henry repeats the location. "This the man's phone, but the woman, she just laying there." He pauses. "Okay. All right. I will." He looks down in his lap, mumbles, "Thank you." On the ground, the woman still looks as if she is asleep: head on her bicep, hands open as if she has just let something go, laying on her side.

"What'd they say?" I ask.

"They want us to stay here with them

until they come. They going to be a few minutes."

"I need to get home," Skeetah says.

Big Henry stares at Skeetah as he pulls to the side of the road to park in the overgrown grass. I am almost afraid he will hit the man, who stands wilted in the ditch again, his toes no longer touching the woman. The man stares off as if he cannot see Big Henry's car sliding past him, inches away.

"The puppies. She don't know how to take care of them yet."

Big Henry turns off the car. I hold myself. The pregnancy test crinkles. Big Henry removes the keys, looks at the man's phone that he has dropped in his lap. He opens the door, pulls himself out of the seat, closes the door, and begins walking toward the man.

"She's hungry. And nursing," Skeetah says.

In every one of the Greeks' mythology tales, there is this: a man chasing a woman, or a woman chasing a man. There is never a meeting in the middle. There is only a body in a ditch, and one person walking toward or away from it. Big Henry is kneeling next to the woman. The man has sunk to a squat so that only his head is visible, which he is holding in his hands. I think I hear him

57

moaning. Big Henry hovers over the woman like a grounded buzzard at the side of the road, awkward and cross-footed. I wonder what the woman with the hair the color of a golden condom wrapper is to the man.

"I don't trust her." Skeetah waits to say this until Big Henry is too far away to hear, so low I think he's forgotten I'm sitting in the backseat.

"You think they family or friends?" I shift to ease the scratch of the test, but I don't move too much because I don't want it to fall out of the band of my shorts. Skeetah doesn't answer. I push the front seat.

"Huh?"

"Family or friends?" I look back toward them to see that the man is wandering toward us. Big Henry hollers at him, but it sounds like he is mumbling.

"Lovers," he says.

"What you mean?"

"You know what I mean," Skeetah says.

I'd always assumed he missed more than half of what went on at the Pit; seemed like all I ever saw around him, once he brought home a pit he told me he stole out of somebody's yard when he was twelve, were dogs. Striped dogs, bald, whitish-pink dogs, fat dogs, dogs so skinny their bones looked like a school of fish darting around under their skin. His voice was a bark, his step the wagging thump of a meaty tail. We lost each other, a little. And now I wonder what Skeetah's seen, what he's been paying attention to when his dogs are sleeping, when he's between dogs, because every dog before China died before they got a year old. Each time, Skeetah waited a week, then got another one. Before China, he never bothered to buy dog food, and he fed them table scraps mixed with Daddy's chicken feed. What does he know about lovers? He's the odd one, the one that always smells like sweaty fur when all the boys are together, the one the girls probably think stinks. But even I know that there's one, always one, who likes the boy like Skeetah. There's always one for everybody. But I don't think he believes that. A hand slaps the door wetly, and the man is there, his fingers trailing red like fishing line. He is squinting at Skeetah, and Skeetah is leaning away from the door.

"Hey, man." I hear the crank; Skeetah is rolling up the window.

"I think I've seen you before."

Skeetah stops mid-roll.

"Don't you cut grass?"

"Can you please get away from the car?" I squeak.

"At the graveyard?"

Skeetah rolls up the window so that it seals. Instantly it is five degrees hotter.

"This asshole," Skeetah mutters. "Why doesn't he go check on his girlfriend?" He wants to open the door, I know. "How he just going to leave her there like he don't see her, walk over her like a pile of dirty clothes on the floor?" He wants to hit the man, the bleeding man, with the door. He wants to cuss the man out.

"He's already bleeding."

"He don't know me. He don't even live in Bois Sauvage."

"Maybe he live in one of them big houses back out on the bayou. Maybe he go to one of them churches upcountry and saw you on his way."

Skeetah rolls on his shoulder so the knob digs into his back; the glass pillows his head. "Big Henry need to come get him." He says it, and Big Henry is shuffling across the grass toward us; he moves gracefully when he runs. All the awkwardness that hobbles him when he is standing or sitting or walking, afraid to crush things, is gone.

"Sir, the ambulance is on the way." Big Henry grabs the man by the elbow with the fingers of one hand. "Come with me."

The man rubs his head, smears blood

across it like a bandana. His eyes twitch from side to side like he's reading a book we can't see.

"Sir."

"He don't deserve it," Skeetah grunts, and slouches further down. "China's waiting on me."

The man walks leaning forward, his head swinging from left to right. He peers from the road to the woods, tangled with switch-grass and swamp myrtle. He doesn't swing his hands when he walks. He stops near the woman and stands, but he won't look at her. Instead, he pulls out his phone, dials, and talks. Big Henry stands on the other side of the woman. He waits. When the ambulance arrives twenty minutes later, the man is still talking. The woman is still sleeping. Skeetah's eyes are closed; every few minutes, his nostrils flare.

Skeetah tosses the bag of dog food over his shoulder like Randall tosses Junior and trots to the shed before Big Henry puts the car in park. Big Henry rolls his shoulders, puts his arm on the back of the seat Skeetah has run from.

"Thank you for the ride," I say.

Big Henry turns, bends his arm, looks at me when he says it. I almost can't hear it

61

over China's excited barking coming from the shed. She throws them like knives. *Rip, rip, rip, rip.*

"You welcome."

My mouth jumps, and I know it's not a smile, but I slide out of the car and away from Big Henry anyway. He's still looking. I got my hands in the pockets of my shorts, and I pinch the test so it won't slide out when I walk.

"You should wash your hands!" I yell over my shoulder on the way to the house. He could have blood on them, that man's blood, breeding things on his hands. The inside of the man's body come out to make Big Henry sick. When I push the door, Big Henry's already at the outside spigot, scrubbing like he wants to peel his skin off.

In the bathroom, the old pink tile that Mama helped Daddy lay feels wet, but I can't see any water on it. The tub is dry. I pull out the test, run the water while I tear the plastic. I've seen movies, know you pee on the stick, which I do. I lay it on the edge of the bathtub, and I climb in, careful not to kick it over on the floor. The tub is some kind of metal, and it is warm. The plastic mat on the bottom of the tub is soft. I watch the stick like Big Henry watched the man. My feet are black against the white, and they leave dirty streaks when I rub them against the tub; it's like I'm rubbing the color off. I sit on my hands; I avoid looking at my stomach, flat in the tub, the way the man refused to look at the woman lying at his feet, sleeping in the long grass.

Color washes across the stick like a curtain of rain. Seconds later, there are two lines, one in each box. They are skinny twins. I look at the stick, remember what it said on the packaging in the store. *Two lines means that you are pregnant.* You are pregnant. I am pregnant. I sit up and curl over my knees, rub my eyes against my kneecaps. The terrible truth of what I am flares like a dry fall fire in my stomach, eating all the fallen pine needles. There is something there.

THE THIRD DAY:
SICKNESS IN THE DIRT

Last night, I dozed and woke every few minutes to wish that I could sleep, could close my eyes and fall into the nothing dark of slumber. Every time I dozed, the truth that I was pregnant was there like a bully to kick me awake. I woke at seven with my throat burning, my face wet.

This is what it means to be pregnant so far: throwing up. Sick from the moment I open my eyes, look up at the puckered plaster ceiling, remember who I am, where I am, what I am. I turn the water on so no one can hear me vomit. I turn it off and lock the bathroom. Lay on the floor. Lay my head on my arm, the tile the temperature of water that's been sitting out on a counter all night, and stare at the base of the toilet, the dust caked up around it like Spanish moss. I lay for so long I could be asleep. I lay for so long that when I raise my head from my arm, my hair has marked cursive I can't read into my skin. The floor tilts like the bottom of a dark boat.

"Esch!" Junior screams as he tries the doorknob, slaps the door, and then bangs out of the back door to pee off the steps.

"Esch?" Randall calls.

"I'm shaving my legs!" I told this to the tile, hoarse.

"Shaving? I'm too old to pull a Junior."

"I'm almost done." I bend over the sink and drink until I don't feel like throwing up anymore. Even after I turn the water off, I still keep swallowing. My tongue feels rolled in uncooked grits, but I still swallow. Repeat *I will not throw up, I will not throw up, I won't.* When I walk out of the door, I follow the baseboards.

"You okay?" Randall stands in my way.

"I rinsed the hair out the tub," I say. "Don't worry."

The sound of Daddy chugging the working tractor through the yard, I ignore. In bed, I pull the thin sheet over my head, mouth my knees, and breathe so hot it feels like two people up under the sheet.

When I wake up for the second time, the air is hot, and the ceiling is so low, the heat can't rise. It doesn't have anyplace to go. I'm surprised Daddy hasn't sent Junior in

here to get me up by now, to work around
the house and prepare for hurricane. Late
last night, he and Junior carried some of the
jugs in, lined them up against the wall while
I made tuna fish. Daddy kept counting the
bottles over and over again as if he couldn't
remember, glanced at me and Randall as if
we were plotting to steal some. If Randall's
told him that I'm sick, he won't care. Maybe
they've scattered: Junior under the house,
Randall to play ball, Skeet in the shed with
China and her puppies. My stomach sizzles
sickly, so I pull my book from the corner of
my bed where it's smashed between the wall
and my mattress. In *Mythology,* I am still
reading about Medea and the quest for the
Golden Fleece. Here is someone that I
recognize. When Medea falls in love with
Jason, it grabs me by my throat. I can see
her. Medea sneaks Jason things to help him:
ointments to make him invincible, secrets in
rocks. She has magic, could bend the natural
to the unnatural. But even with all her
power, Jason bends her like a young pine in
a hard wind; he makes her double in two. I
know her. When I look up, Skeet's standing
in the door looking like he's going to cry.

"What's wrong?"

Skeetah shakes his head, and I follow him.
Inside the shed, the puppies are swimming

in the dirt. They lay on their bellies, their feet sticking out like small twigs, bobbing on the dusty current. They twitch and roll. They are silent. They are pink yawning tongues. All but one paddles toward China, grabs her abdomen like we do sunken trees at the river. They have trouble grabbing her tits, knead her belly with their paws like we do with our feet when we balance on the slimy trunks. All but one swims and sucks.

He is the white and brown. He is the cartoon swimmer, the puppy who dove like Big Henry when he was being born. He lays face down. His mouth opens and closes like he is eating the shed floor. Skeetah's face is so close to the puppy that when he talks, the brown and white fur flutters, and it almost looks like the puppy's moving.

"He was okay early this morning. Ate once and everything."

"When you noticed him like this?" I ask. The puppy turns his head to the side, and it looks like his neck is broken. Skeetah rocks back. The swimmer gasps.

"About an hour ago."

"Maybe it's China. Maybe her milk's bad for him or something."

"I think he got parvo. I think he picked it up out the dirt."

My morning nap on the tile comes back strong.

"Maybe he just sick, Skeet."

"What if it's in the dirt? What if the rest of them get infected?"

The puppy taps the floor with one paw.

"Maybe if you just get him to eat. Maybe he ain't been able to get enough milk."

Skeet scoops up the puppy, puts him in the dirt inches away from China. She lowers her head, pointed like a snake. When the puppy jerks his neck again, she growls. It is the rumbling of rocks across packed earth. The puppy lays still. His eyes aren't even open yet. She growls again, and he slides to one side.

"Stop it, China." Skeet breathes. "Feed him." He pushes the puppy forward inches. The puppy's face plows into the sand.

China's neck snaps out and she barks. She lashes. Her teeth graze the puppy, whose legs twitch outward and draw in tight.

"Skeet!" I yell.

"You bitch!" he hisses, cutting his eyes at her, wounded. He grabs the puppy, wraps it in his shirt, sits back on his folded feet. China ignores him and lays her head along her white, gleaming arms that look like herons' necks. Her eyelids droop, and suddenly she looks tired. Her breasts are all swollen, and the puppies pull at them. She is a weary goddess.

She is a mother so many times over.

"Maybe she just trying to protect the rest of them. You know, if it's serious, she know."

Skeetah folds the puppy in his hand like a baseball. He nods.

"Fine." The bugs outside sing because the day is so bright, it is gold. Daddy guns the tractor; he is pulling plywood in stacks across the clearing, gathering wood from all the corners of the Pit for the storm. Big Henry had told us one of his cousins from Germaine had a whole litter die of parvo; the puppies had just opened their eyes, and then the first one died, and then each day after that, every time his cousin walked out back to his doghouse, he would find another puppy dead, so small and hard that it was difficult for him to imagine that they might have once lived. "You going to come out with me and camp tonight?" The puppy is a black ball in Skeetah's black tee: still, round. Skeetah is not looking at his hands, but he is watching China with something like respect and love in his face. "I need to separate him. Make it easy for him til he dies."

"Yeah." I breathe. My stomach flutters. I will watch Skeet kill his own. "You know

I'm here."

Eating is different now. I hunch over a bowl of eggs and rice in the kitchen and I eat but feel like I am lying to myself and Skeetah, who is stealing food for our night in the woods. Every bite is another lie. Food is the last thing I want. Skeetah pulls more plastic bags from under the sink and wraps them around the one holding the food so that the bundle is opaque as a spider's egg sac, and I can't see the mix of things that would be our hurricane supplies that Skeetah is filching.

"Look good?" he asks.

I swallow. I nod.

"We should take a jug of that water."

"You know Daddy done probably counted them."

"We'll tell Randall to tell him that it was them beers he was drinking yesterday. Made him miscount."

"Randall ain't coming?"

"Don't know. But you know Randall tell Daddy whatever."

Skeetah puts the bundle of bags under his shirt. He looks pregnant now.

I skim the belly of my bowl with my spoon, slide the steel along all the curved places. The rice clumps; the eggs are bundled. It all disappears, and I wonder what I am feeding. I imagine the food turning to mush, sliding down my throat, through my body like water through a storm drain to pool in my stomach. To make what is inside me grow to be a baby in the winter. And Skeet smiles at me and holds the door open, waiting for me to walk through, and he is blind.

Junior is pulling planks of plywood across the yard. He yanks them up and hauls, walking backward through the dirt. Daddy has them scattered all around, pulled from other places on the Pit, and has lain them on the ground. Junior is piling them, and every one leaves a trail of crumbling wood behind him since they are eaten through with black, rotting blotches. Junior is leaving a trail of bread crumbs. He is covered in dust, and it makes him look rolled in chalk. His thin gray shorts sag on him, hanging to the middle of his shins. They must be an old pair of Skeet's. He drops a board, and it claps.

"Where y'all going?" Junior asks.

"None of your business," says Skeet. He walks into the shed, and I follow.

"Go on, Junior." I say. He doesn't need to know that the puppy is dying. He doesn't

71

need to know that young things go, too.

"You ain't the boss of me," Junior says. I try to block his slide into the curtained doorway, but he crawls under me and sees Skeet handling the sick puppy, which doesn't swim now. The puppy's head rolls to the side, and he raises an arm, but I don't know if that is Skeet's fingers pulling him like a puppet, or the puppy, fighting.

"Get out of here, Junior! You so bad," Skeetah says. He pulls down a bucket from one of the high shelves and lays the puppy inside, and then puts it back up so China can't reach it. She growls, and Skeetah places his fingers in the middle of her forehead, shoves. "Shut up."

"I'm telling Randall that you fixing to do something bad to the puppy!" Junior runs outside.

"Oh Lord," I breathe.

China watches, reclining on her side. The puppies feed from her, and she is still, stone. Only her eyes shine like an oil lamp in the light. I should know that's who she is, know that she's often still as an animal ready to attack, but I'm not. Her tail does not wag. I can't help the skin puckering over my stomach, up my arms.

"We'll leave him up here till later tonight. If it's the parvo, hopefully he too far away to infect the other ones." Skeetah wipes his hands on the front of his holey tee. His shirt comes up over his ribs, his thin, muscled stomach. "Shit. The germs. I need to go wash my hands."

I'm sitting on the steps, waiting on Skeetah, when Randall comes out the trees. He bounces when he walks, and it's like the darkness under the green gives him his pieces one by one: a chest, a stomach, hips, arms, and legs. Last, a face. Junior is a voice behind him, riding on his back, his feet flopping over Randall's stomach, leaving white dusty marks like powder with his soles.

"What's this Junior talking about y'all trying to drown one of the puppies?"

I feel a quick wave of nausea.

"I don't know where he got that from."

"He say y'all put it in a bucket."

"The puppy got parvo." I say.

"They was going to drown it in the bucket!" Randall hoists Junior up, so when Junior says this, he is the flash of a face over Randall's shoulder.

"And we wasn't fixing to drown it in no bucket." I say.

"Well, what y'all going to do with it?"

"Take it to back to the pit."

Randall lets Junior go, and Junior hangs on until he can't anymore, until his legs turn to noodles and he is sliding down Randall like a pole. We three are quiet, looking at each other, frowning.

"Go on, Junior." Randall says.

"But Randall —"

"Go."

Junior folds his arms over his chest, his ribs like a small grill burnt black. He needs to put a shirt on.

"Go."

Junior's eyes are bright. When he runs away, his feet make little slapping sounds in the dirt, and leave clouds of smoke. Skeetah grabs the bucket and his nest egg of food that he stole from the house.

"You can't just kill the thing," Randall says.

"Yes, I can."

"You can make it better."

"Nothing can make parvo better. Puppies don't survive that. And if I don't get rid of this one, the others will catch it. And then they will all die. You think Junior can handle that?"

"No. But they got to be another way."

"There ain't." Skeetah hauls the bag over his shoulder along with his BB gun, holds the bucket in one trembling hand. "You know basketball, but you don't know dogs." He walks away. "Tell him something, I don't know what — but this one got to go."

"He too young, Esch." Randall's hands look graceless without a basketball in them. He looks like he doesn't know how to hold them.

"I know," I say. "But we was young, too." He knows who I am talking about.

"I keep catching him climbing up on barrels, looking through the cracks, too scared to go inside. Staring at them puppies. China start growling and I pull him away, and I can feel his little heart beating fast. And thirty minutes later I catch him up there again."

I shrug, lift up my hands like I have something to give him when I know I don't. I start to trot toward Skeetah, who is walking deeper into the shade under the trees on his way to the Pit.

"Come on!" Skeetah calls. Randall strikes at the air; it looks as if he is passing an invisible ball.

"Shit," Randall curses. "Shit."

Skeetah has stolen this: bread, a knife, cups, a half-gallon jug of punch, hot sauce, dishwashing liquid. He sits them next to the bucket, and he dusts off two cinder blocks with a grill laid over it that he and Randall made into a barbecue pit when we were younger. The steel is burnt black, the stones burnt gray. His rifle hangs by a strap from his shoulder, its muzzle digging into the backs of his legs when he walks.

"What do we need that for?" I ask.

In the bucket, the puppy murmurs. It is lonely.

"Come on," Skeetah says.

In the woods, animals dart between the valleys of shadow. Birds trill up through pathways of sunlight. Skeetah cuts through it all, his shoulders curved. He leans forward when he walks, studies the ground. I am noisy behind him, my feet dragging in the pine needles. I kick up my knees, try to set my feet down easy, but I am off balance. What would be the baby sits like a water balloon in my stomach, makes me feel set to bursting. My secret makes me clumsy. Skeetah stops, kneels in the needles and crackling leaves; underneath, it all rots and turns to dirt. Skeetah shakes his head at me and looks up into the trees. We wait.

Before a hurricane, the animals that can, leave. Birds fly north out of the storm, and everything else roams as far away from the winds and rain as possible. The air has been clear these past couple of days. Bright, every day almost unbearably bright and hot and close, the way that I feel when Manny is sweating over me: golden, burning. Insects root under our feet, squirrels leap from tree to tree, crows glide between the tops of the pines, cawing. The beat of their wings sounds soft as the swish of Mudda Ma'am's broom when she sweeps pine needles from her sandy front yard. Skeetah watches them the way he watches China: like any second she might speak, and he's sure when it will happen, she will reveal all the answers to all the things he has ever wondered about. Daddy's crazy, I think, obsessed with hurricanes this summer. He was convinced last summer after one tornado touched down at a shopping complex in Germaine that the Gulf Coast would be a new tornado alley. He spent the entire summer pointing out the safest places in the house to crouch. Every time he caught Junior in the kitchen, he made him practice the tornado drill we were all taught in school; kneel, fold over your thighs, tuck your head between your knees, cover your neck with your bony fingers to protect the soft throat underneath.

Skeetah takes his gun off his shoulder, cocks it. He holds it loosely at first, his eyes moving back and forth like he is reading something written in the air between the trees.

"Skeet. What you fixing to shoot?"

"Wasn't enough cans of meat to steal."

"I ain't cooking it, Skeet."

Skeetah shoulders the rifle. He points the gun at the sky. The wind moves a little in the tops of the trees, and then dies away, like a person leaving a room. The trees are silent with longing. The gun begins to scissor back and forth. Skeetah points, following the squirrels scampering through the trees. They are fuzzy and gray, fat with summer food.

"Shhhh," he says. "We need something to eat."

A branch creaks. The tops of the pines rub together as the wind comes again, but the oaks do not move. The squirrels like the oaks best, run along their black, hard branches highway overpasses. These are their solid houses; they will withstand a storm, if she comes. The smell of baked pine is strong.

"Gotcha," Skeet says, and he shoots.

The shot rings off a pine, making a solid thunk that sounds like a punch. Skeet winces. The squirrels melt in and out of the dark blotches, round the bends of the trunks, disappear, reappear. When one with a half-missing tail appears at the V of the oak and slides over it to scramble down to the ground, Skeet fires again. The squirrel loses its grip, curls into a ball, and rolls down the trunk, leaving a ribbon of red. Skeetah stands and runs toward it, firing again. Its half tail twitches, and it lays still on the earth. It is big for a Mississippi squirrel.

"I'm not cleaning that."

The crows fly away, screaming. The insects scream in chorus in the tops of the trees.

Skeetah picks the squirrel up with both hands, tries to hold the body together so it won't fall apart in pieces. Blood squirts out of it with a pulse. The heart.

"You want him to come tonight, don't you?"

"Who you talking about?"

"You know who I'm talking about. And it ain't Big Henry." He flings a bit of fur away that was dangling wetly like a red earring from the animal's hide. "Ain't Marquise, neither."

"No." I shake my head. Skeetah grabs the rest of the tail and pulls. What was left of it before he shot the squirrel comes away like bristles from a brush.

"Y'all don't look right together," Skeetah says, studying the bloody carcass. He is so hot his nose is sweating. *But we are,* I want to say. *He makes my heart beat like that,* I want to say, and point at the squirrel dying

79

in red spurts. But I say nothing, and Skeetah shrugs and lifts the squirrel up like an offering and begins walking back to the pit.

When we get back to the campsite, Skeetah lays the squirrel on the plastic bag, and he pulls out the knife and cuts the head off. The blood smells like wet hot earth after summer rain. He pitches the head into the underbrush like a ball, runs the knife in a jagged line down the squirrel's chest, and then makes a cross across the animal's arms. He is ruthless, quiet, focused as China before a fight. Skeetah pulls hard, and the skin balloons away from the flesh underneath, stretching, stretching, until it is a wet limp rag, and Skeetah flings it away. Fur booties remain on the squirrel's feet, but Skeet cuts those off and tosses them after the head. The animal is no more than meat, now, thick as two pork chops laid together. Skeetah slices at the stomach, and what comes sliding out is blue and purple, like so much wet yarn.

"Shit," Skeet breathes. The smell of the animal's insides is everywhere. When Daddy used to keep pigs, they shat and ate and rooted in their own filth, growing pink and fat, but the smell of them and their nest was like this animal's stomach: raw, full with shit. Skeetah is right.

He tries to pull the innards out, but they hold, so he tries to cut at the strings holding them, and he cuts the intestines by accident.

"Oh, shit," Skeetah says, and he drops the animal and the innards and the knife on the bloody plastic bag and he steps away, his hands on his knees, his head hanging down. There is sand in my throat, and I cannot breathe.

"Jesus, Skeet." I run off behind a small gathering of trees, as far as I can make it away from that smell and that slime, and I fall and throw up the eggs, the rice, the water, everything I have inside of me until there is no food left, until my throat feels empty and I cannot stop heaving up air and spit, but still I am not able to throw it all up. Inside, at the bottom, something remains.

By the time the meat is done cooking, has turned brown and small with as many hard edges as a jewel, the boys have come. Marquise is slicing at the meat with his own pocket knife, slapping small chunks onto pieces of bread that are turning soggy with hot sauce. Skeetah makes a sandwich, passes it to me, before making his own. The meat is stringy and hard, tastes of half red spice from the hot sauce, which has turned the bread pink, and half wild animal. I bite and I am eating acorns and leaping with fear to the small dark holes in the heart of old oak trees. The sun had set while Skeetah and I were looking for wood for the grill; the sky burst to color above us, and then the sun sank through the trees so that the color ran out of the sky like water out of a drain and left the sky bleached white to navy to dark. I overloaded on wood for the fire; Skeet had to keep grabbing the squirrel out by its foot, his hand wrapped in his shirt, because he was afraid it would burn. But the fire is large enough that I can see all their faces in the dark.

"It's good," Marquise says.

"It tastes burnt," says Skeetah. Big Henry, beside him, laughs.

"It tastes like shit. I can't believe y'all eating that." Big Henry gulps more of his beer, which is so warm the bottle doesn't even sweat water in the hot night. "Might as well give that little bit of nothing to the puppy."

I hardly chew the sandwich, just bite it small enough to get on my tongue, wet with spit, and swallow. Skeetah hands me the half-jug of juice, and I swallow a mouthful of warm colored sugar. I am not hungry, but it is better when I eat because I don't feel so sick. If I throw up again, somebody would ask me what my problem is. And I don't want to have to speak the lie, to be convincing. To have them looking at me and asking. I pass the jug along to Marquise. This is the closest drink to real fruit juice we've ever had in the house. Mama used to put it in the cart while I rode in the basket through the grocery store, wedge the red punch alongside me in the seat so the jug turned my leg cold. But I liked it, because later in the truck that didn't have any air-conditioning, my leg would stay cold, like a piece of ice melting in my hand.

The puppy in the bucket scratches and Skeetah sits over him, his head hanging low, staring. Every once in a while, he'll touch the rim of the bucket like he wants to reach in and rub the puppy, comfort it, but he doesn't.

"You ain't never gave him a name, huh, Skeet?" I ask.

"No." He doesn't look up. "You can give it a name if you want, Esch." He sits with his chin in his hands. "It's a girl."

A name. I knew a girl once in school that was named after the candles you burn to drive the mosquitoes away: Citronella. She always had at least two boyfriends, lip gloss, and all her folders were color-coded to match her books. I used to kneel in the water up to my neck and watch her when we ran into her and her folks swimming at the river. She was golden as those candles, so perfect that I wanted to hate her. And I did, some. But sometimes I would say her name when I was walking along, talking to myself, and I liked the way it sounded, the way it rolled around my tongue like a mouthful of ice cream. *Citronella.* I want to name the puppy this, but I think Marquise, at least, will laugh at me, because he knows her. Probably was one of her boyfriends, walked down the street to the park with her and held her hand.

"Nella," I say. "I want to name her Nella."

Skeet nods. Big Henry tries to pass me his forty, but I shake my head. The hot sauce is still pulling spit from my tongue, but I know I'm probably going to cry when Nella goes, and I don't want any more salt. Marquise shoves a stick in the fire and stabs at the ashes.

"It's a good name," Big Henry says, with a smile half shining and then fading. Skeet looks in the bucket like he didn't hear. Still, the little bit of happiness that was inside me at coming up with the name flutters and snuffs out. What's the use of naming her to die?

There's a breaking sound coming from the woods, the crunch of leaves crumbling underfoot, and Randall and Manny appear. Manny catches all the light from the fire, eats it up, and blazes. He smiles. His scar gleams, and my heart blushes.

"Junior finally fell asleep," Randall says. "Manny say his cousin Rico lost the dog he had before Kilo to parvo."

Manny sits next to Randall at the fire, drinks so much of the punch when Marquise hands it to him that there is only scum left at the bottom.

"You should kill it now," Manny says. "Save it the pain. Rico sliced his dog's throat soon as he saw it getting sick. Right now, you just torturing it."

"No," Skeet says. "It's not time yet."

"You going to shoot it?" Manny eyes the gun. "That's quick, at least."

"No, I'm not."

"Well, how you going to do it?"

Skeetah looks up, but he is looking at Randall when he talks, not Manny.

"You remember how Mama used to kill the chickens?" Skeetah asks.

The cicadas in the trees are like fitful rain, sounding in waves in the black brush of the trees. When Randall speaks, he stares at Skeetah, who grips the side of the bucket.

"She only killed one when it was something special, like one of our birthdays or her and Daddy's anniversary. She used to watch them, like she knew every one, knew which one had eggs to hatch, which one hadn't lain in a while, which one was just getting fat and old. Was almost like the chickens knew it; they'd get nervous. Shuffling around, sticking in groups, staying away from the coop. Next thing you know, she'd grab one, take it behind the house to that big old oak tree stump Daddy'd dragged out of the woods, and stand over it real still while the bird was beating its wings so fast they'd blur. But the chicken wouldn't ever make no noise. And then she would put her hand over the bird's face like she was hiding it from seeing something, and then she would grab and twist. Break the neck. Slice the head off on the stump." Randall doesn't take a breath when he speaks, just lets it all run out of him like a steady stream. He swallows. "Chicken don't taste like that no more." The crickets in the tree closest to us take up a low rumble, almost drown Randall out. I don't really remember Mama killing the chickens so clear, but when Randall says it, I see it, and I think I remember it.

"Yeah," Skeetah says; he is slow to blink.

He lifts the puppy. Her stomach rises and falls, and the wind coming out of her sounds like a croaking frog. I reach out to touch her. "Don't," Skeet says. "It'll carry back to the rest." He glances at me and half smiles, and then looks down at his fingers.

Through the trees, there is a new moon, and Nella is singing to it. I think I see Junior leaping like a squirrel through the shadows, watching and waiting, but when I look closely again, there is only darkness beyond the fire.

When Skeet grabs and twists, his hands are as sure as Mama's.

When Skeetah comes back from burying the puppy, he is shirtless, his muscles black and ropy as that squirrel's. Sweat coats him like oil. He stands for a second in the firelight, still, breathing hard. He throws his shirt into the fire.

"What are you doing?" Marquise asks around the squirrel bone he is sucking on. He slurps and almost swallows it, chokes it back up.

"It's all contaminated," Skeetah says. "Everything."

He shucks his pants, throws them into the fire.

"Are you serious?" Marquise laughs.

"As a heart attack," Skeetah says. His boxers are sagging, the elastic showing at the top. He grabs the dishwashing liquid and walks toward the black water of the pit, bends mid-step to pull his drawers off of one leg and then the other, and then throws them in the fire by looking over his shoulder. But he does not turn back around. All of him is muscle. I haven't seen him naked since we were little and Mama put us in the tub together.

"I can't believe you're going to wash in that," says Marquise, but even as he is saying it Randall is standing, and even though he didn't touch the puppy, Randall is taking off all his own clothes, leaving them in a pile. He is taller, and his arms and legs are rubber bands. Big Henry grinds his bottle into the dirt until the earth holds it still. He kicks off his shoes first, and then peels his socks away and folds them in half before shoving them into his shoes. His feet are large and soft-looking with long black hairs curling down the top like baby's hair.

Where my brothers go, I follow.

I walk into the water with all my clothes on. When I am all wet, I grab the soap from Skeetah and rub suds into my clothes, too. I make them white before I pull them away, one by one, until I am naked in the water, my clothes a dirty, slimy pile on the mud bank.

"Y'all niggas crazy," Marquise says, but he takes off his clothes anyhow and follows us to the water.

"I was hot anyway," Manny says, and he throws his white tee near where I was sitting along with his pants and strips to his underwear. He runs and dives in the water and comes up behind Randall and tackles him so that they both sink. They wrestle, giggling, looking like fish yanking against a line. Marquise is swinging from a rope that hangs from a high tree, and Big Henry is moving through the water with a slow stroke, his hands cutting in so straight they don't make any splash. Randall and Manny keep dunking each other, laughing. I want Manny to touch me, to swim over and grab me by my arms, to pull me up against him, but I know he won't. Randall slips away from Manny, swims over to Skeetah, who has been treading water off by himself.

"Watch out. You know they got water moccasins under that brush," says Randall. Skeetah's scrubbing like he could rub his skin off.

"I'm all right. They ain't studying me."

"I ain't sucking the poison out you," Randall laughs.

"I ain't getting bit. They can smell it, you know."

"Smell what?"

"Death."

Randall stops his forward glide and treads. I can't see his face in the dark.

"Shut up, Skeet." He splashes water that catches firelight and turns red. Drops, like fireworks from the sky, hit Skeet. Under the cicadas, I imagine that I should be able to hear it sizzle. "Now you really talking crazy."

Big Henry is grabbing at Marquise's feet, trying to pull him off the rope. Marquise kicks, and Big Henry tugs so hard on the rope, the limb it's tied to cracks so loud that it sounds like a big bone popping.

"Oh, shit!" Marquise yells, and then he's letting go of the rope, but it is too late, because it's all falling on Big Henry's head. I am laughing so hard my ribs hurt, but when Manny surfaces like a jumping fish next to me, popping up out of the water like the best kind of prize, I stop. The laugh turns to a scratch in my throat.

"What's up, Esch?" Manny's looking at Big Henry and Marquise struggling with the branch in the water, Randall swimming over to help. He talks to me out the side of his face. Skeet is still scrubbing his skin off, not watching us. Manny dives under the water and comes up on my right, still staying far enough away from me that I can't reach out and touch him.

"Nothing." I swallow the words.

"You was scared to take off your clothes in front of us?" Manny is grinning, but he's not looking at me, and he's swimming in slow circles so he's orbiting me like the moon. Or the sun.

It's a little noise that comes out of my throat then.

"Scared to let everybody see what you look like?"

I shake my head.

"It ain't that bad," he says.

"Not bad?" I breathe, and I am ashamed because I am repeating what he says.

"Something like that." He jams a finger into his ear and then shakes his head so fast water comes flying off him like a dog. His bottom lip is pink and full, while his top is a shy line. I have dreamed about kissing him. Around three years ago, I saw him having sex with a girl. He and Randall had talked her into coming back to the Pit with them when Daddy was out, and I heard them all laughing when they passed underneath the window. I followed them into the woods. When they got to the pit, Manny grabbed her butt and rubbed her stomach the way a man pets a dog's side, and then the girl laid down for him. He was on top of her, moving his hand up and down in between her legs, and then he kissed that girl. Twice, three times. He opened his mouth so wide for her, licked her like he was tasting her, like she was cane sugar sweet. He was eating her. I wonder when he stopped kissing girls like that, or if he just doesn't want to kiss me. Now he circles, half looking at me, half looking at Big Henry and Marquise. He grabs my hand and pulls it toward him, wraps my fingers around his dick.

"Not too bad," he says. I want to know what it feels like, so I reach out under the water to touch his chest, his nipples the size of red grapes. They are much softer than that. The skin in the seams of his muscles is the color of Sugar Daddy caramel candy. Manny pulls away. "What are you doing?" His dick slides out of my hand, hot in the cool water: then gone.

"I just wanted —"

"Esch." Manny says it like he's disappointed, like he doesn't know who this girl who reached out to touch him is. His profile is sharp, and it shines like a polished penny in the fire. His bottom lip thins when he smiles. "You crazy?"

My hand is still tingling from where he grabbed it and pulled it toward him.

"No." I meant to say his name; this is what comes out instead.

"Naw, Esch." He kneads the water, pushing himself up and kicking away from me. "You know it ain't like that," he says, and the pain comes all at once, like a sudden deluge.

Manny swims to Randall, who is walking up to the shore, pulling on his clothes. Manny's back is a shut door. His shoulders are beautiful. I imagine myself on his back now, him swimming me across the deep water, carrying me to solid ground. How the other Manny would turn to kiss me in the water, to eat my air. How he would hold my hand on land instead of wrapping it around his dick underwater. When I tell him about my secret, will he turn to me? I push out all my breath and sink, my head hot. Is this how a baby floats inside its mother? I cup my stomach, hear Daddy say something he only says in his sober moments: *What's done in the dark always comes to the light.* I loved Manny ever since I saw him kissing that girl. I loved him before he started seeing Shaliyah, skinny, light-skinned, and crazy, who is always trying to beat up other girls that she thinks he's messing with. Once she broke a bottle over Marquise's cousin's head down at the Oaks Club on teen night. *Shaliyah.* She has the kind of eyes that always move fast back and forth like a cat's. He talks about other girls with Randall, but he always comes back to her: complaining about the way she checks his phone, the way she calls him all the time, the way she only cooks once a week, the way she leaves his clothes in piles around the trailer they share so that he has to do his own laundry so he'll have something to wear to his job at the gas station. I saw her once at the park, and her crazy cat eyes looked right over me: neither prey nor threat. I loved him before that girl. I imagine that this is the way Medea felt about Jason when she fell in love, when she knew him; that she looked at him and felt a fire eating up through her rib cage, turning her blood to boil, evaporating hotly out of every inch of her skin. I feel it so strongly that I cannot imagine how Manny does not feel it, too.

My belly is solid as a squash, because there is this baby inside me, small as Manny's eyelash in mid-sex on my cheek. And this baby will grow to a fingertip on my hip, a hand on the bowl of my back, an arm over my shoulder, if it survives. I think it is for Manny; he is the only person I have been having sex with for the past five months. Since he surprised me in the woods while I was looking for Junior and grabbed me, knew my girl heart, I have only let him in. Once we had sex for the first time, I didn't want to have sex with anyone else. I either shrug and pretend like I don't hear Marquise or Franco or Bone or any of the other boys when they hint. They ask, and I walk away because it feels like I'm walking toward Manny.

There is a sound above the water; someone is shouting. When I surface and breathe, my lungs pulling for air, Skeetah is the only one left, and he is silent. Bats whirl through the air above us, plucking insects from the sky while they endlessly flutter like black fall leaves. Skeetah watches me swim to him and the dirt, watches me dress in my soapy clothes, and says nothing before turning to lead the way through the dark, naked.

THE FOURTH DAY:
WORTH STEALING

Fleas are everywhere. Walking toward Mother Lizbeth and Papa Joseph's house, I wade through scummy puddles of them. They jump and stick to my legs like burrs, biting, until I stand on what's left of the porch: a couple of two-by-fours leaning at a slanted angle against the house like an abandoned pier sinking below storm-rising water, the tide of the earth rolling in to cover them. The screen door has long disappeared, and the front door hangs by one hinge. I have to push the wood, which flakes away to dust in my hands, and squeeze sideways through cobwebs tangled with leaves to get into the house.

The house is a drying animal skeleton, everything inside that was evidence of living salvaged over the years. Papa Joseph helped Daddy build our house before he died, but once he and Mother Lizbeth were gone, we took couch by chair by picture by dish until there was nothing left. Mama tried to keep the house up, but needing a bed for me and Skeet to sleep in, or needing a pot when hers turned black, was more important than keeping the house a shrine, crocheted blankets across sofas as Mother Lizbeth left them. That's what Daddy said. So now we pick at the house like mostly eaten leftovers, and Papa Joseph is no more than overalls and gray shirts and snuff and eyes turned blue with age. I remember more of Mother Lizbeth alive. I'd sit on her lap and play with her hair, gray and straight and strong as wire. I would help her take her medicines: two handfuls of pills she had to take every day, by handing them to her one by one. She would feed me sweet figs, still warm as the day, we picked from a tree behind the house. She'd laugh at me, said I ate figs careful as a bird; her smile was black and toothless. And sometimes she was sharp, didn't want to be hugged, wanted to sit in her chair on the porch and not be bothered. When she died, Mama told me that she had gone away, and then I wondered where she went. Because everyone else was crying, I clung like a monkey to Mama, my legs and arms wrapped around her softness, and I cried, love running through me like a hard, blinding summer rain. And then Mama

97

died, and there was no one left for me to hold on to.

I bend and slap away all the fleas. In the kitchen, Skeetah is panting and pulling in the corner, his whole body straining. Where yesterday he had a short 'fro, today his head is shaved clean, and is a shade lighter than the rest of him. His scalp looks like fresh turned dirt.

"Junior told me you was in here. What you doing?"

"Trying to get this linoleum."

"For what?"

Skeetah was trying to peel it from the corner. A big piece flapped over in front of him like a dog ear.

"It's in the dirt." He pulled. I expected he would grunt, but no sound came out. His muscles jumped like popped gum. "The parvo. It's in the dirt in the shed."

"So what's Mother Lizbeth's floor going to do?"

"It's going to cover the dirt." He pulled, a loud pop sounded, and the tile gave. He threw it back and it landed in a pile with four or five others.

"You giving China a floor?" Daddy had started on our house once he and Mama got married. Hearing the stories about him and Papa Joseph when I was growing up, I always thought it was something a man did for a woman when they married: build her something to live in.

"No, Esch." Skeetah slices at the underside of the next tile with one of Daddy's rusty box cutters. "I'm saving them puppies. China's strong and old enough to where the parvo won't kill her." He yanked. "They're money."

"Why'd you cut your hair?"

"I got tired of it." Skeetah shrugs, pulls. "What you doing today?"

"Nothing."

"You want to go somewhere with me?"

"Where?"

"Through the woods." Skeetah gives another yank, and the next tile comes loose. He throws it wide. "You gotta run." I've always been a fast runner. When the boys and I used to race when we were smaller, I was always in the top three. I beat Randall a few times, and almost beat Skeet once or twice. "I need your help."

"Okay." He needs me. Before China had these puppies, I'd go days without seeing him. Days before I'd be walking through the woods looking for eggs or trying to see if I could find Randall and Manny, or walking to the Pit to swim, and I'd stumble on Skeetah, training China to attack and bite

99

and lock on with an old bike tire or a rope. They'd play tug of war, send up clouds of dust and leave dry rivers in the pine needles. Or China'd nap while Skeetah ate razor blades, sliding them between the pink sleeve of his cheek and tongue and back out of his lips so fast I thought I was imagining it. I asked him why he ate them once, and he grinned and said, *Why should China be the only one with teeth?*

"Yeah." I say.

The sound of Daddy's tractor growls in the distance, comes closer. Skeetah picks up the tiles and begins pitching them through a window at the back of the house, where he knows that Daddy won't come because the back door has been grown over with wisteria and kudzu for years. The front door is the only way in. He pitches the last tile and the box cutter just as Daddy is shoving his way inside, the sound of the wood like a gunshot ricocheting through the room so that I think he's broken the hinge, but the door stays upright. The cobwebs leave a gray trail and there's a leaf stuck in his hair. His T-shirt is dark at the pits and neck and down the middle of his back. His boots hit so hard on the floor that he sounds like he's going to go through the rotted wood. He's not that much bigger than us. Is this what

Medea saw, when she decided to follow Jason, to flee her father with her brother? Did she see through her father's rich robes to the small-shouldered man beneath? Even though he doesn't work much anymore, picks up odd jobs working on oyster boats or towing scrap metal, he's worn the same work clothes every day for as long as I can remember: steel-toe work boots, pants, two T-shirts, two pairs of socks. Mama laid his outfit in clean layers for him on the chair sitting in the corner of their room every night, and Daddy would come up behind her when she was bending over the chair, put his arms around her waist, whisper in her neck. He'd tell us to go watch TV, to go to our rooms, to get out the door. Now Daddy looks up, surprised.

"What y'all doing in here?"

"Nothing," Skeetah says, quick and loud, and he begins walking toward Daddy and the door.

"Hold up," Daddy says. "I need y'all help."

"I got to see after China."

"Not yet," Daddy says. He grabs Skeet's arm as he tries to pass him. "She'll hold."

Skeetah walks into the step he was taking and pulls away from Daddy with his stride. Skeet seems surprised at the way Daddy's fingers slip from his arm, and Daddy looks at me, just for a minute, like he's confused. Skeetah stops and turns, and Daddy points up to the attic.

"Gotta new storm in the Gulf. Named José. Supposed to be hitting Mexico."

Skeetah's eyes open like he wants to roll them, but he doesn't.

"You see them pieces of plywood up there? Them two that don't look too rotten?"

Skeetah nods. I'm surprised that Daddy doesn't have that sweet bread scent of morning beer on him.

"Yeah."

"I need you to take this hammer and pry them up off the wall and throw them down. Me and Esch will carry them outside and put them on the tractor."

The ceiling in the living room fell in years ago, so now it's easy to see through it to the attic above, where the beams of the roof are showing in snatches. Skeetah tries to jump and hoist himself up, but even though he can jump that high, he can't grab the beam because the plaster that sticks to it like barnacles makes it difficult for him to grab it.

"Esch, let your brother climb up on you."

Skeetah looks at him like he's crazy, but he doesn't say anything.

"I can do it."

Daddy could be a ladder for Skeetah if he wanted to, hoist him up with his hands tough as rope, but he won't. We all know it.

"Come on, Skeet."

I lunge like I see the cheerleaders do at school when they climb all over each other to make their pyramids, a human jungle gym: my front knee bent, my back leg straight, as solid and steady as I can make them. Daddy's got his arms folded, looking up into the attic.

"Naw, Esch. I can jump."

"No you can't," Daddy says. "Go on."

Skeet puts one hand on my shoulder. I'm surprised by how hard his skin is; his calluses are like pebbles embedded in the soft sandy skin of his hand, where Daddy's whole hands are like gravel. When Skeetah isn't smiling, the corners of his lips turn down. Now that he's mad, his chin looks hard, and his mouth is a straight line.

"I'm going to step and grab, okay? Quick as I can."

I nod. Skeetah looks at me for a moment more, and says it again.

"Quick as I can."

When Skeetah steps, his sneaker bears down on my thigh and the rubber grooves feel like cleats. It hurts. I can't help but let a little sound come out of my throat, but then I close it off so that I can't even breathe. He stands and grabs a ceiling beam behind the plaster. My leg is shaking.

"Right there," Daddy says.

When Skeetah pushes off my leg and pulls with his arms, it feels like his foot is grinding into my skin. Another noise surprises its way out of my throat, and I breathe hard, ashamed. When we were little and we would fall and skin a knee and cry, Daddy would roll his eyes, tell us to *stop. Stop.* I straighten up and rub my leg.

"All right," Daddy says. Daddy throws up the hammer and Skeetah moves over to the side of the attic where I can't see and starts wrenching. I huddle over my leg, rubbing at the marks Skeetah's left in my skin. The first board comes away fast. I look up to see Skeetah flinging it through the hole in the ceiling, and it lands too near Daddy's feet. I jump out of the way. "Watch out, boy."

Daddy hands me the plywood and motions toward the door. The other piece of plywood cracks and comes away, and I look back to see Skeetah sending it sailing through the ceiling like a paper airplane, directly for Daddy, who ducks.

"Shit!"

"Sorry," Skeetah says as he jumps down,

landing like a cat. The board has clipped Daddy, bounced off the wall to clatter to the floor. Skeetah is smiling.

"Gotdamnit, boy."

"I said I was sorry." Skeetah's not smiling anymore, but when I push my board through the door, I smile into my shirt, because he has that same look on his face as he did the day he mastered the razor eating, and I know it's for me.

Into the woods to the east of us, about a mile through pine and oaks so big and old their arms have grown to rest in the dirt, there is a pasture full of grazing cows. A wooden and barbed-wire fence rims the pasture. In the middle sits a big brown barn, and next to it, a small white house with a high sloped tin roof and small windows. White people live there.

Skeetah found the place one day by accident while we were playing an all-day game of chase in the woods, running in circles, hiding and seeking for hours in teams. He stumbled into a clearing where the pines had been cut brutally away so that stumps dotted the field beyond the fence like chairs that no one would ever sit on. Egrets picked their way through the grass, attentive and showy as fussy girlfriends at the cows' sides. When I came crashing out of the woods, I forgot to touch Skeetah, startled at the way the sky opened up at the field, the way the land looked wrong. There was too much blue. A pickup truck slid soundlessly out of a shadow in a gap in the woods, which I figured must've been their driveway, and a cow lowed. An older white man and woman got out of the truck when it parked, waving away the cloud of dust they'd kicked up. Off in the distance, we heard a dog bark.

"Come on, Skeet," I said.

He stood a moment longer, squinting at the house, his head to one side.

"I'ma leave you," I said, and I turned to trot off back into the soft underside of the woods, the green reach of the trees. It wasn't until I was deep in the gloom of the forest that I heard him running so quickly to catch up with me that I looked back scared, thinking the white people who lived in that house on the edge of the black heart of Bois Sauvage had come after us, but saw only Skeet jogging, his face so calm. He wasn't even breathing hard.

This is where Skeetah says we are going when he comes into my room, changed out of the jeans he was wearing in Mother Lizbeth's house into a T-shirt the color of pine needles and dark brown Dickies that have holes in both of the knees. He doesn't have any socks on under his tennis shoes.

"You got to change," he says. "Wear something green or brown or black. Don't wear nothing white or tan."

"Why not?"

"You got to blend in." Skeetah leaves to wait in the hallway, and I dig through my drawers until I find a black T-shirt and a pair of black basketball shorts that Randall gave me because they were too small for him. They originally had the St. Catherine high school logo on them, which means he stole them and that they were practice shorts, but they're so old that the dragonfly blue writing at the bottom that would have made them unacceptable to Skeetah has flaked off and left a faded gray shadow where it was. I pull my hair back into a ponytail, put on some black socks and my tennis shoes, smooth my big T-shirt over my puffy stomach. Skeetah knocks on the wall twice, and I know this is his way of telling me to hurry up.

"Let's go."

We run out the door, scatter the chickens before us, and they whirl about like crape myrtle petals blown loose by summer rain. Brown and rust red and white, the only sound the swish of their wings. China interrupts, barks.

Away from the Pit, the pine trees reach skyward, their green-needled tops stand perfectly still. Once in a while, they shiver in the breeze that moves across their tops. They seem to nod to something that I cannot hear, and I wonder if it is the hum of José out in the Gulf, singing to himself. The breeze doesn't touch us down here. Down here, the air is thick and hot. The trees are so dense that there's only a little undergrowth, and the bushes fight for their bright spots on the hard-packed, shadowy earth. There are birds, like yesterday, but these are small and brown, so small that they could fit in the middle of my hand or in the maw of China's mouth. They are following us. As we walk through the wood on an unseen trail, the tiny birds fly from tree to tree, chattering sharply with each other, keeping pace with us. In the dense air, the oaks stand apart from the piney clusters: solemn, immovable. Spanish moss hangs from their arms, gray as an old king's beard. Skeetah grabs my hand, and I almost jump away from him, surprised at the feel of it around mine, his fingers hard, the small calluses on his palm from China's leash now dry and scratchy as old bread. He pulls and we run through a corridor of pines, oaks, birch, birds. I can't help it. I lean back against his pull, and I laugh.

We fall into a pace. My face feels tight and hot, and the air coming into my nose feels like water. I am swimming through the air. My body does what it was made to do: it moves. Skeetah cannot leave me. I am his equal. Skeetah sprints a little faster, and when the slack in my arm is still there because I am still at his side, he looks back at me quickly and smiles widely. There, silver. He has a razor in his cheek. Is this how Medea ran with her brother, hand in hand, away from their father's hold to join the Argonauts? Did every step feel like the running leap a bird takes before flight? When we come to the edge of the clearing, he lets my hand go. I sink to my knees, lean forward, and bury my face in the pine straw, breathing in the baked sap of the fallen leaves, feeling the sweat dripping off of me everywhere. I need to pee; there is a wet weight that makes me think of the baby. I find a bush. When I come back, Skeetah is flipping the razor over his scarred knuckles, his shirt in his hand. He wipes his pale head, drying stinging sweat. I don't want to bare my stomach, so I don't wipe my face with the hem of my heavy shirt. Beyond the barbed wire and the lolling cows, the barn and house sit, small in the distance. The house must have been added on to over the years because it is uneven: on one end of the house there is a lean-to shed, and with the roof of the sloping front porch, it looks like a ship manned by rowers on each side. We are here.

"You got to keep watch."

"Where you going?"

"I'm going to see if I can get into the barn. See that little window on the side? The one right above that trailer?"

"Yeah."

"I bet you they don't even lock them."

"Why do you want to go in a barn?"

"They got cow wormer in there. I know it."

"You can't give your dogs cow wormer."

"Yes, I can. Rico was talking about it when his dog and China was mating. Say that's the best kind of wormer to give a dog. Make them a little sick, but it knock all of them worms out. Everybody does it."

"So you going to steal it?"

"I can't lose no more."

"Well, how I'm going to let you know if somebody's coming?"

"You see that group of stumps right there? Them three all huddled up next to each other close to the middle of the field?"

"Yeah."

"You going to lay there, and if the white people come, you going to whistle. And then you going to keep low and start running to the woods."

"What if they get you?"

"Don't stop," he says, looking me in the face, his head forward and down like a dog standing across from another at the end of his leash, straining, ready to fight. "You hear me? Don't stop."

We pick our way around the edges of the field, circle the eye of the house and barn, fight through the wooden lash. Skeetah is still holding his shirt in one hand, but he's eaten the razor. He moves through the wood carefully, folding branches in his hands like dog chains, holding them lightly so he doesn't break them, and letting them go with two fingers. He holds them for me, but even then he still catches me with several of them, and the branches feel like popped rubber bands when they hit me on my arms, or in my forehead. I make a noise.

"Sorry," he says, glancing back.

I shrug even though he can't see it as he

peers toward the house. We are working our way toward the house side of the pasture, Skeetah looking for cars, for movement. In the shadow of the house away from the barn, a puppy lolls. A mutt. Skeetah pauses, drops to his knees. He puts on his T-shirt and wets one fingertip, holds it up to the air. His head is to the side with one ear up as if he is listening to the trees, the insects droning in waves. I shrug at him again, this time with my hands up.

"What are you doing?" I whisper.

"Seeing if we upwind or downwind."

"Okay, Crocodile Hunter." I expect him to laugh, but he doesn't even grin. He wets two more fingers, holds them up. "You know he's dead, right?"

"Shut up, Esch." Skeetah's quiet, wipes his hands off on his pants. "That must have been the dog we heard that first time." He licks his finger and holds it up again, but soon drops it. "I can't tell."

We are standing in the middle of a patch of blackberry vines. Their barbed-wire twine catches on my ankles, fingers a shin, draws blood in short, deep lines like a child's scratch. I knee the air, trying to pull away, only to get caught up in more on my calf, around my toe.

"Hold still." Skeetah grabs them as he'd

grabbed the branches and pulls. "They can smell blood, you know."

"Not from this far, Skeet."

"Fine, don't believe me." The vines peel away. Skeetah wets his fingers again, but this time he wipes away the droplets of blood that have gathered on my legs like summer gnats. He wipes them away in dabs, licks his fingers again, wipes. He has the same patient look Mama had on her face when she used to find us crusty in public, smears of Kool-Aid along our mouths, crumbs on our cheeks. She cleaned us like kittens. He bends to wipe the seams of my socks, and his bald head gleams with sweat. He picks up my leg and I balance with one hand on his head. His shaved skin reminds me of scales when I rub against it, and it is cool like a puddle of water that has been turning dark and dry at the edges in a tree's shade.

We worm our way through the woods as we watch the house for movement. We slide on our stomachs under bushes so tangled and overgrown that we cannot crouch or crawl through them. We slither like snakes, grab dirt and pine straw with our elbows, and pull. Skeetah stops often, straw and twigs sliding off his slick head to catch on his shoulders like holiday tinsel, and he

113

listens. I stop, too, try my hardest to be so still, to hear the threat, but the blood beats through my ears so strongly I cannot hear anything over that and the whooshing of my breath. Skeetah crawls through a stand, and we start again. Dust turns to mud on our arms, leaves us striped. Bits of sunlight bite through the tops of the pines, that murmur once and twice and are quiet. There is nothing but us creeping through the underbrush. A rabbit sits, watching us, as we make the halfway mark around the circle of the field and its quiet house. It twitches its ears, stares at us in profile, one large black eye like a wet marble in its face, wide and glazed as if it is seeing something supernatural. We keep walking, and it stays put, even after we leave it sitting in the little clearing we'd broken through, even after we leave it for the road.

The path to the road is less thick. Here the trees are mostly the kind that lose their leaves in the winter, but they are green and full with summer. The wind makes them clap as we pass. The road is narrow, and from what I can see of the house, we only have around three-fourths of the field between us and where we started. A vein of oyster shells runs down the middle of the road, but the rest is paved with small rocks that look like they come from the river. Sand rises up in little hills at the road's edges, and Skeetah and I kneel next to them as he squints down the drive, his right hand up to me. *Wait,* his lacy knuckles say.

Insects sizzle and answer us. Heat. A little further down the drive, a snake sleeps. Skeetah waves me forward, and we run across the road. Our feet over the stones are light as skipped rocks.

The drive is endless, winks out in the distance where the trees on either side meet in the middle. For a year, we were very unlucky, and St. Catherine schools changed our bus route so that we were picked up at 6:30 A.M. and for the next hour we rode up and out of the black Bois that we knew and into the white Bois that we didn't that spread out and upcountry, past churches and one-room stores selling cigarettes and hot fries, chips and cold drinks in glass bottles and penny candy, the kind of stores that have one gas tank out front with the writing scratched off. Randall would sleep with his head on the glass, Skeetah would do homework, and I would study all the other houses in other lonely fields; the trailers, the long low brick homes, small wood shacks that looked slapped together, that couldn't be bigger than two rooms. And all the kids we picked up were white: broad-shouldered, thick boys with wiry hair on their lips and little girls with red cheeks and eyes watery blue, their faces scrubbed rough. I wonder if they have their own Skee-tahs and Esches crawling around the edges of their fields, like ants under the floor-boards marching in line toward sugar left open in the cabinet.

The house is plain from all angles: its white is faded to tan by the sun, and all the windows are shut with white curtains drawn over them. It's a blind house with closed eyes. There's a raised concrete porch run-ning across the front of the house, and some rocking chairs, painted bright blue, the kind of bright blue I've seen on the lizards that live in the seams of our walls, that crouch still on the front porch. The barn is un-painted and tall, and the doors are shut. The wood is old and dark, like the kind of wood Papa Joseph used to build Mother Lizbeth's house. It looks similiar, as if all the walls are so old they're about to peel away from each other at the edges.

"Shhhh," Skeetah breathes, and I don't know if he's telling me to be quiet or calling my name. But he is standing still, so I stop behind him. He points. There, in the cove of trees where we first viewed the house and barn, in the cove of trees that leads to the Pit — someone is there.

Skeetah moves with his back curved, his fingers touching the ground as we scoot forward from shadow to shadow. We hug the trees. It's not until we're laying on our sides, peeping over a red dirt hill, that I see things I think I know, like the rubber band swing of an arm, a careful sway and settle of limbs. Randall and Big Henry. And then a piping. Junior.

"Who house is that?"

"Some white people's, Junior," Randall answers.

"You sure you saw them heading this way?" Big Henry asks.

"Soon as me and Junior jumped the ditch to the yard, we saw them running off back in here. Fast."

"How you know they came here?"

"I don't," Randall breathed. "But this all they got back here, and they ain't got enough people for chase. If we find them, I bet they're going to want to play."

"I want to go see the cows," Junior says, jumping up again and again, trying to bounce level with Randall's face. He gets as far as his chest. "Please."

"No," Randall says. "You can see them

from here."

I push up from the hill, ready to walk over. Skeetah grabs my arm, stops me mid-rise, and it hurts almost, the way he pulls at the shoulder. He is shaking his head, and I cannot understand what is in his face. He points to the ground, tries to pull me down next to him so I won't let them know where we are, what we're about to do.

"They can help," I whisper. "More eyes."

He still has my wrist, pulling it tight to him like a rope to his side, as if he can make me heel. I snatch my hand from him, and it slides through his grip like a wet fish.

"Yes," I say, and I start walking. He doesn't have any choice but to follow, so I don't even look back. There is a rustling and a wet crunch of pine needles, and I know that he is following.

Randall, who is all edges and honed sharp to see what others can't, hear what others can't, is the first to hear us.

"I thought I saw y'all coming back here."

"Yeah," I say.

"Why y'all was running so fast?" Randall asks. Big Henry is resting on a tree, bent over so that he is sitting on air, the trunk his chair back.

"I don't know," I say.

Behind me, Skeetah speaks.

"You need to take Junior home."

"What's wrong with him being out here?"

"I got to get something." Skeetah folds his arms.

"From where?" Randall asks. And then he looks at Skeetah, and his head nods and his mouth opens so that he looks like a gulping fish. "Oh," he says, and he is quiet.

"What?" Big Henry asks.

Skeetah breathes hard, once, and then pulls his arms tighter across his chest.

"For the dogs," I say, because Skeetah will not speak.

"No," Randall says.

Skeetah just looks at him, his muscles ropes in his crossed arms.

"You don't know what them white people got up in that house. They could have a gun," Big Henry says.

"We ain't going in the house," I say. "We going in the barn."

"We ain't going in no barn." Skeetah speaks up, his lips tight. "I'm going in the barn and you keeping watch like I said."

"Neither of ya'll going nowhere." Randall spreads his fingers, long and skinny, shakes his head, snatches at Junior's arm, who is watching beside him. "Y'all coming home with me."

"Aw shit," Big Henry breathes.

"We ain't going nowhere." Skeetah un-lashes his arms and they come whipping out from his sides, and his voice is loud, and he's like those little firecrackers we get on the Fourth of July that throw out sparks from all sides and jump in bright acid leaps across the hard dirt yard. "First of all, me and Esch done walked all around this field and watched the house for damn near an hour. Ain't nobody home, and all they got is a puppy on the other side of the house, over by that driveway. And I know what I need and I know where it's at. And it ain't like you won't get nothing out of this. If my dogs live, I can make eight hundred dollars off them. *Eight hundred dollars.* Do you know what we can do with eight hundred dollars? You won't need to beg Daddy for the rest of the money for basketball camp week after next, and you won't have to stress over playing good enough in the summer league to get one of those scholarships for it either. I know you want to go, just like you know Daddy don't have it." Skeetah fizzles, his hands down by his side. Now he's just trailing bitter, sulfurous smoke. "You ain't the parent," he mutters.

"This is stupid," Big Henry says.

"I'm the fastest," Junior says as he yanks on Randall's arm.

"Shut up, Junior," I say.

Randall pulls Junior to him and puts his hand on his head the same way I put mine on Skeet's when he was wiping off the blood. Junior quiets, turns to face us, and Randall's arm is around his neck like a scarf. Junior's still smiling; he still thinks he's about to run with us.

"You ain't running nowhere, Junior." Junior's face pulls. Randall's arms cradle him by the chest. Randall looks down at Junior's head, wipes away moss caught in his hair. "You'd do that for me?" Randall speaks to Junior's head, so at first I don't know who he's talking to, and then I remember Skeet, who is nodding next to me now. With each dip of Skeetah's head, sweat drips unimpeded from his crown, past his strong nose, his downy upper lip, to fall from his chin like a weak summer sprinkle.

"Yes," Skeetah says, still nodding. "Yes."

Skeetah sketches the plan. It is what makes him so good with dogs, with China, I think, the way he can take rotten boards and make them a kennel, make a squirrel barbecue, make ripped tile a floor.

"You too big to be out there in that field."

"Wasn't going to go anyway," says Big Henry. Skeetah shrugs.

"So you stay here in the woods with Junior. Shut up, Junior. This is serious. You ever heard of Hansel and Gretel? Well, that's who own that house, and they want to fatten you up like a little pig and eat you. So shut up and stay in the woods with Big Henry. And if you sneak out like you did last night — shut up, Junior, I saw you — I'm going to catch you and whip you. That's if the white people don't eat you first."

"You want me to help you get in the barn?" Randall asks.

"No, I don't need no help. Besides, you too tall. You going to be at the edge of the field, right by the fence, and keep watch on the whole field. You see anything, you whistle."

"What about Esch?" Randall says.

"Esch going to be in the middle of the field, laying down by them stumps right there: she got a better shot of the driveway than you 'cause she going to be closer. If she see something, she going to whistle. And loud, Esch. No baby whistles."

"I knew how to whistle with my fingers in my mouth before you did, Skeet," I say.

"I know," he says. He glances at me when he says it, and he and I both know that he is telling the truth. "Well, all right. Is everybody ready." He says it like that, like a statement rather than a question. Skeetah is not giving us any room to not be ready. "All right, then. Once you see me come out that window, I want everybody to start running. Don't look back. Run."

There is a line through us all, stringing from one to another across the field; Skeetah with his knees bent, his back a black ball, running toward the barn window. Me on a low rise, grass tufted up unevenly around me in bunches, lying like a snake in wait behind the tree stumps. Randall hidden in the woods behind me, crouching behind a large, low bush with leaves the size of my fingernails. And Big Henry and Junior, even farther back behind Randall. When I left them, Big Henry was bouncing back and forth on his feet, and Junior was squatting on the ground away from him, his feet splayed out in a Y, digging with a stick to raise the pine needles into peaked roofs.

The cows rip bunches of grass away, feed steadily, chewing and swallowing and yanking. The egrets flap, walk in small couples. One leaves its mate to wander over to me, pecking between each step so that his beak is another leg. It walks him closer. I hiss at it so it stops. It is whiter than the other egrets. Its feathers are soft, downy, as if it is

123

younger, recently born; a fluffy, warm body beats under the down. I hiss again, and it is a flailing pillow, beating away. The cows ignore Skeetah as he runs by unless he brushes too close to their salad plate, and then they skitter away a few feet to settle. Skeetah crawls under the other edge of the fence and sprints to the window he showed me, a leaping shadow. His hand moves to his face and away again, and I know that he must be taking out the razor. He jumps and pulls himself up onto the window's ledge, balancing with his feet braced against the wall, and he begins to fiddle with the window. My underarms feel flushed and swampy.

"What is he doing?" I talk myself into hurrying him. "Now, Skeet, do it."

He wrenches it, but the window will not open. He slides down the wall and puts his hand to his face again. Grabbing the hem of his shirt, he yanks it over his head, wraps it around his arm, and jumps back up on the ledge. With one arm holding him up, he elbows the window with the T-shirt. It breaks. He elbows it again, and it shatters. Skeetah is all forearms and knees, truncated thighs and twisting shoulders, and then he is black as the shadowy interior of the barn, and then he is gone.

"Thank God," I whisper to the egret, who will not leave me, and pecks in a suspicious circle near my foot.

What I can see of the road is empty. The trees are moving so it seems like they are a green, shimmering curtain in the distance, the road fading to a dark green velvet line in the middle. I stare at it, try hard to see something, run my tongue over my lips again and again, twist it into a wave to ready it. My arm feels like it is going dead, so I roll to the side, glance at the road. Is that blue, a flash of metal like a dying star? But there is nothing. I hiss at the bird again, wonder why Manny didn't come by, wonder when he will come again, if he will want more from me next time. If I can get him to look at me in the eye again. To not walk away from me.

The pain is sudden, sharp. It shoots through my hips and I squeeze my legs together and wonder why my bladder feels like a soaked sponge. I can't help it. I have to pee. Again.

"Shit, Skeet," I say to the side of the barn, the empty shimmering road. I will hold it. It shoots again, and I rock my hips side to side in the grass, squeezing my legs. Sometimes when I move like this, squeeze like this, it helps. The pressure eases. It lasts for

125

a shake of my head, a nod at the still empty road, and then it is back. Unbearable, a tadpole grown to the confines of its egg. Pressure. I can hold it. I can't.

I stand up, look back toward where I know Randall is crouching in the green. Maybe I can pull my panties and shorts to the side and pee that way. I pull the elastic at the crotch, but they are too tight. I cannot face the road and pee. It is impossible. Randall and Big Henry, and farther back, Junior, will see me. I can deal with them seeing a flash of shoulder, of leg, even a nipple, but I cannot bare myself in this field, my butt facing them, and pee. It will only take a moment, I tell myself. Jumping into a squat and facing Junior and Randall and Big Henry in the woods, I put my butt as low to the ground as I can and yank my shorts down in wedges until I feel the air on my skin. I force the pee out, and it hits the grass as strongly as a rush of water out of a water hose. It beats the grass low. The baby and the pee are one, there when I forget they are there, when I forget so well I think they might be gone. I start to inch up my pants, but they are stuck, and I'm trying to miss the wet-pee grass when I hear it, and I wish I hadn't. Randall's whistle, high-pitched and sharp, short. I yank my shorts all the way

126

up, fall forward on my hands, and turn my head to see a silver grille, a dark blue blur, growing to fill the driveway.

They're here spasms through my head like a bat, but I put my fingers in my mouth, and I blow and blow and blow until I hear Randall scream, "Esch!"

Skeetah's arm is the first thing to break the surface of the window. The truck is pulling up the driveway and rounding the side of the house, and I am crawling backward on my hands and knees, the cows nervously shuffling away from me, the birds waving them on, my egret familiar making squeaking sounds at my side as it abandons me, when the door to the truck opens and I rise up on my legs, still bending low, still backward. There is a dog in the bed of the truck, and it is leaping like a doe, barking to call attention to itself, again and again and again, its fur long and shaggy, the color of the cloud dark sky above me, its dark head pointed toward me in the field, its nose intent on our line.

The white man is the first to get out of the truck. He slams the door behind him, waves his hands at the dog as if he is casting out a fishing net for perch in the shallow tides on the beach at night. Someone has bound my feet with barbed wire: I can-

127

not run. Skeetah's upper body is hanging out the window when the dog leaps from the truck, growling to a bark like a shovel dragged along asphalt wearing away to stones. Skeetah falls face forward, lands on his forearms and his head, crumples to a roll and then rises. His feet kick backward behind him and he is running as the man looks toward the other side of the barn that he cannot see, follows the dog, who is bounding around the barn, the color of a storm wrapped in rain. Skeetah is running with one arm above his head, back and forth as if he is beating the air with his palm, and I realize that he is telling me to run, and I turn to sprint while the man behind us is yelling, "Hey! Hey! What are y'all doing in my field? Hey!" And while he is too old, hair the color of his dog's, has arms that are too short and a belly, and his face is already red from trying to sprint so that he has given up on running in the middle of the field, his dog is all fire, combustion and spring. Skeetah catches me, wheezes, "Run," so I stop looking at the man, the woman who's out of the truck now, her hands on her pink-clad hips, her hair bright red, and the man walking toward us through the field, swinging his right hand as if there is a cane there, limping. I run. The dog yelps excitedly, yards from us.

"Hey!" the man yells to the dog. The last I see of him he is turning, still gesturing with no cane, toward the house. The wood opens and swallows us. Big Henry and Junior are gone, as well as Randall, who is all bounding grace ahead of us, his head low, his legs flying out back behind him like black ribbons. The dog's bark catches in the back of its throat, rips on its teeth on the way out. My heart is gushing, and my arms and legs are stinging. I feel the pee weight at my center. I would run it away.

"Hey!" We hear the man yell again, his voice muffled in the blanket of the woods. Then rifle shots. "Twist!" he calls. "Twist!" The voice dwindles to nothing in the threads. My feet catch, hold, and kick the earth. Skeetah runs next to me in the funny way he's always had, his hands like blades. Every time the dog barks, it's as if his teeth are grazing my neck. My skin is tight with fear.

"Come on," Skeet says, and he is moving in front of me, leaving me. I stretch my legs, reach with my heels, to gain ground. The dog rumbles behind me. Slipping through a clutch of pine trees ahead is Big Henry: Junior clings to the bulk of him, his head turned backward to watch us. His face is

129

immobile except for the jarring of Big Henry's run, which shakes his mouth open with each running step. I expect him to be crying or screaming, but he isn't. He knows this frantic run before this ruinous dog. Big Henry pounds the earth now, footsteps heavy for once as he tears through low bushes like a startled bear. Randall dodges the trees like a point guard. The dog snaps and I swear I can feel his saliva on my legs, and then I see that Skeetah has scooped a branch in his hand, holds it like a bat but then swings it backward like a golf club.

"Faster than this," Skeet stutters all at once. I know I am, the secret in my stomach be damned. I stretch through my toes, my arches, my heels, my tendons, my calves, unlock the hinges of my knees, the fulcrum where my thighs meet my hips. This is that other thing that I can do. *Run.*

"Halfway!" Skeetah yells as we pass a cathedral of oaks, leaving clouds in the dusty chapel at their middle. The dog yips with each bound. Still there. I expected it to lose interest, to bound off, but it will not, inexorable as hovering thunder.

"Get!" Skeetah yells, and swings the branch again at the dog. I am even with him now, but still we cannot lose it. We come to a hill, barren of pines but slick with needles;

at the bottom, Big Henry is picking himself up, one arm grabbing at the ground and one hand in a white grip on Junior, who has not let go through the fall.

"Go!" I yell. Randall is prying Junior from Big Henry, who is still soundless, and now we are a pack, Randall our lead, signaling us through the widest gaps through pines, over the smallest bushes, around the staunchest oaks. The saw palmetto cracks like whips at our shins. The dog's barks turned high-pitched: *Success,* it says. The pit is below us, and we hug its edge, sprinting ever faster to the house, to a slammed back door, to a car's roof, to escape. The woods between the pit and our house and the shed pass with a sigh, and then we are in the backyard, and Skeetah flings away the branch. The dog skids to a stop. He barks loudly in pleasure, calls the florid man excitedly. *Here, they are here!* he says.

China is the shushing sound, the finger laid against the lips in admonition. She is on him, a white blur against gray, snow on cloud, the biting cold. Unforgiving. She is one great tooth. Twist's growl meets with hers but already he is turning, rolling to a ball, screaming. Randall runs to the top of the steps with Junior, who is still staring, his mouth still open, and I have stopped at the foot of the steps, Big Henry on the roof of his car, to watch Skeetah lurch out of his run, his arm still outstretched, and pivot to watch. Twist screams again, and there is a frantic lick to it. China grips him and arches her back, digs in as her whole body jerks toward the other dog. It looks like she is giving birth again. Twist's scream turns to a squeal. She has him by the neck. Skeetah is smiling.

"Skeet!" I yell. I slap him on the back, his muscle like dinner plates between the flat plane of his shoulder blades. He looks at me, surprised, the smile startled from him.

"What?"

"She's going to kill him."

He looks back to China, who is curved in two, a fang, and is jerking moans out of the other dog, who is in fits against her, bleeding.

"Stop it," I say.

Skeetah puts his hands in his pockets, fingers what I now see are shapes there, big as curled fists. The cow wormer.

"He's going to hear it hollering, and he's going to follow it here," I say over the grunting and the squealing. Twist is rolling like a tornado.

"Stop!" Skeetah barks and lunges toward China. "China!" He yells, "Hold!" and he grabs the thighs on her two back legs and pulls. She jerks her head once, viciously, and then lets go, flinging her head backward so that blood rises and glitters through the air before falling to droplets in the sand, a light shower of red. Twist jumps and runs, limping like his master, away to the pit and past, his panicked yelp like a siren receding in the distance, off to some other emergency. Behind him, he leaves red rain.

THE FIFTH DAY:
SALVAGE THE BONES

Bodies tell stories. This is what I realize when I burst in on Skeetah in the bathroom in the morning, bladder full with early morning pregnant pee, and see him standing in front of the mirror. Skeetah is shirtless. He is tracing cuts across his stomach with two fingers, the way he checks China's mouth after a fight for tears, missing teeth: lightly, sensitively. The way other people put their fingers in cupcakes to lick the icing.

"Come on," he whispers, pulling on a shirt. The light in the bathroom is gray because the sun is not yet up. We slide past each other and he stands outside the doorway, which I leave cracked, as I pee. I flush, put the toilet seat down, and sit, pushing down on my stomach, feeling it push back against my hand. Hoping but knowing all at once that it was not a dream. Skeetah shuffles in the hall, and when he realizes I'm not leaving, he comes back into the

134

bathroom. I'd seen his shirt ripped after Twist ran away, but I didn't know how badly he'd been cut.

"When did that happen?"

"When I came out the window. I was in a hurry."

I push my stomach in, and nausea moves through me. What should I tell him?

"I'm sorry," I say. "I had to pee."

He picks up an Ace Bandage so old it's faded white and pulls the hem of his shirt over and behind his neck so it hugs his shoulders like a shrug. He's so skinny it's loose on him.

"It's all right," he says.

The wrap is one of Randall's, probably used on his knee, which he's troubled so much his coach told him he needed surgery. The school will pay for it, but Randall keeps putting it off because he doesn't want to lose any playing time. After games, his knee swells up like a water balloon.

"I whistled once I saw them."

"I know." Skeetah is holding the wrap with one hand, trying to wind it around his torso with the other. The wounds are angry; there are four of them gouged into his stomach and side. He is failing.

"Let me," I say, and I grab one end. Skeetah lets it fall. His head is closer to the color of the rest of his body now. When I fell asleep last night, he was in the shed with China, laying her floor, resettling them in. The kennel is still three pieces of wood hammered together at bad right angles, rooting into the dirt. "You put something on it?"

"Just took a shower." Skeetah mumbles this into his underarm. "Then I poured some peroxide on it. From China's bottle." That's the other thing he does with her after fights, wipes at her cuts with a towel he's washed, bleached, and dipped in hydrogen peroxide. She smiles lazily like a woman in a new Fourth of July outfit being complimented.

"This clean?" The wrap looks dirty, worn thin.

"I washed and bleached it last night," Skeetah sighs. I wrap the bandage once, and I expect him to flinch from the cloth, but he doesn't. For once he doesn't smell like dog. He smells like the constant wind that pushes the tide in over the Gulf of Mexico, but not the tide at the beach. The tide at the Bay of Angels, which smells of the oysters fresh dug from the mud. Daddy used to take us swimming there when we were younger, in a little cove. The water was murkier than the river, and colder, and the bottom was a landscape of oyster shells. We dug up oysters, threw them out farther away from the cove. Marsh grass waved at the edges, and pines leaned out over the water. Pelicans floated in rows. Daddy would fish off a sinking pier, and sometimes on a ledge on one of the support pilings under the bridge with some of his friends, and most of the time, at the end of the day, he'd be left with an empty cooler of beer and one or two croakers bleating in the icy water. His friends caught fifteen-pound redfish they'd have to wrestle from the water. Daddy'd call us out at the end of the day, more drunk than mad, the sunset turning through the sky behind us like a top. Our feet were always a snarl of cuts.

"Tighter," Skeetah says.

Mama went with us swimming in the bay sometime. She circled Daddy and his friends, sat in a sagging plastic and aluminum yard chair Daddy'd found on the Pit. She laughed at their jokes sometime, but she didn't drink any beer. Mostly she just sat with a fishing pole braced between her legs. She was the one that caught a baby shark; it was the same color as the water, as long as her arm, and strong. Daddy tried to take the pole from her and she wouldn't let him. His friends laughed, tried to get her to

137

give it to them, but she held it in both hands and walked the shark up and down the oyster-shelled sand, in the biting marsh grass, under and out from the bridge. She walked it tired, her arms big and round, strong under the woman fat. She coaxed it to death. And when it gave up, she hauled it in and let out a laugh that swooped up into the sky with the pelicans and flew away, wind-ready and wide as their wings. She cooked it in butter that night, soaked it in buttermilk to take the wild out of it. When we ate it, it was tender, sea salty, and had no bones.

"Almost done?" Skeetah is watching my hands. I wonder if he sees the wounds underneath the bandage already, if he imagines what they will look like once healed. His own fight scars.

"Yeah," I say.

The last time Mama went with us to the bay, Daddy flipped his line backward to cast it out over the water and caught her palm with his hook. The barbed needle sank in deep. She pulled it out and rinsed it off in the water we were swimming in. Her stomach was big with Junior. It healed crooked and purple, puffy, and she had to go to the clinic to get an ointment for it when it started to leak pus. Whenever she would walk me through the store or through a crowd when we were out in public, holding the back of my neck with her hand, I'd feel the scar and see those pelicans. Up close, their beaks were etched with dark like the barnacles on a ship's hull, the same color as Mama's hand, and they were sharp as knives. They didn't like us swimming close to them. Her hand was special, her own, one. Mama.

"You ran slow yesterday."

I hold the bandage close. Skeetah grabs a rusty safety pin from off the sink and pins it shut.

"Only in the beginning," I say.

"Why?"

"I don't know." The light is creeping into the bathroom like fog.

Skeetah pulls his shirt back over his head, looks down at my body to my chest, my stomach, my feet. What does he know? I shift, barely help myself from folding my arms.

"Maybe you're gaining weight."

"You're saying I'm fat?" I am trying not to cry. I don't want him to know, but I can't tell him, because I can't say it. I haven't said it to myself yet, out loud. Just chased it around in my head since I saw the lines.

"No," Skeet says. "Just growing up,

maybe." The light is thick in the bathroom; it suffuses everything after he walks out, the smell of the bay going with him, leaving me and a smell like fried food that makes me turn on the water in the sink and vomit as quietly as I can, my face in the bowl.

I am kneeling on the sink. The bowl is hard metal, and where it meets the plastic of the counter, there is a ridge. It is cutting into my knees. I want to see how big I am, to see if you can tell. This is the only private mirror in the house. A big mirror with a fake gold-worked frame hangs in the living room, but I cannot do it there. I have to see myself as Skeetah, Randall, Junior, Daddy, and *Manny* do, have to see beyond my hands for eyes, hands that cup my stomach in my sleep so that I wake with them in the top of my shorts.

I tuck the hem of my shirt up through my bra. My breasts are full, turgid and tender the way they get before my period comes on. But I can still keep them smashed down in my bra. There's the flat Y of my torso leading into my waist. Dark marks over my stomach like small black beans, old chicken-pox scars from when I was little and lay on the sofa, delirious with pain, for three days. Me, Randall, and Skeetah had it at once, and Mama must've rubbed us down with chamomile lotion every hour, but it felt like an endless dark day, like the kind they have in Alaska midwinter, between each time she'd lay my head in her lap, lift my shirt, and rub ease and sleep into my skin. I even had small burning bumps on my tongue.

Before I became pregnant, my stomach had been almost flat, the belly button an outie: an eye squeezed shut. The skin dark and spotted darker. I don't look fat so much, now, just a little past full. The eye is open to a slit. There is a layer of meat around the belly button. I turn to the side, my feet braced on the sink bowl, my toes on the bottom, my butt on my heels, my knees down, and I sit up as straight as I can. There it is. It is not a watermelon curve. It is not that large. It is not a cantaloupe curve; it is not that insistent. The closest I can get to it is a honeydew curve; it is long and slight. I push with my hands, and it will not sink to dense pearls like fat. It pushes back, water flush and warm. I unpin my shirt. We all share clothes, so it's mostly men's T-shirts for me, loose jeans and cotton shorts. They cannot tell, but it is there. Perhaps Skeetah saw when I walked from the water and put on my clothes. I do not know, but I will not give him the chance to see again now. I will not let him see until none of us have any choices about what can be seen, what can be avoided, what is blind, and what will turn us to stone.

The piles that Daddy has been building like birds' nests all over the yard for the hurricane are not growing today. Daddy is secreted like a snake in the dirt under his dump truck, his legs in dark blue pants, the hems tucked into his work boots that used to be brown when Mama bought them for him years ago for Christmas and are now black. Junior is sitting next to Daddy's feet, digging a cluster of holes in the dirt. He smoothes the dirt away so that there is no evidence of digging, only holes.

"Hand me that wrench, boy."

Junior doesn't hear or he doesn't want to move. He palms the sand gently, the way he used to pat the stray dogs that lived on the Pit before Skeetah bought China home. They were always mottled the color of dried sticks, of leaves sinking into earth and darkening, and they followed Junior around the Pit, licked his face when he had it out with Randall over not wanting to take a bath, or because he'd failed another test. They boiled around him like a rain-swollen creek when he'd run out into the bare yard,

142

the trees, and cry. They nested with him under the house. But China had been settled in for two years now, and the dogs had disappeared. I do not remember if she killed them, or if they slunk off one by one in the night once she took on weight and could rip rubber tires in two. Junior's forever the puppy weaned too soon.

"Junior!" Daddy yells. I'm walking through the ripped net of the shade, trying to edge past them unseen. I want to find Skeetah. He has medicine to give.

"Junior!" Daddy beats the rim of the dump truck with whatever tool he has, and it clangs like a bell. Junior startles, drawn from his holes. "The wrench!"

Junior picks up the wrench. He is strong for a little boy. When he grabs it and curls, I can see his muscles bunch. He is skinny in the way of picky-eating little boys before they reach puberty, when they either turn lean or get fat, and then grow into their man bodies. He lets it rest on Daddy's leg.

"Here," Junior breathes. I move too quickly, and he sees me. I shake my head, but he's already saying it. "Esch. Where you going?"

"Esch! Where your brothers at? I need they help." Daddy is a voice billowing from the bottom of the car like smoke.

"I don't know."

"What?" he bellows.

"I said I don't know." Junior is rising to follow me. I walk faster.

"Where Skeetah at? Randall here?" Junior asks.

"Hold up!" Daddy yells. "Come here."

Daddy is wiggling from underneath the truck. It bulks over him like the rest of the detritus in the yard: refrigerators rusted so that they look like deviled eggs sprinkled with paprika, pieces of engines, a washing machine so old it has an arm that swished the clothes around and looks like a hand-held cake mixer.

"I want you to get up in the driver's seat. When Junior come tell you, I want you to try to start it."

"I can go find Skeetah if you want."

"No." Daddy's already putting one shoulder back underneath the truck. "I got to get this fixed today. Now. They going to be money to be made after this storm come through by a man with a dump truck. José hit them folks in Mexico yesterday, but they already got another storm out in the Gulf. Tropical depression number ten. And it's so far out and the water so hot . . . ." Daddy trails off, his voice dissolving under the metal. The truck broke right after Mama

144

died, and Daddy got disability checks from it since it was an accident. I don't ask him how he's supposed to be able to drive a big dump truck after the storm without somebody asking him about it. Junior crouches next to Daddy. In the dirt next to him, a beer bottle, half full, is screwed into the sand.

There are multiple levers, and I don't know how to work any of them.

"Tell Daddy I don't know how to start the truck," I yell to Junior. The seat is peeling away at the seams like plastic Kraft wrappers, and the foam padding underneath is damp. The dash and the steering wheel and the glass are coated in dust turned candy shell hard.

Up close Daddy smells like vinegar, like salt. That is his fresh alcohol smell.

"You see that there?"

"Yeah."

"That's the clutch. That's the brake. Put this here in neutral. You don't need to do nothing to this. But when you turn the key, press the clutch and the brake at the same time."

"Okay."

"Don't touch nothing else." His hands are like mine, like Skeet's. That's where we get these flat wide fingers from. But I look at his face and his collarbone punching up through the neck of his shirt like knuckles, and I can't see anything else he ever gave me. He walks around the side of the truck. Minutes later, Junior clambers up the side of the truck.

"He say start it."

I press and turn. There is a click and then nothing. Junior drops and runs, reappears climbing.

"He say again."

Again I press and turn. This time there isn't even a click. A fly buzzes into the truck, decides to try my arm. I wave it away.

"Shit!" I hear muffled through the machinery.

"Ask him if he want me to do it again."

Junior doesn't even bother climbing down; he leans out and yells. His little muscles stretch out like shoestrings. When he was a baby, Randall held him the most, and I did the rest of the time. Daddy fed him until he figured out me and Randall could do it. He taught Randall the right ratio for the formula, how to heat the bottle up in a pan of water so that the milk didn't get too hot, and then he went back out in his pickup, trying to find yard work and odd jobs. Afterward, Randall mixed the bottles, kept them filled in the refrigerator so he or I could feed Junior. Whenever Skeetah held him, Junior would cry. When we went to school, Daddy brought Junior to Mudda Ma'am, who had white hair she'd braid into pigtails and loop over her head, and who I never saw wearing anything other than a housedress. She watched kids for money while their parents were at work. She watched Junior until he was old enough for Head Start, which is when her memory started going, so she let the kids go with it. Tilda, her only daughter, moved back in with her to take care of her, but mostly spent her time wearing a dirt path between Javon's house and her own for crack. I wonder if Junior even remembers Mudda Ma'am. He never talks about her, never says her name even when we walk down to the park and see her wandering amongst her azaleas like a child losing at hide-and-seek. Sometimes I wonder if Junior remembers anything, or if his head is like a colander, and the memories of who bottle-fed him, who licked his tears, who mothered him, squeeze through the metal like water to run down the drain, and only leave the present day, his sand holes, his shirtless bird chest, Randall yelling at him: his present washed clean of memory like vegetables washed clean of the dirt they grow in.

I press, turn, wait.

"Stop!" Daddy is waving the wrench in the air, but the truck is so large that I cannot see his head over the hood, only his black hand, the dirty tool. "Get out. It ain't ready. Go."

I jump down, Junior already tailing me.

"Go get me another beer, Junior."

"Y'all always leaving me, Esch. Wait!" Junior says, and he runs to the house, leaving a dust ghost trail behind him.

"She need some time to herself." Skeetah is saying this. China is beside him. She is snapping at gnats. And with his arms crossed over his chest and a baseball cap high on his head, there is Manny. Every time her mouth shuts, he tries not to, but he flinches. I see it in the balls of his shoulders.

"You should give her a bath or something." Manny tosses out the comment. Shrugs and justifies the jump when China snaps and shakes her head at what she has missed.

"I will." Skeetah kneels, runs his hand down China's chest. She looks up and her whole body shimmies like a woman dancing down at the Oaks, a blues club set on six acres of woods and a baseball diamond in the middle of Bois. They host baseball games for black town teams every Sunday during the summer. Once, when the outside bathroom stalls were broken when we were younger, Randall walked me into the blues club during a baseball Sunday to use the bathroom. He and Skeet and I had spent the day begging quarters from our friends to buy pickles and soda at the concession stand, hanging from the chicken wire that backed the dugouts, watching the away team clap and whistle and kick at their bats and throw practice shots while Mama and Daddy were in and out of the blues club.

"I think that's the dirtiest I've ever seen her," Manny says.

China has a little blood from the other dog, Twist, on her still at the corners of her mouth like lipstick. The red dirt of the Pit has given her a pink gleam, like a barely cooked shrimp still gummy with sea. Manny ignores me and Junior, who is trying to jump at a tree branch and touch it like a basketball goal. The lighter Manny carries in his pockets to smoke his cigarillos dances over and under his knuckles. That is his nervous habit, the thing that he does but does not realize that he does when he is do-ing some things and thinking of others.

"I'm waiting until right before the fight to

clean her. So she be shining on them."

On the day Randall walked me through the Oaks, all corners and smoke and the bowling of beer bottles hitting tables, he had gripped my shoulders so hard they hurt. Mama had been on the dance floor; I'd never seen her dance before that, and I never would again. She was dancing with a man, not Daddy, while Daddy sat at the edge of the floor and watched. She had shook like China, threw her head back so water glistened down her throat, and her body ran in curves when normally she was all solid. She was beautiful.

"I thought you wasn't going to fight her, her fresh with milk and all." The lighter stops, and Manny flips it up in the air and catches it. He lights a cigarillo and wedges it in the corner of his mouth and talks around it.

"I ain't. But I'm going to take her. Can't let niggas forget who she is."

China lays down in the sand indolently. Her breasts, still swollen but maybe a little less now, lay flat before her like a pillow. The skin where her breasts separate from her rib cage is wrinkled — her nipples are a pale pink so colorless they are almost white. I haven't ever touched her chest, but if I did, I would imagine that her teats would be soft and cool against the heat of the day. She does not lay her head in the dirt and huff like other dogs, but stares at Manny and me instead. Like she knows.

"You know Rico going to be there. Fighting Kilo."

Manny begins flipping the silver and red lighter again when he mentions Rico. The image, which looks like a tattoo, reads *Hearts on Fire,* and pictures two hearts diagonal to one another, going up in flames. His lips kiss the cigarillo and he pulls. China blinks and yawns. There is a movement behind my breast that feels like someone has turned a hose on full blast, and the water that has been baking in the pump in the summer heat floods out, scalding. This is love, and it hurts. Manny never looks at me.

"Well, I hope Kilo ready. Marquise told me some of his cousins from Baton Rouge been talking shit about how they got a boss dog, and they bringing her out to fight, too." Skeetah rubs China on her side, smoothing her fur over her ribs as he squats over her. Her tail thumps once, raises dust, lies still.

"Kilo always ready."

Rico is Manny's cousin, the boy from Germaine who bought his dog, Kilo, to mate with China. Rico's big red muscle of a dog with a killing jaw. It was Manny who talked up Kilo to Skeetah. As China grew older, her pulpy puppy muscle hardened like a pearl in the stomach of an oyster, and Skeet's devotion was the living muscle. She grew lean and strong. Manny would talk shit whenever we were all out under the trees as if he could lessen the wonder of Skeetah's prized dog. He thought he could dim her, that he could convince us she wasn't white and beautiful and gorgeous as a magnolia on the trash-strewn, hard-scrabble Pit, where everything else is starving, fighting, struggling.

Manny would sit on a milk crate or a tree stump and say, *My cousin Rico got a fire dog. Probably about the same age as yours, but bigger. More muscle. Got a killing jaw.* Skeetah would ignore Manny, or glance at him while he was dragging China through the sand, around the junk by her teeth locked in a bike tire, and say, *Really. Yeah,* Manny would say, and his white teeth would flash in his glass-burned, beautiful face. *Yeah.* China would squeal a dog's squeal and bear down with her haunches, make Skeetah stumble toward her. *We'll see,* Skeetah'd say.

Rico called China small-time until he came to the Pit with Manny one day and finally saw her: knee-high, stout as any boy dog but still sleek with muscle, and her long neck and head like a snake's. Skeetah had her climb a leaning tree and then shred a half of a car tire, pulling it so hard the wire in the rubber made Skeet's hands bleed. When they mated, China had let Kilo lick her from behind, let him mount. Smiled like she liked it. The tendons had stood out in Skeetah's neck, and he squinted so that it looked like his eyes were closed. Kilo had placed his big mouth on her neck like he was kissing her and slobbered on her. She'd snapped at him, figured it for a hold. Hated the submission of it. She nicked him, snapped at him until she threw him off. She'd drawn blood: he hadn't.

"What's the dog name? From Baton Rouge?"

"Boss," Skeetah laughed. China snorted into the dirt.

"Well, Kilo been fought from Florida to Louisiana. Broke a dog leg once. *They* better be ready."

"You seen it?"

"What?"

"The break?"

"No, Rico told me." Manny waves away a gnat, inhales strong on the cigarillo, and blows smoke in a fog in front of his face.

153

"Y'all need to start a fire out here. Why y'all always got so many bugs up here on the Pit? Gnats so bold they out in the middle of the day. Fuck the evening time." He drops the cigarillo; it smokes a pencil thread and then smothers in the sand.

"We savages up here on the Pit. Even the gnats. Mosquitoes so big they look like bats." Skeetah nods at me and Junior. "You better watch out. Junior look puny but he'll sucker-punch you in the neck and leave you choking. And Esch —" Skeetah stands when he says it, and China circles him, sniffing in the dirt, "You see how boss China is. You think the other girl on the Pit going to be weak?"

"I ain't saying either of them weak." Manny still hasn't looked at me. "But you know China ain't as boss as she used to be."

"What?" Skeetah's tendons are showing.

"Any dog give birth like that is less strong after. Even if you don't think it. Take a lot out of an animal to nurse and nurture like that. Price of being female." Finally Manny glances at me. It slides over me like I'm glass.

Skeetah laughs. It sounds as if it's hacking its way out of him.

"You serious? That's when they come into they strength. They got something to protect." He glances at me, too, but I feel it even after he looks away. "That's power."

China is licking Skeetah's hand like she licks the puppies. Skeetah pushes her head away but she keeps at it, and he looks away from Manny. The tendons in his neck smooth. The menace leaves him; if he were a dog, his hair would flatten.

"To give life" — Skeetah bends down to China, feels her from neck to jaw, caresses her face like he would kiss her; she flashes her tongue — "is to know what's worth fighting for. And what's love." Skeetah rubs down her sides, feels her ribs.

"You wormed her yet?" I ask. Does Manny think that of me, that I am weak? That there is a price to this body that swallows him, that pulls at him and takes him until he has nothing left? Is Manny glad because he will never have to pay it?

"Naw. She wouldn't take the Ivomec earlier. Spilled it."

"You know how to mix it?" Manny slid his lighter into his jean shorts pocket. His muscle shirt was white as his teeth. Shaliyah must have washed. I wonder if he ever told her that about weakness. If he ever called her female, bit it off at the end like underripe sugarcane when he said it?

Skeetah looks up at Manny, his hands

155

dropping, his jaw loose.

"What you mean, mix it?"

"Fuck, you going to kill the dog." Manny smiles like he wants to laugh. I swallow and realize that I want to push him, to place my hands flat on the muscles of his chest and shove him for looking that way at Skeet, for insulting him. For saying things he doesn't know he is saying about me. I want him to fall over backward, straining his bad arm, and then I want to bear him down in the dirt. Make him touch all of me, for once. "You supposed to mix the Ivomec with cooking oil and then give it to the dog. And don't try doing it with water if you ain't got no cooking oil. Then it won't mix good."

"She didn't take none of it this morning." Skeetah is holding China's head still, prying her eyes wide, peering into them.

"You sure?" Manny is still smiling.

"I'm sure."

"And she only need a little bit. You got a medicine syringe?"

"Yeah, I . . ." Skeetah pauses. "I got one yesterday." Looks at me. I figure Randall done told Manny what happened with the farmer and the wormer and the dog, but I know that Skeetah doesn't want everybody to know either. Less people that know, the less people that talk if the farmer ever

156

wanders through the wood our way, asking questions. We live in the black heart of Bois Sauvage, and he lives out away in the pale arteries, so I don't think he will ever come here, swinging his cane like an axe, his dog foaming, probably a rifle in the back window of his gleaming, tinted pickup truck. But I know Skeet would say, *But still.*

"You need half a cc for every twenty pounds. What, China about sixty-five pounds? Give her one and a half." Manny pulls his arm across his chest, shrugging his shoulder as he does it. Stretching out the wound. This is what he does when he is bored. He looks away from Skeetah and China, beyond Junior, who is peering into the dark shed where the puppies are dozing on their new tile floor, to the woods. Never at me. "Any more than that and she could go blind. And any more than that, she could die."

Skeetah pulls China to him by her haunches and pries open her jaw, sniffing at her tongue. He has turned from lover to father. She, his doting daughter. I draw a line through the sand with my toe, pull my hands from the pockets of my shorts where they had crept to cup my stomach, trying to expose me so that Manny will look at me like he looks at China. Junior begins whis-

157

tling into the darkness of the shed, like he would call the puppies to him, lead them into the light, to a new brother, and burrow with them under the house like his lost dogs.

"Get away from the door, Junior," Skeetah says. China licks his breath, tasting his words. "Esch, we got oil, right?"

Daddy keeps a two-gallon jug of vegetable oil in the cabinet for frying oysters or fish when he can catch them or his friends give them to him, but I don't think China will like the taste of it. I stick a finger into the oil and rub it across my teeth. Too metallic, too bland. But the bacon grease Daddy keeps on the counter in an old coffee can, the metal waxy with residue: that tastes like drippings. That tastes like the next bite is going to be salty crunchy bacon, tender in the middle, burnt at the edges, stiff as a twig. This she will like.

Skeetah has found a big cardboard box, cut it in half, and lined it with material, and I can't tell whether the material is old clothes or old sheets or old towels, because under the dogs they are just dark gray rags. The bottom of the box reads *Westinghouse.*

"I took it from behind the hall at the church," Skeetah says. He is sucking the Ivomec into the medicine syringe. It is colorless as water. He is sitting on a toolbox rusted and kicked to bad angles, the Ivomec bottle between his knees. When he shifts, the toolbox crunches against the metal inside like a mouth grinding its teeth. He recaps the bottle, slides it into his pants pocket. Manny is gone, but Junior is standing in the corner, his hands folded behind him, leaning against the shed wall.

"Where's Manny?"

"Said he had something to go do." Skeetah holds the syringe in one hand, the coffee container of bacon grease in another. He wobbles.

"He said he'd be back," Junior pipes up. He rocks on his feet and slams against the shed, shaking the tin.

"Junior. Stop it. Shit, I need a bowl." Skeetah turns to me. "Can you get me a bowl, please?"

"Junior, go get him a bowl." Even though I have to pee, the melon under my shirt ripe, I still don't want to leave the shed.

"He asked you," Junior says quietly, intent on the puppies. They are blindly pitching themselves out the door of the box, headlong.

"Junior, go 'head."

"No."

"Esch, please."

In the house, I hardly sit on the toilet. I lean over and mouth my knees, feel the tender skin above my kneecaps with my lips. Outside, the rooster crows at the middle of the day, his call cutting through the hazy buzz of the insects. Nausea digs at me. Manny has left; I don't want to think of him, to know he is somewhere out there eating up all the sunlight, smoking a cigarillo, passing purchases to customers at the gas station, his hands brushing Shaliyah soft as marsh grass, but I do. I walk in shadow on the way to the shed. Where I can't avoid the sun, where it touches me through the branches, it burns.

Skeetah pours a palmful of the bacon grease into the bowl and then squirts in the Ivomec. He mixes it with his finger. Even though we are in the shade, the heat is worse in the shed, like the inside of a hot fist. Junior and Skeetah are both glazed with sweat, and Skeetah blinks like he's about to cry because the sweat runs like water from his scalp to his forehead into his eyes. I am trying to see whether the Ivomec is mixing well in the bowl when there is an eclipse of light in the doorway and Skeetah looks up and past me, pissed.

"Move out the way of the door. You blocking all the light."

160

It's Manny. Both of his hands are on the top of the doorsill, and he leans into the door, stretching his body like taffy. All I can see is the shadow of him and the white of his smile. It feels wrong to not be able to see his face, seems wrong that he is as dark as me now, that he would be washed dark by the sun behind him like ink set to bleeding over waterlogged paper.

"Anybody seen my lighter?" Manny's voice is as distinct and sharp as the corners of the toolbox Skeet sits on.

"No." Skeetah is stirring the medicine with his finger. "Move."

"You, Esch?"

I shake my head.

"You put it in your pocket," Junior says, and Manny leans on the doorjamb, fishes in his pockets. Light diffuses through the room. I see Manny's profile, his glass-burned side, and then he stops fumbling and turns to us and his face is dark again. I want him to grip my hand like he grips the dark beams over his head, to walk with me out of the shed and away from the Pit. To help me bear the sun. To hold me once he learns my secret. To be different.

"I didn't see you over there, Junior," Manny says.

"Thank you," Skeet says. The oil has

161

absorbed all of the Ivomec. The mix is off-white, creamy. Skeetah tastes it.

"You shouldn't do that," shadow Manny says.

"Don't you have somewhere to go?"

"I'm just trying to help you out."

"You could help me out by moving out of my light — in or out."

"I'm out." Manny shrugs. "I'm going to look up under the trees. Ain't no way I'm coming in; China don't like me." China is sitting before Skeetah, ignoring how close I am to him, intent on the bowl with the bacon grease in it. She is panting, her tongue dripping water.

"China likes everybody." Skeet is sucking the mixture back up into the syringe.

"Okay." Manny laughs. His smile again. Each time I see his teeth, nausea elbows me. Manny steps away and the light floods in and I want him to leave, to come back, to never have been. China is dancing on her hind legs because Skeetah is standing, the syringe in his hand.

"Here."

I press the bowl to my stomach.

China is hopping on her hind legs. What tore through the gray dog yesterday is now a woman approaching her partner on the floor of the Oaks, the first lick of the blues guitar sounding from the jukebox, a drink in her hand. China lands on her front paws and pushes back up. Skeet crouches, places one arm around the back of her neck, twining his hand around her jaw, tilting her head up.

"That's my girl," he says.

China grins. Her tongue flashes out like a wet, whipped rag.

"I know my girl," Skeetah breathes. With his other hand, he tilts the syringe to her lips.

China barks, nods. Her front legs rest on his chest like a lover's. She flings her head back in submission, supplication.

"Good bitch," Skeetah says.

China nuzzles the syringe, licks.

"That's my bitch." Skeetah closes his fingers, the medicine disappears, and he withdraws. The puppies twitch and nuzzle at their feet. China accidentally steps on the orange one, and it yelps.

"Always my bitch," Skeetah says.

Outside, Manny is pacing the yard, running his feet through the sand.

"*His* bitch must've gave it to him." Skeetah breathes this into China's coat; from the doorway, she is the dusty lightbulb in the room. Junior is creeping along the wall, trying to get closer to the puppies. In the

163

yard, the dust from Manny's searching feet billows up and obscures him, turning his white shirt, his golden skin, dark as a bruised peach.

I've heard girls at my school talk. These are conversations I snatch from the air like we take down clothes that have crusted dry on a clothesline. The girls say that if you're pregnant and you take a month's worth of birth control pills, it will make your period come on. Say if you drink bleach, you get sick, and it will make what will become the baby come out. Say if you hit yourself really hard in the stomach, throw yourself on the metal edge of a car and it hits you low enough to call bruises, it could bring a miscarriage. Say that this is what you do when you can't afford an abortion, when you can't have a baby, when nobody wants what is inside you.

In the bathroom, I bend over standing and knead my stomach, knead the melon to pulp, but it just keeps springing back: ripe. Intent on bearing seed. I could find something big enough and hard enough to jump on: Daddy's dump truck hood, Daddy's tractor, one of the old washing machines out in the yard. We have bleach in the laundry room. Only thing I wouldn't be able to find is the birth control pills; I've never had a prescription, wouldn't have money to get them if I did, don't have any girlfriends to ask for some, and have never been to the Health Department. Who would bring me? Daddy, who sometimes I think forgets that I am a girl? Big Henry, one of the few of our friends who has a car? Manny? Teeth-in-the-dark Manny? *If I took care of it, he would never know,* I think, *never know, and then maybe it would give him time. Time to what?* I push. *Be different. Love me.*

These are my options, and they narrow to none.

The sun set hours ago, and I am sitting on the toilet seat, pulling the towel that Randall tacked up for a curtain to look out in the yard. I see Skeetah dragging wood to the door of the shed. The bare bulb burns outward, shining on the dirt he kneels in. He is prying nails from wood. Insects swarm at the edges of the light. The frame for the kennel that sat for days, wedged into the dirt like a fallen scarecrow, is upright again. He is building her a house. He is watching over her, gauging her for sickness. He knows love.

"Gotdamnit."

Daddy's pickup eases into the yard so slowly that I can hear him curse above the gurgle of the engine. This is how he drives when he is bombed-out drunk. Very slowly, and with his brights on. His headlights break the golden bubble that encases Skeet and flood the yard with light. Skeetah raises the arm with the hammer and shades his eyes. Daddy parks parallel to his dump truck, which has sat rust-barnacled and silent since I attempted to crank it this morning. Daddy leaves his headlights on and gets out of the truck.

"I said, gotdamnit!"

Daddy tries to punctuate this by slamming the door of his truck, but he fails. His hand slips from the metal, and it closes so quietly I can't even hear it from my seat on the toilet next to the window.

"Gotdamn Van's Salvage," Daddy mutters, "didn't even have the part I needed." He leans against the side of his truck like it's a human being, speaks this almost as low as he used to on the nights he came home dazed drunk when Mama was alive. Mama would walk out to meet him, gather him to her like a child. She was only a few inches shorter than him and could bear all of his weight. He would whisper to her as they walked up the concrete slabs that made up the steps to the front porch. We never heard what he said to her. I imagine that he told her that he loved her, soaked tender with moonshine.

"You left your lights on," Skeetah says.

"Now how I'm going to make money after the storm?" Daddy slaps his truck, but it is awkward, at odds. It slides into a caress. "What you say?"

"I said you left your lights on." Skeetah is prying at a reluctant nail, his head down, concentrating. He watches Daddy out of the corner of his eyes.

"Oh." Daddy reaches into the truck and pushes the knob to turn off the headlights. He walks toward Skeetah slowly. This is his drunk walk: purposeful, plodding. "What you doing?"

"Nothing." Skeetah stills, stops pulling at the nail, but stays bent over.

"Nothing?"

"At all."

"I see you doing something, so you can't be doing nothing."

"Ain't you tired?"

"What?"

"You been busy trying to get parts for that dump truck all day."

"Damn right," Daddy says. "The U-Pull-It, the Salvage, all looked at me crazy. No dump truck parts. No help when I was looking through the cars. Look at me like they

167

don't know when a man's talking when I tell them a bad storm's coming."

Skeetah straightens, balances on the balls of his feet, preparing to outwait Daddy. The hammer is on his knee.

"Them's boards. You been in my piles?"

"Naw."

"I got them gathered for the house. You always meddling. You want the windows to shatter?"

"Daddy, I ain't mess with your wood."

"Well, where you get it from, then?"

"Found it off up in the woods." Skeet is running the hammer back and forth on his leg. He is waiting for the step that turns Daddy mean.

"You ain't found shit in them woods." Daddy is waving his hand in the air as if he is waving away night beetles startled to flight, wading through the glossy brown bugs with shells as hard as butterscotch candies. He spits. "Did you?"

"Yes." Skeetah is very quiet. The hammer is still.

"Bullshit!" Daddy yells. "Everything I do for y'all and y'all don't appreciate shit!" He raises his arms again, as if he has stirred more bugs to motion. He reaches to grab Skeetah's arm, to pull him to standing and then shove him, probably. This is what he does when he wants to manhandle, humiliate; he pulls one of us toward him, shakes, and then shoves us hard backward so that we fall in the dirt. So that we sprawl like toddlers learning to walk: dirt on our faces and our hands, faces wet with crying or mucus, ashamed. Skeetah is rigid, as straight as the hammer hanging at his side. Daddy tries to shove him but he is slow to let go; it is as if his hands are deaf to what his brain wants them to do, and they grip Skeetah's shoulders, hard. He shakes Skeetah.

"Let me go, Daddy." This is so quiet that I can barely hear it.

China is standing in the doorway of the shed. She does not growl. She does not bark. She only stands, head cocked to one side, her forelegs locked wide, her breasts adding more bulk to her, the rest of her lost to the darkness of the shed. She is still.

"Let go!"

"All I do!" Daddy shoves Skeet so hard that Daddy lurches backward with the force of it, but he catches himself before falling.

Skeetah stutters backward but lands crouching, still on his feet. China darts forward. Skeet holds the hammer like a baton.

"Hold," Skeetah calls. "Hold!" There is wetness to his voice. China stops where she is. She is one of the flaking statues at the graveyard next to the park, an angel streaked by rain, burning bright.

"I wish she would," Daddy says, his arms straight as his sides. "I wish she would."

Skeetah edges sideways to China, lays down the hammer, and puts his hand over her muzzle. She is marble under his fingers.

"I'd take her upcountry and shoot her."

"No."

"Call the county pound. Make you watch them take her away."

Skeetah has his arm around China's back, tucked over and under her stomach, his hand lost somewhere in her breasts. China does not turn and lick him. She watches Daddy still. Skeetah rubs her chest with his other hand, smoothes the fur in broad downward strokes again and again.

"I'm trying to save us," Daddy says. Skeetah crouches. "Y'all need to learn to appreciate me. You hear me?"

The nightbugs answer back *yessssssss*. Skeetah ignores Daddy, rubs China, glances back and forth between them.

"Put them gotdamn boards back where you found them. You hear me?"

China's tail lowers, but her ears are still laid back down her skull like a crest of feathers. Skeetah is whispering to her, murmuring.

"You hear me?" Daddy yells, takes a halting step toward Skeet. China's tail rises.

"Yes," Skeetah says. He is facing Daddy, staring at him plainly, his face smooth and open, only his mouth barely moving when he speaks. "Yes."

"Good." Daddy steps back. Skeet leans on China to stop her from moving. Daddy turns to walk into the house. He shuffles sideways, slow and deliberate, watching Skeet and China watch him leave them to the abandoned hammer, the fallen frame, the dark expanse sounding of bug and wood and wind spreading out and away from the two of them like a bride's train.

THE SIXTH DAY:
A STEADY HAND

Daddy is knocking down what is left of the chicken coop. The chickens and rooster have long abandoned it. After summers of heavy rain the wood grew soft and rotten, and then the short, knuckle-freezing winters dried it up and hollowed the woody pulp out, and it began to sag and buckle into the earth. It used to have Mama's clothesline tied to it with the other end fixed to a pine tree. After Mama died, Daddy moved the clothesline to a closer tree, but he didn't tie it tight enough, so when Randall and I wash clothes and hang them out with wooden clothespins, the line sags, and our pants dangle in the dirt.

Skeetah slept out in the shed with the dogs after he faced Daddy with the hammer last night. I have been sitting on the sofa near the living room window, waiting for him to come into the house, because I know he will circle around and enter the front door to avoid passing Daddy in the back. But Skeet has not surfaced. He could always hold his breath the longest when we first began swimming in the pit, crouched on the silty, junk-reefed bottom; we would circle him like anxious boats, calling him to the surface, but he would remain still and bubbling below. I take breaks and sneak cans of Vienna sausages in the bathroom, swallowing all five quickly. They are so light they could be air. I tried to read this morning, but I stopped in the quest for the Golden Fleece, distracted again by Medea, who can only think of Jason, her face red, her heart aflame, engulfed by sweet pain. The goddess struck her with love, and she had no choices. I could not concentrate. My stomach was its own animal, and thoughts of Manny kept surfacing like swimmers in my brain; I had my own tender pain. I slid my book between the wall and my bed and slunk to the kitchen, filching Daddy's hurricane supplies. I eat, and nothing touches my stomach, nothing tells me it is full with food, with something more than food.

Thwack, thwack, thwack, sounds the hammer. The wood creaks. One panel falls off. Daddy begins cussing, calling down sonofabitches, fuck this's, and gotdamnits. I am tired of waiting. I grab another can of

173

sausages, stick it in the pocket of my shorts. I will go to Skeetah like Medea went to her brother when they fled on their great adventure with the Argonauts. I will offer my help.

Skeetah looks like somebody's punched him in both eyes. The sound of Daddy's hammer in the shed threads through the door, and it steadily pulses like blood. China is reclined, the puppies squealing at her tits. Her head is laid on her paws, and she does not look up when I step over the threshold. Junior is a crow, perched on a metal drum beside the door, eating a pack of peanut butter crackers. It makes me hungry.

"Something's wrong," Skeetah says. He is sitting on the floor, his back against the wall. He lets his head roll back, and his Adam's apple bulges so prominently it looks like bone.

"What's wrong?" I say. His eyes burn like he has fever.

"She been too — easy. Usually she let them suck and then fight them off when they done had enough, but they been sucking for almost an hour and she ain't moved."

"Maybe she just tired, like you said yesterday."

Daddy's hammer beats at the room.

"That ain't it."

"Well, then what?"

"I think I gave her too much."

"You did what Manny said."

"How you know Manny knew what he was doing?"

"Rico probably showed him how."

"And who say Rico going to show him the right way to do it if he know Manny going to show me?"

"He wouldn't do that."

"Who?"

"Manny." I swallow his name. He has to be better than that. I know it.

Skeetah speaks to the ceiling, his eyes wide, his elbows hanging from his knees with his hands clasped; this is his prayer.

"You don't know," he says.

"Everybody ain't always plotting against you and China, Skeet."

He crawls across the floor, waves his hand in front of China's face. She follows him with her eyes, sighs so hard she raises dirt on her linoleum floor in a dusty wave.

"Ain't nobody said that, Esch." Skeetah puts his hand on China's neck, as careful as Mama used to take biscuits from the oven. China breathes hard again, pushes one of the puppies away from her desultorily. "That's my girl."

"She probably just need to eat something."

"I can't lose her." Skeetah's bald head looks muddy from sleeping on the dirty floor of the shed. Mama's arms would look like that when she was pulling greens in the small garden plot she kept behind the house. It was fenced off with wooden slats from an old baby crib Daddy had found at the side of the road. There is danger in what Skeetah says, in even thinking China could die. Reckless to say it aloud, to call it down, to make it possible.

"Why don't you go take a bath?" I imagine the gashes at his side, seeing them turn red with infection under Randall's old wrap. We catch boils on the Pit as easily as we used to catch stray dogs, and I know enough about them to understand that they are bacterial infections. He's not going to want to go to the hospital, and Daddy isn't going to want to take him if it comes to that. "Your stomach."

"I'm all right." He is rubbing China's head to the beat of Daddy's hammer.

"You need to be clean at the fight. Healthy. So do she. If you hurting, what she going to do?" This is the way to his heart. His pride. He stops petting China, lets his hand rest on the warm globe of her skull. She sighs and kicks another puppy away. The triangle of sunshine disappears and appears again on the floor, hidden by clouds and then free again; when Skeetah looks up at me, he squints.

"Fine. Watch her." Skeetah stands, walks to the door, shoves Junior in passing so that he almost falls off the barrel.

"Scab!" Junior yells.

"And don't let Junior touch nothing."

China feebly kicks at the puppies. She scoots along on her back to get away from them, and only stops twitching when her back is against the wall. The puppies make little squeaking noises, paw the air, roll helplessly on their sides. Their eyes are slivers of fingernails. There are four: the white China clone, the red one that looks like Kilo, the brindle runt, and the black-and-white one with patterns on the fur. They wobble away from China. I crouch in the door, my belly pushing out so that it pushes against my thighs, my knees; I pull my T-shirt away from my stomach. China eyes us all lazily, and then puts her head to her paws, closes her eyes, and, as far as I can tell, falls asleep.

"Esch?"

"What, Junior?" The puppies are flailing across the floor. Junior jumps down from his perch, lands with a thud in the dirt next to me, and crouches.

"They need to go back by China," he says. He lets his hands hang across his knees and dangle down, but even then, it still looks as if he is reaching out to them. "They going to go out the door."

"How they going to do that with us sitting here?"

"They got gaps." Junior brushes his hand between us. "Here."

"Don't touch them." I pull at my T-shirt again. Junior's breath smells like peanut butter. I'm so tired; it washes through me like blinding, heavy rain. China's ear twitches in her sleep. I wish she could talk.

"Aw, Esch." Junior leans forward on his haunches, tipping over toward the puppies, slowly. "I'm just going to put them back. See?" He grabs the white one by the nape, pinches it with his whole hand, and moves it a foot back so it is closer to China. She breathes sleepily. Junior looks back at me, smiling, his lips closed over his teeth, the multiple gaps, the digs of decay in the crevices. "See?"

"You do it, but quick." China's tail jerks in her sleep, and then she is still. "Before she wakes up."

"Okay." Junior picks up the red puppy, drops it next to its sibling. His lips part over his teeth, and he is really smiling.

"Hurry," I whisper. I want to sleep like China, lie down on the cool dirt of the shed.

"All right," he whispers. The spotted one wiggles a little in his hand, feeble and blind as an earthworm, before he sets it down.

"You can't touch them again," I breathe. A muscle spasms in China's side: a white sheet flapping in the wind on a clothesline. "Hear?"

Junior grabs the last puppy, the brindle runt, around the belly. His thumb and middle finger touch as he grabs its rib cage. The puppy is skinny, not growing milk fat like the others. Junior brings it to his nose; this close, its fur looks like it's moving. Fleas thread their way through its downy hair. Its head falls to the side, and it yanks it back in the other direction. I'm surprised its neck is so strong when it is only a child's handful of fur and skin and bones.

"Hear?"

"Yeah." Junior is not moving.

"Put it down!" I hiss. I want to slap Junior, but I know it will wake China. Junior is sniffing the puppy, and I swear that if I weren't there, he would lick it. China lets out a mewling sleep growl.

"Gotdamnit!" I grab the slim stick of his arm hard. Dig my fingernails in. Hope he can feel the fear in my hands.

"All right, Esch!" Junior whines, pulling from me, still clutching the puppy. China kicks.

"Do it!" I dig. I am sweating, hot under my arms. I am burning. "Junior!"

"All right."

Junior's smile is gone. His mouth pulls tight at the corners, baring his bottom gums. That is his crying face. His back is narrow and hard as a ruler. He leans over, lets the puppy roll from his hand. It tumbles on its side, stops, and sweeps its head along the floor. Junior yanks his arm away, cradles it to his chest, and refuses to look at me. Instead he gazes at the puppies, whispers furiously through his downturned lips.

"That hurt, Esch. That really hurt."

"What if Skeet had come in? What if China had woke up?"

My hands feel weak now that they are not gripping Junior. When he was a baby, Randall and I would pass him back and forth on the sofa, feeding him, rubbing his stomach, palming his head. Randall said that he frowned like Mama.

"You made me bleed." Junior spits on his hand, rubs it back and forth across his forearm where I have left red marks that look like winking eyes. "You didn't have to do it so hard."

"You don't listen," I say. Junior never cried when he was little.

"Still." He wipes his spitty hand across his eyes.

"You never know," I say. China huffs in her sleep again. "You know that Junior, don't you?" My hand flops in China's direction. "You know her."

China sleep-growls again, high and sharp. I touch Junior's back, feel down the marble chain of his spine. He yanks away, still holding his arm, and looks at me, his eyes like the dark heart of an oyster. I look back to China to make sure she is asleep, make sure that her puppies aren't straying too far away, make sure that my shirt is still pulled away from my stomach. I am tired again. Junior sits on his legs in the dirt, far enough away from me so that I can't grab him, but still next to me. I had expected him to run under the house.

"I'm sorry," I say.

Junior bends over and braces himself on his arms in the dirt, his butt in the air. He nods at the puppies. When he was a baby, this is how he would fall asleep on the sofa, in the bed with Randall. The puppies are swimming blindly, as if through very deep water, away from China, toward him again. I wonder if he has been sneaking into the

181

shed when we are gone with China, whether he has already been playing with them.

"Can we go to the park today?" he asks. Daddy beats the coop twice, then swears. He is hung over. He will be mean. I peel back the top of the sausage can, take one out, and hand it to Junior. China rolls on her back to face the wall, to escape her puppies in sleep the best that she can, and I nod.

"Yeah, we can go."

When we were younger and Mama had to get us up in the morning for school, she would touch us on our backs first. And when she felt us twitch under her hands, felt us move toward morning, she would softly tell us to wake up, that it was time for school. When she died and Daddy had to wake us up, he wouldn't touch us. He'd knock on the wall next to our door, hard: shout, *Wake up.* When Skeetah comes back out to the shed in a black wife-beater and jean shorts, he's already sweating. He wakes China like Mama used to wake us. The puppies roll away from him. He puts them in a larger box, where they scuffle and scratch unseen.

"She needs to get up," Skeet says. When we tell him that we are walking to the park, he is resolved. "She needs to work it out."

Skeetah puts her on a leash and then picks her up, slinging her over one shoulder. Her hind legs tangle in his thighs and make it hard for him to walk. He hasn't done this since she was a puppy. Then she would smile over his shoulder, licking the salt from his ear and neck. Now she frowns, her eyes half closed, nodding to sleep. A thin line of spit stretches to his back. Skeetah hoists her up again and again, and it is only when we have rounded the house, circled an old tub, the husk of a car I never remember seeing run, and jumped the ditch to the ragged asphalt road does he set her down. Pines sway on both sides with a sudden wind, and China lists with them. She is shaking. Her white hair dusts Skeetah's shoulders, which look hard. He is frowning. He yanks at her leash.

"Come on."

Junior bumps me in the side.

"I'll be right back." Junior says, and then he is running away toward the house.

China looks desultorily after him. Skeetah yanks her leash, again, and begins walking. She drags herself into motion, pads after him. The chain pulls at her ears, circles her head like a garrote. Skeetah walks leaning forward and doesn't look back. A hawk circles over our heads, riding a draft. It glides down in a spiral and then flaps off and vanishes in the feathery tops of the trees. Our house is the color of rust, nearly invisible under the oaks and behind the rubbish, lopsided. The cement bricks it sits on are the color of the sand. I follow Skeetah, who is walking so quickly, his figure dwindles in the high, hot day. I expect Junior to come back with a ball, but then I hear the grab and grind of bike tires, and he is peeling down the road, standing up. The dull black bike wobbles from side to side with each pedal. It is too small even for Junior to ride. When he swerves next to me, I realize it has no seat. This is why he is standing. I laugh.

"Where did you get that from?"

"Found it," Junior huffs. His smile is more like an exhale, and then he is huffing again, wheeling away from me to ride circles around Skeetah. Where China would have usually chased anyone on a bike, she saunters, head down, and ignores Junior. Skeetah ignores her in turn, walking straight ahead, his back curved, his silhouette one tense, worried line. The leash remains taut. I run to catch up with them.

As we walk into the center of Bois Sauvage,

away from our Pit, the houses appear gradually, hidden behind trees, closer to one another until there are only ragged lots of woods separating them. We walk past Big Henry's incongruously narrow shotgun house. Marquise's small pink house, which has only three windows and sits in a yard so clustered with azalea, seems like one more faded flower. Rich boy Franco's house is green, and for some reason, someone in his family has painted the bottom two feet of the tree's trunks in his yard white. Some older boys named Joshua and Christophe have a blue-gray house with a screened-in porch along the side with bougainvillea grown to riot under the oaks in the yard, and then there is Mudda Ma'am's yellow house faded to tan, choked with wisteria. Manny's trailer is on the other side of Bois Sauvage, away from this side of the neighborhood: the small Catholic church, the haphazard cemetery Skeetah mowed, the county park with the dirt parking lot, which strives to impose some order, some civility to Bois. It fails. The woods muddle the park's edges. Mimosa trees arch over it with a basketball player's long, graceful arms and drop pink flowers like balls. Pines sprout up in the ditches along the edge of the park, aside the netless basketball goals, under the piecemeal shade of the gap-toothed wooden play structure sinking into the earth, beside the stone picnic tables with their corners worn smooth by rain, even in the middle of the baseball field overgrown with grass. Maintenance workers, usually county convicts in green-and-white striped jumpsuits, come out once a year and halfheartedly try to trim back the encroaching wood, mow the grass set to bloom, the pine seedlings. The wild things of Bois Sauvage ignore them; we are left to seed another year.

Junior whoops away from me, the rubber of his underinflated tires sounding like a saw grinding through a stump. He swoops down in the ditch and upward, his bike sailing for a moment in the air before he lands, with a jolt so jarring it almost pinions him to the non-seat. He glances back and crows in pride, and then fishtails into the park. Skeetah still resolutely drags China, whose tail and head hang low in shame. He does not follow Junior into the park toward the basketball goals where people are playing.

"What you doing?"

"I'm making her walk it out."

"Y'all done already walked damn near two miles to the park. You don't think she sweated it out yet?"

"No." Skeetah snaps China's chain and

sets off at a trot, away from me and toward the graveyard. The heat is a wet blue blanket. I turn, follow Junior toward the court. Under the trees in the small, warped wooden bleachers, there are people sitting; I see long dark shadows framing their faces, long glistening legs crossed at the thigh, small shorts: two girls. Clouds trail the sun, and there are clear faces: Shaliyah, her cousin Felicia. I stop where I am, on the periphery of the court, opposite the shade under the oak tree and the bleachers, and I sit ungracefully in the grass. It feels like falling.

Manny is on the court, spinning, unfurling like a streamer to fling the ball into the basket. I wonder if she can tell his injury like I can, see it in the way his arm snaps back down after he lays up the ball too fast, as if he cannot extend it far enough. I wonder if she notices the way he swings his arm back and forth across his chest when he runs, as if he still holds hope that he can work past the rip, heal it, make his body as seamless and perfect as it used to be. I wonder if she notices that he favors it during sex, that he places most of his weight to his left so that he is always at my right ear, breathing. An ant crawls over the bone of my ankle, smelling with its antennae. I wave it away into the spiky grass. Sweat has bloomed on my shirt between my breasts, which throb gently. They always hurt now. My skin feels like the darkness of it is pulling heat, so I cannot help but glance toward the shade, see the bit of metal that Shaliyah wears on her arm catch the sun through the tree and throw it back gold. I will not sit there.

Big Henry, Marquise, Javon, Franco, Bone, and Randall are all on the court. They breathe in sobs. Cut curses. All shirtless except for Big Henry, they elbow each other, fall and let the concrete peel the skin of their hands, their knees, their elbows away like petals. There is an openmouthed excitement on each of their faces, the same kind of look that Skeetah has when he is wrapping China's chain around his fist, pulling it so that it indents into his skin, when he says, *Watch 'em, watch 'em — GET.* It's the same kind of face that most of them have when they are fucking. Under the oak, Shaliyah waves at her face with a candy box, fanning. She rubs one arm and then the other, and flips her hand as if she is flinging off the sweat she finds there. She is calm and self-possessed as a housecat; it is the way that all girls who only know one boy move. Centered as if the love that boy feels for them anchors them deep as a tree's roots, holds them still as the oaks, which don't uproot in hurricane wind. Love as certainty. It is the way I imagine China feels, even as I look back and see Skeetah running the perimeter of the baseball field, the leash still taut.

Manny calls a time-out, walks over to the goal nearest me, his eyes closed, his breath catching. He leans on the pole, stretches his arm, pulls back with his hips. Randall stares out at the road, his hands locked behind his head, at Skeetah and China running in the distance. Manny waves his arms in wide arcs, stretching out the muscles in them, eyeing the sidelines, and when he sees me sitting in the grass, feet away from him, his mouth twists.

"Come on," Manny yells.

The game begins again and Manny is like China when she is beset by mites in her ear. She runs in circles, chasing her tail, lashing her head against bushes, hoping to shake them out until Skeetah clasps her between his knees, holds her head, and treats them. Manny runs like that up and down the court, weaving through Big Henry and Marquise for layups. He pulls up for jump shots on Randall, who inevitably slaps them away and out of the court, and even though

189

Manny's shots begin falling short because of his bad arm, he still shoots, ignoring Franco's calls for passes. The look on Manny's face becomes China's the first time she caught the ear mites; she was still half grown, still short in the torso and long in the leg. When the ear mites became more agitated in the heat and began biting her frantically in her ear, she turned on the last stray dog of Junior's, black and brown and missing an ear, and she tore the other ear off. Bone passes Manny the ball, and Manny catches it, wincing at the pull in his arm, and he rushes Big Henry under the goal, even though Bone is the other big man inside, and even though Big Henry is easily half a foot taller than Manny and twice as big. Big Henry locks his knees, and they both fall. They slide across the concrete.

"This ain't football!" Marquise squeaks.

"Foul!" Manny yells, jumping to his feet.

"What the hell you talking about?" Big Henry asks, bewildered, picking himself up by his toes and fingertips.

"Just play!" Randall says. He waves his arm out toward the road, to where Skeetah has disappeared in the distance. "Let's just fucking play." He puts his hand on Manny, who is on his toes before Big Henry, and with a squeeze to Manny's shoulder, he is

Skeetah to China. Manny calms. The pace is slower, and when he calls his last time-out, he rests on the pole opposite Shaliyah. He waves his fingers, and she laughs.

The game fades away to a lazy, trickling finish, which is Randall pulling up from half-court and sinking the ball with a three-pointer. Marquise trots to the water spigot, Franco behind him. Randall lets the ball roll to a stop in the grass and walks over to me before putting his hands on his knees. Sweat drips from him like water, and he is winded as a horse. Big Henry alights in the grass next to me, graceful as a heron, and then falls back and throws his arms over his eyes because the sun surfaces from behind the clouds and blinds us.

"Good game," Randall says.

"Thanks," Big Henry breathes.

"What the hell is Skeet doing?" Randall spits sweat when he speaks.

Manny is walking over toward the bleachers, toward Shaliyah.

"Running China."

"I see that. But what for?"

"He wormed her yesterday and he say she sick today."

"Yeah?"

"I think he afraid he gave her too much."

Randall screws his mouth up like he's eating a sour scupadine; he is chewing the pink inside of his cheek.

"What can he do." It is a statement. I shrug and look under the bleachers. Shaliyah must have bought Manny a sports drink because he is standing under the oak and tilting the bottle back so that the liquid runs down straight into his throat. The sun is shimmering through the oak leaves and catching his skin, so his whole body shines fractured as the glass scar on his face.

"What?"

"What can he do?" This time Randall asks it as a question.

"Nothing," Big Henry says. His arms are flung out at his sides. He is looking at me. He's not really fat, but the bigness of him is all over: his hands like baseball mitts, his head like a melon, his chest like a steel drum barbecue pit, his legs like branches reaching from an indomitable trunk. "Can't do nothing," Big Henry says. I feel like he can see through my shirt to my swollen breasts, my stomach that pouches just too far when I sit so that it is more than fat. He grins, tentative and gentle as he moves, but it is like an afterthought.

"Well, shit." Randall folds himself in half and wipes his face on his basketball shorts. "Shit."

"You ready for the summer league game tomorrow?"

"Yeah." Randall's voice is muffled in his shorts; the cloth makes it quaver.

"They going to pay for basketball camp this year?"

"Don't know. Coach say it's between me and Bodean."

"Nervous?"

"They only choose one, and I score two to Bodean's one every game. I work harder than him."

"You already imagining all them scouts at the camp, ain't you?" Big Henry laughs.

"Figure I look best in a black jersey." Randall leans back and cradles his skull in his hands. "Or baby blue." Randall smiles, but I know that a part of him is serious, that he already knows what college he wants to go to.

Big Henry pushes himself up off his elbows. Manny sits down next to Shaliyah on the bleachers, leans over to her, rubs his sweaty shoulder into hers. She squeals and tries to jump up, but he clutches her to him. She squirms and squeals again, laughing. The sun is bearing down on me, burning, evaporating the sweat, water, and blood from me to leave my skin, my desiccated organs, my brittle bones: my raisin of a body. If I could, I would reach inside of me and pull out my heart and that tiny wet seed that will become the baby. Let them go first so the rest won't hurt so much.

"That grass going to make you itch."

"I know," Randall says. He stretches the waistband of his shorts. "Water." He walks to the spigot across the grass, and he is fluid and tall and black.

"I know you hot out here." Big Henry touches the back of my hand with two fingers, presses.

"Yeah." Manny is rubbing the sweat from his forehead into Shaliyah's cheek. Her squeal becomes a shriek. Her teeth are so white.

"You want to come sit in my car? It's parked in the shade. Windows down." Big Henry glances over at the bleachers and then rolls to his side and stands in one quick motion. Sometimes I forget he was an athlete.

"Okay." The clouds are slower now, hang off in the distance above the tree line as if they are wary of the sun. "Okay." I look at the ground when I rise, when I turn away from the court, when I walk. Barely resisting the urge to look back. I don't even see when Junior barrels up next to me, whooping, swerving at me on his bike. He is laughing. Under the trees in the dirt parking lot, Javon is parked. His car gleams like the approaching sunset. Marquise is leaning on his bumper. Randall runs over behind us, reclines on Big Henry's hood and the front windshield so that his wet back looks like pudding. Inside the car, Big Henry and I sit with the doors open, one leg out, heads back. Big Henry plays Outkast.

Randall makes jokes and Big Henry laughs. When the sun rests on the rim of the trees, we leave, and Manny is on the court now with his girl. They are playing a game of one-on-one, and he is taunting her, knocking the ball out of her hand so that it ricochets across the court. Her laughter carries on the softening pink wind. Big Henry closes his door. I slam mine, and Randall scoots over to the passenger side of the windshield. Junior holds the top of the door, still standing on his bike, and Big Henry folds his big paw over Junior's. Big Henry taps the gas and then eases, and this is how we follow Skeetah and China, who are both running now, both sucking dark and blazing bright under the setting sun and the scudding clouds, all the way home.

The puppies are whining for milk. They have been listening to Daddy hammering at the coop, dismantling it nail by board, into the pine-black evening. They writhe against each other. Skeetah lifts them out one by one by their necks, sets them on the floor before China, who is still nosing the ground. He has not taken off her chain yet, so it pools in the dirt next to her, as heavy and sharp as a bike chain. She breathes through her mouth, but something wet seems to catch at the back of her throat with each exhale. She nods with each breath. Her legs are still, but the sweat Skeetah worked up on her catches the red dust on her coat, channels it so that it runs down her back like watercolor paint. Under the bulb, my arms seem blacker, seem dirtier than I've ever seen them. I pull my hair back, tie it by taking a tendril of hair from the bottom and knotting it around the rest. I want it out of my face. Mama was wrong: I have no glory. I have nothing.

"Randall!" Daddy yells. It is strange to hear the night without his hammering.

"Yeah," Randall says from the doorway of the shed. Big Henry is beside him. Junior is clinging to Randall's back, grasping at his shoulders, his biceps, losing his grip and sliding with the sweat. Skeetah looks toward the door, shakes his head at Daddy's call, China's chain slack in his hands. She looks as if she is eating the earth.

"Come here."

Randall sighs, grabs Junior's forearms while he bends over and hoists him back up.

"Yeah, yeah."

I slide into his place in the doorway next to Big Henry so I can see everything. Junior is licking his fingers as Randall walks, swiping them in Randall's ears.

"Ugh. I told you to stop." Randall rubs his ears, but I know he can't get the wet out. "I'm going to put you down."

"No, Randall. Please."

"Well, then stop. That shit is so nasty." Randall stops, links his long arms into a seat under Junior's butt, and hoists again. "What?"

Daddy has only knocked down one of the chicken coop's walls. The chickens wander drunken and bewildered around his feet, seemingly mystified that he is dismantling their house, even though they haven't roosted in it in years. In the half-light from the bulb from the shed and Daddy's headlights, they look black. Daddy lets his hammer fall, and the chickens scatter, fluttering away like leaves in a wind.

"The storm, it has a name now. Like the worst, she's a woman. Katrina."

"There's another storm?" Randall asks.

"What you think I been talking about? I knew it was coming," Daddy says. *Like the worst,* I repeat. *A woman.* He shakes his head, frowns at the coop. "We going to try something."

"What?"

"I want you to get on my tractor and I'm going to direct you to this wall right here." Daddy points at the longer wall. "And we going to knock this damn thing over."

Randall hoists again. Junior's face rests on Randall's shoulder.

"I can't drive that thing."

"All you got to do is put it in gear and press the gas. You know how to steer."

"We got to do it in the dark?"

Daddy steps to the side and I can see his head, barely coming up to Randall's shoulder. His face says he is smiling, but his voice says he is not.

"What you mean, 'We gotta do it at night?' That depression out in the Gulf done became a hurricane. We ain't got enough wood to board the windows up and you going to sit here and ask me why we gotta do this at night?"

Randall is silent. Junior is sliding again.

"She headed toward Florida. She come

198

up slantways and who you think she going to hit?'

"Florida," Randall sighs. "Don't they usually fade out after they hit?" Randall doesn't hoist Junior, who is trying to clutch at Randall's waist with his feet. Junior is losing. Junior's chin disappears behind Randall's shoulder, and his head sinks to Randall's shoulder blades. "All's I'm saying is that you could drive it better than me."

"I know I can." Daddy waves away the compliment. Usually when Randall gives them, they work. "But I can't see to get it at the right angle. If you do it, I can tell you how to hit it so that the whole thing comes down at once."

Junior's feet are at Randall's knees. Junior comes down in the dirt and barely catches himself. I want to call him back to the shed because I know he's getting on Daddy's nerves and will only make Daddy worse, but I don't. He is the Patroclus to Randall's Achilles tonight.

"Come on." Daddy walks into the darkness without waiting to see if Randall follows. Randall rounds the corner with his hands linked behind his neck, shaking his head. Junior shadows him.

Skeetah releases China from her chain, and then loops the metal around and around his forearm and shoulder until it is a solid silver wing. China pads to her corner, flops down all at once, instead of her usual graceful sitting first, the gentle roll onto her flank, her side. She lays her head on the linoleum that Skeetah must have swept clean, because she does not raise dust. Skeetah walks toward the door, lays the chain on the oil drum, arranges it just so, lingers over the links. He cannot bear to look at her.

"You think that did it?" Big Henry asks.

"I don't know," Skeetah says.

"Maybe she just tired," I say to them, because I hope the words will pull Skeetah's brow smooth, untangle the yarn-knotted furrow of it. Hope that they will make him stop looking at his hands. Big Henry shifts from foot to foot, leans on the door jamb. When he moves, the locusts and cicadas and grasshoppers sound loud, disgruntled.

"You ran her for a while."

"Yeah." Skeetah plays with the links the way he used to play with liver, with oatmeal, with beets from the can shaped like tubes of cranberry sauce. This was before he grew older, before his knees gained muscle and his shoulders knotted and he began shoveling his food, lima beans or mushrooms or chitterlings, as if he didn't care what he ate anymore.

"And she still nursing. She probably just tired."

Daddy's tractor growls from the darkness, bullies the insects. It rolls over branches, discarded plastic garbage cans, detached fenders. They crack and break. Daddy leaves splinters. Randall and Junior follow in its wake, stumbling through the detritus. Skeetah shakes his head.

"He's going to have them out there all gotdamn night." Skeetah grabs China's bowl from where he has secreted it high on a shelf; it is so high he has to stand on his toes. Randall or Big Henry could have grabbed it without even reaching. Daddy leaves the tractor running and swings one leg over and is down. Skeetah pours China's food, sets it on top of the drum. "Hold on."

Big Henry moves to let Skeetah walk out of the doorway, and then he smiles at me. The moon shines like a fluorescent bulb behind his head. A piping wind blows, and where my hair escapes and touches my face, it feels like a spider's web unanchored, adrift. Randall climbs up the tractor and sits. Junior hoists himself up and begins scaling the metal.

"What you doing?" Daddy asks Junior.

"Helping Randall."

"No you're not. Get down."

"I won't be in the way."

"Get down."

"Please."

"I said no."

Randall scoots forward on the seat, motions behind him.

"He can sit behind me. He won't be in the way."

Junior is leaning back to please Daddy, to make him think that he is on the verge of obeying, of jumping off, but still he grips the seat with his hands, and he does not step down.

"Please, Daddy."

Daddy clears his throat and spits. His T-shirt has a gaping hole at the neck, and it is uneven at the hem, as if someone has been pulling at it.

"Hurry up," Daddy says.

Daddy waves Junior up to the tractor, and Junior climbs up, slides behind Randall, wraps his arms around Randall's waist with the expectant look of a child on a carousel ride. Skeetah bangs out of the back door of the house with a cup of something in his hand. Moths flit about his head like mussed ash. He walks by and I smell bacon drippings.

"She has to eat," Skeetah says as he dribbles the drippings, the color of pine sap, over China's dried food. China looks at him, then away. He slides the bowl toward her, but she ignores him. His eyes are a darkness in his face. "Come on."

China grimaces at him, a showing of tooth and red gum. The puppies are twitching toward her over the linoleum, as if they smell the milk through her breasts, through the pink meat of her. Her nipples look like chewed-up gum.

"Come on." Daddy waves the tractor forward. "This the corner. Right here."

"All right," Skeetah breathes, heedless of the creeping puppies as he pushes China's bowl so close to her that she could lay her head down in it. The lines between Skeet's muscles looked filled in with charcoal.

"All right!" Daddy yells. "Now keep coming straight forward, right there." Randall guns the tractor and it surges forward. Junior's head snaps back, but he hangs on. There is a crack of wood and then a metal whine as Randall presses the gas again and the tractor jerks forward. "Hold it! You got chicken wire stuck in the grille."

Daddy tugs at the wire, pulls at the grille and hood. He yanks, leans forward so far he almost puts his face in the grille, detangles,

203

and then he begins pulling at the wire again. Randall is still.

"Do it," Skeetah commands China.

China's ears are flat as plastic knives laid on her head and her mouth is wet and pink as uncooked chicken, except here the bone shows. She is quivering, her muscles beset by a multitude of tics. She is shaking all over, now eye to eye with Skeetah, seemingly ignoring the dirt-red puppy rounding her bowl, waddling for milk. He is the one that is a model of the father, of Kilo; he is the fattest, the most well fed, the bully. Turgid with the promise of living. When their eyes eventually open, I think that his will be the first.

The tractor idles and the engine turns, sounds as if it going to move.

"Don't do it!" Daddy yells against his tugging, but his grunts eat the *Don't,* and I don't know what Randall hears, but he lets up on the brake and slips it in gear, and the tractor eases forward. "Stop!" Daddy yells. He is pulling back, his hand clenched in the wire, and he twists so hard his arm looks long and ropy.

The red puppy creeps forward, rounds China's bowl, noses her tit. China is rolling, rising. The rumble of the tractor is her growl. Her toes are pointed, her head raised.

Skeetah falls back. The red puppy undulates toward her; a fat mite. China snaps forward, closes her jaw around the puppy's neck as she does when she carries him, but there is no gentleness in it. She is all white eyes. She is chewing. She is whipping him though the air like a tire eaten too short for Skeetah to grab.

"Stop!" Skeetah yells. "Stop!"

Randall puts the tractor in gear, switches it to park, but the small hillock the coop is on pulls the tractor back as the engine idles.

"No!" Daddy calls.

Daddy flings his hand free. There is oil on it. He holds to his chest. His shirt is covered in oil. Daddy's jaw is slack. He is walking toward the light of the shed. The oil on his T-shirt turns red. The sound coming out his open mouth is like growling.

"No!" Skeetah calls.

The blood on Daddy's shirt is the same color as the pulpy puppy in China's mouth. China flings it away from her. It thuds on the tin and slides. Randall comes running. Big Henry kneels with Daddy in the dirt, where what was Daddy's middle, ring, and pinkie finger on his left hand are sheared off clean as fallen tree trunks. The meat of his fingers is red and wet as China's lips.

Skeetah kneels in the dirt, feeling for the

mutilated puppy; he knocks into metal drums and toolboxes and old chainsaws with his head and his shoulders.

"Why did you?" Skeetah wails.

"Why?" Daddy breathes to Randall and Big Henry standing over him, the blood sluicing down his forearm. They are gripping Daddy's wrist, trying to stop the bleeding. Skeetah is punching the metal he meets. China is bloody-mouthed and bright-eyed as Medea. If she could speak, this is what I would ask her: *Is this what motherhood is?*

THE SEVENTH DAY: GAME DOGS AND GAME MEN

There were too many of us in the car on the way to the hospital. Daddy, with his hand wrapped in a red-blooming towel, sat in the front seat. Big Henry drove. Junior and Randall and I sat in the backseat, the smell of blood like the Gulf when the tide's low. That and the smell of dog, like China was in the middle of the driver's seat, licking her whiskers with her bloody tongue, nosing the absent Skeet. Daddy sounded like a larger version of the puppies, his breathing whining in and out. I wondered if he noticed it through the pain. His neck was stringy and long as a cooked turkey's. We took the back way to the hospital, through miles of woods, lonely houses like possums in the dark, half caught and then left behind by the headlights. Junior let me hold his hand. When we arrived at the hospital, Randall and Big Henry half dragged, half carried Daddy through the doors to orderlies who were standing there as if they were waiting for us, and they put him in a wheelchair. We sat in the lobby. The orderlies wheeled Daddy next to us. They left us to whisper with the night admitting nurse, who rose from behind her desk, her scrubs pink with red hearts on them, wearing red Crocs, carrying a clipboard. Daddy bent over in the wheelchair, and the blood ran like a starving stream down his thigh, soaked into the seat, and the nurse began to ask questions and looked at Daddy as he sat up, his head rolling back, and saw his hand. The nurse had a gap between her two front teeth like Mama. She tucked the clipboard under her arm, grabbed the handles, asked Daddy's name. Randall answered as she wheeled Daddy away and followed.

Junior fell asleep sitting upright in his chair and sagged over on Big Henry, who sat slumped over, his elbows on his knees, trying to rub the blood off his hands. It pinked and spread over his skin like a jellyfish. A white couple sat three chairs down from us; the man was bald with wispy hairs like dandelion fluff around his ears, and the woman had red hair that stood up in a curly thin afro the way that older white women's hair often does. Their clothes were clean and faded along the ironed edges. Every few minutes, the woman would rub the gold crucifix at her chest, and the man would take off his silver-framed bifocals and polish them. They studied the receptionist station the whole time we were there and never looked over to Big Henry and his hands, Junior's feet that kicked in his sleep as if he were dreaming of falling, and me. I wondered who they were waiting on, but I never found out because a nurse came for them and they disappeared. The waiting room was scrubbed clean and pale; it smelled of Pine-Sol, coffee, and weariness.

When Randall and Daddy walked out of the long hall, it was three o'clock in the morning. Randall looked older than Daddy under the lights, and Daddy's eyes were glazed as if he was drunk, clear and shiny as the glass water jugs I'd filled, but he was not mean. He shuffled along next to Randall, his hand wrapped up to the wrist in gauze and tape so that it looked like a webworm moth nest wound tight in a pecan tree, a yarn of larvae eating at the ripe green leaves beneath to burst forth in black-winged flurry in the throat-closing heat of fall. Only Daddy's hand would not emerge whole and quivering. Daddy's hand would be not the moths but the bare branches, like bones, left under the husk.

Now Daddy sleeps. He hasn't slept this late since the week after Mama died, when I found him at the table, on the sofa, beside the sink in the bathroom, in the hallway, his torso over the threshold, his legs out. Cans and bottles, mostly beer, lay about him like smaller versions of himself wherever he was. The sun is over the tops of the trees, flooding down into the small clearing around the house. All of the fans are blowing at all of the windows, so the house hums as if it is alive. Big Henry sleeps on the sofa. Randall is snoring in his room. Daddy's door is closed. The chicken coop stands with three walls still, the tractor lightly touching it as if providing a thick, rubber-muscled shoulder to lean on. Junior is watching a rerun of *Reading Rainbow,* the volume so low it is barely louder than the fans. He does not turn it up.

We left Skeetah in the shed last night. He did not run with us to the car. When we came back to the house, he was asleep in his bed in the room he shares with Randall, wrapped up in his sheet, so I only saw the lump of him. He wore his shoes still, and they stuck out of his blanket like bristles on a toothbrush. In place of the curtain he'd dragged a piece of tin he'd salvaged, probably from Mother Lizbeth and Papa Joseph's roof, and wedged it across the doorway of the shed. China was a lump, as pale as biscuit dough, laying out in the dirt, her chain attached to a car's half-eaten skeleton. He'd separated her from the puppies. When I woke up this morning, he was gone. And so was China.

Daddy is propped up on pillows when I walk into the bedroom, a bowl of chicken noodle soup on a potholder before me, a little of it dribbling around the edges. He is eating crackers one by one, placing them between his lips and then pulling them in. His chewing sounds like crumpled notebook paper. I put down the bowl and the spoon on the night table, cluttered with a glass of water from the tap, a Budweiser can he's been using as an ashtray, and his medicine for pain and infection. His arm is resting on a hill of old blankets and crocheted pillows, which Randall piled last night. Daddy is watching the thirteen-inch black-and-white television sitting on the wide, mirrored dresser across from the bed. He hasn't changed a thing here since Mama died: there are small glass candleholders with tall peach candles wedged into them, and two small bunches of fake flowers in squat vases that look like cups that Mama placed at both ends of the dresser. There are pictures of us, Polaroids, which Mama wedged between the glass and the frame of the mirror. There is one picture of her and Daddy standing chest to chest, in a frame. Her hands are on his shoulders, her hair ironed straight and pulled back smooth, her dress cut open in the front so that it shows her collarbone, as dense and burnished and beautiful as a brass doorknob. She smiles without opening her mouth. Daddy doesn't smile at all, but his hands are around her back, and he has that serious, prideful tilt of his head that Skeetah has when he is standing with China at a dogfight, showing her off before the mad scramble, the cutting barks and teeth.

"Play with the antenna," Daddy says. His voice sounds dry as the cracker. He leans over and pulls a wicker tray from next to the bed and drags it across his lap. The bowl wobbles in his left hand. He spills some of the soup on the potholder when he sets it down.

There is only static. I grab the right antenna, yank it up.

"Down," Daddy says.

The box fan in the window is not pushing any air in the room. Every day seems hotter than the last. I grab the left antenna, split

212

them one from the other like a wishbone.

"There."

"Katrina has made landfall in Florida . . . miles from Miami." It is the local news. The weatherwoman is speaking with the anchor, and she is pointing at the interactive screen before her, but the television is so old and the resolution so bad that the map looks like concrete, and the storm, an oil stain.

"Early reports say that there are some dead. Does anyone . . . idea of where . . . projection of storm?" Mike's voice is even, smooth, when we catch it through the static.

". . . unclear. The storm is currently a category one . . . could weaken . . . could change." The woman's hair is light; she may be blonde.

"So what would you advise our listeners to . . . Rachel?" The TV gives a static moan, so I split the two parts of the antenna further.

". . . prepare as well as they can for the storm. Katrina is on the . . . if it does not weaken . . . moving northwest, they should also prepare . . . government will issue orders for mandatory evacuation."

"So what does this mean?"

"This means that our viewers may . . . preparations to remain in their homes for the hurricane, and instead may want to begin . . . possible evacuation." Rachel appears to be smiling.

"I can't see, Esch."

I step aside. Mike turns to the camera.

". . . highways will be open for evacuation. It is better to leave earlier . . . hours . . . stuck in traffic."

"You're still in the way," Daddy says. He blows his soup and stirs it with his spoon, but he does not eat, and instead he lets his good hand drop behind the wicker across his lap.

Mama smiles serenely from the photo. She has no idea that three years later, she will be bleeding to death in the bed that Daddy now lays in with three of his fingers missing. In one of the Polaroids, I am dancing in the kitchen. It is at one of Mama and Daddy's parties where his friends, and one or two of hers, would gather to drink beer and eat oysters and potatoes, fried golden in the same oil and silt and salt. Mama would plug in the cassette deck radio in the kitchen, put in tapes by Bobby "Blue" Bland, Denise LaSalle, and Little Milton, and I would dance while the crowd clapped and laughed at my jerky hand-swinging, all of us sweating in the kitchen. Mama would say, *That's my baby, my dancing girl,* and I would kick extra or wave my arms harder.

214

The music would wring me dry. Now I look at myself and at Mama, at the leaping Randall and the dark-eyed and grinning Skeet, who looks in his picture as if he is worm-ridden, and barely resist snatching the pictures from the mirror, taking them to my room, laying them across my bed to attempt to decode them, to fit them together like a jumbo puzzle.

"Preparation . . . key," Rachel says.

I shut Daddy's door.

China is breathe-barking. Every time she inhales, she exhales with a bark, flat and strong as a slap. The sound is carrying through the woods. On the back step, I hear her as if she is drawing closer, but I do not see her appearing with Skeetah at her side. There is only the day, hotter than the one that came before it, dense as water approaching boiling. And then her voice catches. There are other dogs, in the woods near the house, on the other side of the Pit, down the winding, gravel-eaten length of the street, and they bark with her. They ring her like a chorus. Their voices crackle across the sky, all places at once. Somewhere out there, I know, Skeetah is in the middle of these dogs, pulling them to him. He is the hand on the leash. He is the palm. He flexes and they come, he looses his grip and they spread to the red dirt, the pines, the creeks, the oaks. They howl. They hack.

China gives a great shout, and all at once, they are silent.

Randall's game is today. I wipe the bathroom mirror with my palm, and the glass cracks at the edges, the reflective surface flaking away like glitter. I oil my hands, rub them through my hair, which calms into ringlets. I pick two bobby pins that Mama left in a plastic case under the sink, and I slide them into my hair behind my ears, so that it frames my face like a pillow. Junior is singing along with the television, the words indecipherable, his voice higher pitched than a girl's. I smile, turn my head to the right, to the left. This is what I look like, I think. This is the lie. Skeetah is a smell before I see him: the oily sweat of dog, pine needles growing green, and an unwashed stink like milk set too long out in a hot kitchen. He stops in the doorway. I run Vaseline across my lips, rub them together, try to make them glossy.

"What was that noise?"

"What you talking about?"

"China, barking like crazy."

Outside, Randall is dribbling. I can see

him out of the window, shooting, throwing the ball at the house when it rebounds, catching it, throwing it again. The sun is directly overhead, pouring down into the clearing where he practices. He is warming up. The ball is not full with air, so each time that he touches the ball, it is more like a slap.

"Nothing."

The neck on Skeetah's shirt is stretched as a bib. He looks down at it, shakes his head, grabs it with both hands, and pulls. The shirt rips. The newly sprouted hair on his head is prickly as Velcro.

"It didn't sound like nothing."

The shirt is black, so what is wet on it is sweat. It could not be blood. I would know. Skeetah drops the tee, and it slaps wetly on the tile. The smell of him moves through the room like smoke from burning wet leaves.

"She forgot."

"Forgot what?"

"Who I was yesterday."

"Don't you mean she forgot the puppy?"

Randall catches the ball each time it springs from the backboard and throws it back up. He is not letting it touch the earth. He is saving it from making that flat, collapsing sound, again and again. His lips turned down at the corners, smiling.

"No. She forgot me."

Skeetah bends, turns on the tap in the tub, lifts the hook for the shower. The spray from the water is cold, a fine mist.

"How long you going to keep China on the chain?"

"Long as it takes." Skeetah kicks his shoes across the floor; once, twice. "As long as it takes." He peels his socks away like banana peels, and the smell of them is rotten. My stomach shudders.

Big Henry is perched on the hood of his car. Marquise sits next to him, leaned over almost double so that he looks like a crab, all back and arms and legs, as he rolls a blunt on the blue metal. China faces Big Henry, tongue lolling pink and straight as an exclamation mark. She smiles and then grimaces, over and over, so that she has two faces. The pink of the Pit on her coat is overlaid by a brown scum, which etches the lines of her muscles in her shoulder, haunch, and back clean and clear as marker. Big Henry lists sideways, tipping lightly as if he is on the verge of running. I put my hands in my short shorts, look down at the tennis shoes that I have scrubbed until they are as close to white as they can get: off white, a dirty cream the color of egg whites cooked with pepper. Big Henry turns away from China, who is grimacing again. I sit close to Big Henry's windshield on the other side of Marquise, who scoots forward to make room for me.

"You think he ready?"

"Who?" Marquise asks.

"I wasn't talking to you, fool." Big Henry laughs before biting it off with glances at China and me.

"Skeetah?" I ask. Big Henry shakes his head across the careful shifting and picking and measuring that Marquise is signaling with the hitch of his back.

"Randall."

Right now Randall would probably be squeezed into the bathroom with Skeet, either hissing at him to hurry up and get out of the shower, or washing off with a rag and soap over the sink, dripping suds all over the counter, the floor, the toilet, taken to ignoring Skeet, probably thinking about the game. He has been too tall to wash in the sink for years.

"He fast. He'll be ready soon."

"I mean the game." Big Henry smiles a little then, just a dimpling at the corner of his lips.

"Oh." I nod, my face hot. "He been

practicing all day. He ready." My sweat is making the backs of my thighs slick; I am sliding along the metal like mud gone downhill in a bad rain, coming to a slow, sticky stop on Marquise's back.

"Well, damn, Esch, I didn't know you wanted me like that." Marquise turns and smirks around the blunt he is licking shut. He winks at me, his tongue white at the edges, bits of the cigar paper flaking off and sticking like food. I know that wink, that grin. He smiled like that when he was done when we had sex for the last time about a year ago, when he was wiping himself, turned away from me; he threw that smile like salt over the shoulder. I grip the seam where the windshield joins the hood, and I pull myself away from him so that we are no longer touching. I do not like his smile.

"Leave her alone, Marquise."

"I'm just fucking with her."

"Too hot out here for you to be fucking with anybody."

I slide down the side of the car, stand, look down so I can pull my shorts so they are not bunching in my crotch, showing me. When I finally look up, Big Henry is looking at me with the same dazed half intensity he showed China, as if he is staring but thinking of something else. I shrug, and then when I realize there was no question asked, I shrug again.

"I'ma get Randall." I break into a walk and stutter to a run. Feel them watching.

When we leave for the game, Daddy is asleep. I leave a full cup of water and a packet of crackers on the bedside table and push his bottles of medicine closer together so they are easier for him to reach. He sleeps with his mouth open, his face slack with medicine, and drools. Where Junior's or Randall's sleep faces are babyish, fat and smooth, Daddy's sleeping face is Skeetah's: puckered, the skin pulling: the face frozen in fight. From the dresser, Mama beams at me, hands caressing Daddy, smiling.

I am glad to be sitting in the backseat by the window in the car, Junior's bony rump squirming on my lap, Skeetah in the middle pulling at the blunt, Marquise next to him at the other window, opaque through a cloud of smoke. Big Henry's head could be any other boy's head under his baseball cap, and Randall leans on the headrest, his eyes closed, everything still but his eyelids jumping like dragonflies. I do not think that he is dreaming. Junior shifts, and I hold him tight; he is my shield.

The summer league game is in the gym at

St. Catherine's elementary school. Ms. Dedeaux told us once that the elementary school used to actually be the black school for the district before the schools were desegregated in 1969, after the last big hurricane, when people were too tired finding their relatives' uprooted bodies, reburying them, sleeping on platforms that used to be the foundations of their houses, under tents, biking or walking miles for freshwater, for food, to still fight the law outlawing segregation. Daddy went to this school when it was all black, and Mama, too. On one of their blues nights after I had danced myself to shaking, Mama told the story of how they met, that Daddy would not stop pulling her hair in the hallway, making fun of her little-girl pigtails since the rest of her was so grown, and of how she turned around one day and hit him in the chest so hard he lost his breath. Then he stopped pulling her hair, but started leaving her presents in her desk, instead: pieces of pecan candy he'd stolen from his grandma, whole pecans wrapped in newspaper, blackberries dusted with ditch dirt, hot from the sun, leaking black juice. That was their beginning.

Now there's construction paper taped in makeshift galleries along the wall by the door. They flutter in the wind driven by the industrial fan, and at the concession stand a woman with finger waves, a gold tooth, and lips the color of azaleas rolls her eyes at Junior, who drags his feet when we pass her. Moles fade to freckles in a messy paint splatter across her face. Bags of potato chips are laid out on her folding table in rows, one against the other, orderly and even. I grab Junior's bony shoulders and push him to the top of the stands where we sit.

The inside of the gym is dark, the steel ceiling beams lost in a humid haze like cloud cover; it is hotter here at the top of the bleachers. Big Henry sits next to Marquise, who sprawls on one elbow and tries to wheedle a sports drink out of him. Randall is already on the court doing drills, tossing the ball to his teammates as they weave in and out of each other in knots and make lay-ups, palm rebounds in lazy arcs. Skeetah sinks into the bleachers until his butt is resting on the floor, his legs kicked out so that his soles are to the court, his arms spread wide across the seat behind him. The corded gather of him eases. He wipes his forehead with the hem of his shirt and it beads again. He nods languidly. He is smiling, his teeth white and even: glistening bone. He is high.

"You're surprised I came." Skeetah speaks

to the court, his smile grown slack. He blinks solemnly.

"Yeah."

"What's been done been done." Skeet shrugs, his shoulders rise and settle like sleek feathers. "China going to come back to me. To herself. Soon."

"You bring them back by her to feed yet?"

"Yeah. I held her muzzle shut. Every time she move her head toward them, I pop her on her nose."

"You think the other three puppies going to make it?"

"Fucking right they going to make it." Skeetah lays his head back on the bleacher behind his shoulders. He swallows and his Adam's apple slides like a mouse down the gullet of a snake. "This ain't beating me."

Junior is tapping me on my leg, beating out Morse code.

"Esch?"

"Go 'head. Stay away from the concession stand."

Junior smiles, teeth missing in the front, and then swallows it and tries to look trust-worthy enough to stay away from the snack table.

"And don't try to steal nothing, neither."

Junior squeals, his mouth turned down at the corners to plead.

"No."

"Here." Big Henry is reaching into his pocket, cupping loose change like marbles. He drops the coins in Junior's hand, which Junior cups and holds before him. He leaps down the stands. His T-shirt billows behind him like a limp flag.

"Not even a thank-you." Marquise rubs his braids.

"Thank you!" Junior screams.

Big Henry rests his elbows on his knees, shakes his head. Huddled over, his face a surprise emerging from the broad bowl of back. He glances over at me, and it is as if he passed the money to me, as if he dropped it in my hand like chalky pecan candy, like mealy pecans, sun-blackened blackberries. Skeetah is blinking half-lidded at the game, where Randall and his team-mates are already glazed with sweat, shining darkly in the dim light like the rain-drenched stone that lines the muddy beach of the pit. Big Henry asks the air in front of him, but everyone knows who he is speaking to.

"You want something?"

His hands are so different from Manny's, so large, and they are slow-moving as the sheaves of the stunted palm trees planted at odd places along the beach, alien to the Mississippi Gulf, as they bear the dragging wind made slow by the barrier islands.

"No," I say. I have to go to the bathroom.

I maneuver around clumps of boys and girls, some I go to school with, some from Bois Sauvage and St. Catherine, until I reach the bottom of the bleachers. Still, the gym is more than half empty. All of the parents, six or seven of them, and their toddlers sit on the first row only. Girls slap and slide along the benches while still sitting; boys wear white tees, sleeveless shirts, caps, basketball shorts. There is laughter, shrill calls. Everyone is flirting, saying in nudges and jokes and blushing what they would do in private.

On the court, Randall is already blinking hard at the sweat blinding him. His shirt sticks to him on the sides, close as a bud. He goes up for a rebound, rises up out of the cluster of players, but they buzz angrily, and he falls. The referee whistles, and Randall walks to the foul line, bouncing on the balls of his feet. Nothing about him seems to touch anything else: the court, the ball, his shirt that he picks at so that his skin can breathe. He is a bayou crane, alighting so he doesn't even sink into the black marsh before taking off in flight.

"Excuse you."

Bumping into him is a shock. He is solid, stocky, with the kind of chest men get when their bulky muscles start softening to seed. His fresh fade has a tinge of red in the brown, which lights up when he tilts his head at me as it catches the light coming in through the door. He has a gold grill in, the same grill that he had in on the day that he and Skeetah mated China and Kilo. He opens his mouth further, and the letters are stamped in spit-shined jewels, one on each tooth, into the gold: R-I-C-O.

"Sorry."

Manny stands to one side behind him. He is wearing blue, and he and Shaliyah and Rico must be fresh from the barbershop, for his curls have been cut close so that they are only black waves, but his face stands out without the hair framing it, beautiful: the strong nose, the jaw leading to a hollow where there is a fresh purple mark, the shiny scar on his face making the rest of the skin even more vivid. He jerks his head up, raises his eyebrow in the easy *whatsup* way boys acknowledge each other. To me. Shaliyah is in sandals and a miniskirt next to him, all dips and swells like a badly rutted road worn smooth by the rain. She wears gold earrings, bracelet, and a necklace even here, where we don't have to pay for admission.

"What's up?" Rico says, and I am veering over the edge of the court as he barrels past me. Manny pulls at Shaliyah's hand, and they follow Rico. I wade through a tide of kids at the door, all Junior's age or younger, trading small candies they are sucking from wax paper and salty cheesy chips and neon cold drinks they've scraped the labels off of with their small, bony fingers. The bathroom is around the back of the gym in a separate, smaller building, and I run to it.

The bathroom is dark, darker even than the gym, and it is small, with only one sink and two dark green stalls. The walls are gray cinder block. I go in the stall farthest from the door, lock it behind me, pee while squatting and then flush, wipe down the seat, and sit on the bowl, which is narrow enough to feel like a seat. I wedge my nose between my thighs and breathe. My stomach and my shirt, bunched together, feel like a pillow wedged in my lap. I wish I could pull it out. My eyes burn. Inside my chest, a machete swings, back and forth, up and down, breaking the living, clearing a pulpy path behind it where green things lie, leaking. My face is wet against my leg. I stay like that until it stops, until the toilet stops ticking, the door creaks open, and the machete pauses, smelling of sap and metal.

I wipe my face with my shirt, open the stall, and he is standing there, pulling the outside door shut behind him, sealing the darkness.

"This is the girls'," I say weakly.

"Been thinking about you," says Manny, and then he has pushed me back into the stall, closed it behind us, grabbed my arms and turned us so that he is sitting on the toilet. He unzips his pants, and I grab his dick hard enough to hurt. I want it to hurt. He doesn't wince, intent on my loose shorts. He pulls me down on him so I am straddling him, and then he is inside. It is easy and wet. He grips my shoulders, pulls me down hard, rolls back away from me, pulls me down again, his face in my chest. It is the first time he has grabbed me over my waist, kept his hands on me closer to my face. Touched me.

"Wait," he says, and then he is making me stand up, pulling off my shorts and underwear, bearing me back down on him. My clothes catch on one ankle, hang like they're half-pinned from a clothesline. We have never done it like this. His hands are on my ass, and he tries to look down, to see, but it brings us face-to-face. Sweat gathers at his hairline, catches on the red grooves left by

the clippers, like ant trails, across the top of
his forehead. He grimaces, looking down,
away, over my shoulder, up to the ceiling.

I grab his face.

Under my hands, his jaw, freshly shaved,
feels like a cat's tongue. My fingers are
black as bark against his paler skin.

He will look at me.

He shrugs, twists his head to the side.
Flipping like a caught fish. I roll my hips. It
is too sweet.

He will look at me.

He snorts, puts his head down into my
shoulder. I pull hard, and my hands slide
along his face. I grab again.

He will look at me.

He grunts, grabbing at my sweaty sides,
his eyes closed. His lashes are longer than
those of any girls I know. Beautiful. The
thumbs of his long hands press into my
stomach, so he can pull again, but then they
stutter. He presses hard again: my belly
pushes back. He looks down and back up,
eye to eye: all I have ever wanted, here. He
is looking. He is seeing me, and his hands
are coming around to feel the honeydew
curve, the swell that is more than swell, the
fat that is not fat, the budding baby, and his
eyes are so black they are all black, and they
are a night without stars. All I have ever

wanted. He knows.

"Fuck!" Manny yells, and he is throwing me up and off of him. I hit the door behind me, the rough cat tongue of his face gone, and I grip steel, air, nothing. The bathroom smells like the salt of marsh mud, like tadpoles dying in their shrinking shallows, and he is zipping his pants, folding me into the corner of the stall when he opens it, leaving me standing in the dark bathroom, runny at the legs, breasts aching with bloom, one of Mama's hair clips hanging from one string of hair before it falls into the toilet, lost in the scummy bowl. I wipe myself, flush the toilet, watch the water spin in a spiral, a baby storm, as it sucks the clip down and down and away.

I've crossed the threshold out of the bathroom three times, and each time that I think I am done crying, that I can go back into the game to sit next to my brothers as if nothing has happened, my eyes start leaking and my chest burns, hotter than the bright air with the bees drowsing in the crape myrtle, and I have to go back into the bathroom. I go in the other stall, pull my feet up, squat on the toilet. Smash my face into my salty knees. When I can breathe, I leave the stall to splash cold water on my face, but my eyes still look red, my eyelids swollen in the funhouse mirror. And then I think that Manny saw me, and that he turned away from me, from what I carry, pulling his burnt gold face from my hands, and then I am crying again for what I have been, for what I am, and for what I will be, again.

"Esch, you all right?"

"I'm all right."

"Big Henry told me to come check on you. I told him that I didn't want to come in the girls' bathroom, but he said . . ."

"I'm coming. Hold on."

At least my face is dry. Maybe everyone will just think that I am high. I want to let Junior go ahead of me back around the building to the gym, so I walk slowly, but then he walks slower so he doesn't leave me, and it takes us ten minutes to walk around to the front.

"You okay, Esch?" Junior asks.

Desultory claps flit out like small evening bats. Occasional whoops. It sounds empty.

"Yeah." I am breathing through my mouth. In the bathroom, I cried so hard I felt nauseous. Kids are milling around the gym door like our chickens, and I expect Junior to run off with them, to leave me to duck into the gym alone, but he doesn't. He loops his arm around my elbow like he is escorting me, and I keep my head down, my eyes half closed so all I see are anonymous legs, tennis shoes, gold-sandaled feet as Junior leads me up the bleachers. We circle Big Henry, sit up and to the side of Skeetah so that Junior and I are farthest away from the crowd and the floor, up here in the dark. It is only after I sit that I realize that Manny and his girl and Rico are sitting a few seats below us and to the right. Manny is leaning forward, away from her, as if he would run down the bleachers and into the game. His shirt pulls across his shoulders, his tense back, and I look away.

"Esch?" Skeetah asks. He is a little less high now, his eyes a little less dull.

"I'm fine." I try to say it loudly.

"Fuck that nigga." Skeetah touches my knee lightly, punctuates what he says with a nod. It is as if he is touching the sadness in me with his hand, so I move my knee away, smash my lips together. Already I want to cry. He touches my leg again, with one finger this time: lightly, quickly. "Fuck him." He spits this at Manny's back, loud enough for Big Henry to hear.

"What's up?" Big Henry asks. I shake my head and look down.

Skeetah slaps the bench with both hands. It echoes loudly. Rico, who was elbowing Manny and talking, his hands like birds, turns at the sound, smiling to show his gold. Manny shakes his head, but Rico gets up anyway, ascends the stairs two steps at a time, and stops in front of me and Skeetah. In the gloom, his teeth shine.

"I heard your bitch had our puppies," Rico says.

"Our puppies?" Skeetah asks.

"Yeah, ours. I thought we was splitting them down the middle."

"Really."

"They healthy?"

"Why don't you ask your cousin if they healthy?"

"I want to see them."

"Ain't nothing for you to see." Skeetah sits up slowly from his recline. He hunches over when he speaks, his shoulders curved, his muscles gathering.

"What you mean?"

"It was China's first litter. Lot of them born dead, and lot of them done died."

"Manny say one look just like Kilo. That's the one I want."

"It's dead." Skeetah stands, and he is barely taller than Rico, who is standing a bleacher below him, and half Rico's size.

But Skeetah tilts his head to the side, squints at Rico, and I know he's not scared, that he will never be scared. "China killed it," he says, and there is a lyric in his voice. He almost sings it when he says it, gleeful.

"Well, then I want another one."

"All they got left for you to have is the runt."

"What the fuck I want with a runt?" Rico laughs when he says it. It sounds as metallic and hard as his teeth.

"Well, that's all I got. That one and a black-and-white one. Both small."

Skeetah is omitting the white one, the one that is a clone of China.

"Manny?"

"Yeah." Manny walks up the stairs to us, looks at Skeetah and Rico. I ignore his black eyes.

"Thought you said Skeetah got a white one look just like China."

"He do," Manny says.

"Ain't it a little early to be trying to claim one of *my bitch's puppies?*" Skeetah says. He is leaning forward, straining at the leash. "They a week old. You know like I know that if they make it through the first six weeks, then they ready to go. So until six weeks go by, you ain't got no fucking business claiming shit." Skeet is smiling, and he is rubbing his thumbs with his fingers, his hands clenched loosely as if he can already feel the sting of them on Rico, on Manny. I know that's who he really wants: Manny. Big Henry and Marquise move with a loping, easy purpose, to flank Skeetah.

"Y'all little Bois Sauvage niggas really think y'all run shit? I will *fuck y'all up.*"

"Everybody just chill out," says Manny. "It ain't even got to be like that."

"Fuck you!" Skeetah's voice carries, sliding up in pitch, and it breaks his face in pieces. "You a dirty motherfucker!"

"You going to let that little nigga talk to you like that? If I was you, I'd beat the shit—"

It is what Skeetah has been waiting for Rico to say. Skeetah punches Rico. He does it with his whole body, raining down on Rico's wide, sweaty face with the steady fury and quick power of the small: fierce as China. The referees on the floor are blowing their whistles, and people are standing up around us, like they are doing a wave. Manny tries to catch his cousin Rico, and Big Henry reaches out to grab Skeetah, but then Manny has pushed his cousin back into Skeetah, volleyed him like a ball, and Manny is punching Skeetah, and Marquise is on Manny, and Big Henry slides his body

236

in between them as a barrier, to stop it all, but then Rico punches him, and they are brawling, falling down the stairs, ripping the crowd like fabric.

Randall is in the middle of the court, wrestling the ball from the huddle that one referee is screeching into his whistle over, when he stops, distracted by the rumble of the crowd, and sees the boys beating one another down the bleachers, Junior and me arm in arm, running down the edge of the stands for the door. Randall looks lost on the court, the ball cradled in his limp hand. The other referee is blowing his whistle at Skeetah and Rico and Manny and Big Henry and Marquise, who are fighting their way along the side of the court now, the crowd carrying them out of the door in the kind of frothing waves we only get before hurricanes.

"Get out of here, Batiste!" Randall's coach yells at him: the green hand towel he has been using to mop his face snaps like a flag in a bad wind. "That's your people, ain't it? That's you! You're done! Go on!"

Randall lobs the ball at the wall of the gym, and it ricochets back onto the court. Players that aren't frozen by the fight try to catch it. I pull at Junior's arm, and we are the first out of the door; he is fast. Randall jumps in the middle of the fight as it spills out of the door, begins screaming at all of them, calling names, pulling them from their fury one by one until he stands in the middle of them, taller than all of them, black as iron, rigid as a gate.

"What the fuck is wrong with y'all?"

"Who the fuck you think you is?" Rico yells. Manny has him by his shoulder, pulling him backward away from Randall.

"Let me go!" Skeetah says. Small scratches mark his face in beads. Big Henry is holding his arm, and Marquise stands next to them, breathing hard, glaring. "I'm going to kill that motherfucker. He ain't getting nothing from me!"

"I'm going to see your little bitch-ass tomorrow," Rico sneers; his lips are bleeding. "With your fucking dog."

"You know you can't fight no dog just had puppies." Big Henry steps toward Manny and Rico, stumbling forward with Skeetah. Big Henry's lips are swollen at one side, puffy and wet.

"I knew I didn't like this bitch for a reason," Marquise bites out. His forehead is bruised.

"Fuck that," Skeetah says. "Fuck that. He ain't getting none of my puppies."

"Skeetah" — Randall leans in to Skeetah,

his hands still raised — "you fight her tomorrow in that dog fight and Kilo win, them puppies die. You know that."

"Kilo ain't going to win," Skeetah yells, and jerks against Big Henry, who holds him with both arms, hugging him.

"You can't," Big Henry says.

"My cousin coming with his dog, Boss. He'll fight for China. If he win, then fuck you," Marquise says.

"And if I win?" Rico asks.

"Then fuck you," Skeetah says.

Randall elbows Skeetah in the chest, points one finger at Rico as if he would shush him.

"Then you get a puppy," Randall says.

"My choice?" Rico husks.

Randall looks at Skeetah, nods slowly.

"Yeah, your choice."

Skeetah shakes his head.

"Fuck them," Skeetah says.

Rico smiles; his name is etched into his golden teeth in blood.

Skeetah spits.

"Yes," Randall says. "Yes."

THE EIGHTH DAY:
MAKE THEM KNOW

"Esch?"

Junior touches me, and I roll away from him.

"Are you going to the fight?"

I woke up this morning and I hurt.

"Skeetah say I can't go if you don't go."

Someone has been beating me.

"He fixing to wash China."

They have been beating me in my sleep.

"Him and Randall got into a fight because Randall say he shouldn't be taking her. Say it ain't her place to go."

I will not get up for the bathroom. I don't want to eat.

"Say Skeet always being stupid, and we always ruining things. Like his game. Say the only way he could go to camp now is if Skeetah came up with the money."

I curl. Under pillow and sheet, I curl around the hurt, around the slipping secret, like a ball.

"Randall dunked the ball so hard this morning he tore the basket down. He made Skeet fix it." Junior taps my shoulder.

"He broke it. Esch?"

I want it to stop.

I try to read the entire mythology book, but I can't. I am stuck in the middle. When I put the book down and wipe my wet face and breathe in my morning breath, ripe to the afternoon under the sheet, this is where I have stopped. Medea kills her brother. In the beginning, she is known by her nephew, who tells the Argonauts about her, for having power, for helping her family, just like I tried to help Skeet on the day China first got sick from the Ivomec. But for Medea, love makes help turn wrong. The author says that there are a couple of different versions of how it happened. One says she lies to her brother and invites him onto the ship with the Argonauts as they were fleeing, and that Jason ambushes him. That she watched her brother die, her own face on his being sliced open like a chicken: pink skin cut to bloody meat. The other version says that she kills her brother herself, that her brother runs away with her and the Argonauts, assuming that he is safe, and that she chops him into bits: liver, gizzard, breast and thigh, and throws each part overboard so that her father, who is chasing them, slows down to pick up each part of his son.

I read it over and over again. It is like she is under the covers with me, both of us sweating to water. To get away from her, from the smell of Manny still on me a night and morning afterward, I get up.

Junior is sitting on the floor in the hallway outside of the door.

"What you sitting out here for?"

Junior shrugs, looks up at me.

"I was going to go outside, but Skeetah getting ready to wash China, and it be getting muddy under the house. Why you didn't wake up?"

"I was tired."

"Daddy asked why you didn't bring him something to eat this morning. Randall told him you didn't feel good."

"Randall made Daddy some eggs?"

"Yeah."

"What he doing now?"

"Sleep. He was hollering about the hurricane; say it ain't stopping, that the woman on the news say it's coming straight for us. Randall told him to calm down. Him and Big Henry went to the store and got some beer and then Daddy went to sleep."

Junior follows me down the hall to Daddy's room. Randall has nailed up a blanket over the window, folded it in half over the box fan, which hums and lets in light. Daddy is asleep, sitting up, slumped over like I left him yesterday. The TV is low, a buzzing firecracker. On the screen, there is a map of the Gulf, and Katrina spins like a top, as if the long arm of Florida has just spun it loose. There are two beer cans next to the bed, one open, both of them sweating. I close his door to a crack.

"You going to the fight?"

Junior touches the back of my arm, and I stop outside the bathroom. He pinches me, and I look down at him, his big dark eyes, his missing teeth, his long eyelashes. He opens his eyes wider, looks hopeful.

"Huh, Esch? Please?"

"Who cut your hair?"

"Randall shaved it this morning. Said it's too hot for hair."

"He's right." I palm his lightbulb head, shake it.

"Esch." He grins, and he looks like Skeet in the picture in Daddy's room. The air is close, close as the water in the pit.

"All right," I say. "We'll go."

I sit sideways on the toilet, rest my arms on

the windowsill; my body feels stung all over by catfish, my stomach the lead sinker.

In front of the shed, Skeetah is testing the water from the hose with one hand: it is so hot that I know the water boils fresh out of the faucet. He will wait until the water runs cold for her. When Skeetah first sprays China, she shakes. She is standing, legs wide, back straight, her head up. She is licking at the water, and it is as if she was never sick. She is coy as a girl with a lollipop, lapping at the hose. She sneezes and closes her eyes, and the dirt starts to run in sheets down her sides. It is the first time that I have seen her off leash in days.

"Come on," Skeetah says. "We gonna make you shine."

Skeetah cuts off the water and picks up a mostly empty bottle of dishwashing liquid and empties it on her back. He begins scrubbing, and the soap turns a pink gray. He rubs the soap up the flat, wide length of her head, down her face. He pulls her fur back so that her clenched teeth show, her fangs curving down sharp against her pink gums. Her eyes are slits, half closed in pleasure. She is stretching into Skeet's hands. He is pulling her limber, massaging her. Her nose is up to the air, and she is long and beautiful as an outstretched wing.

He kneels in front of her, swipes his hand down her chest, and she licks him, happy.

"You came back to me," he says.

"You shouldn't be taking her."

Randall rounds the corner of the house. I expect to see a ball in his hands, but there isn't. It's like he's missing his nose.

"Randall, you can kiss my ass."

"You ain't got no reason to be mad. I do."

"She's my dog. Those are my dogs."

"You was steady fucking up. I had to do something."

"Fuck that coach." China is grinning against the pull of her skin again. Skeetah's scrubbing hard. China looks striped. "And fuck Rico. Ain't nothing about China weak."

"You still ain't thinking about the puppies."

Skeetah turns on the hose. China walks in circles in the water.

"Stay!" Skeetah yells, and she stands frozen. "It wasn't your dog to give."

"And it wasn't your game to fuck up. What am I going to do about camp?"

"If he would've said that shit to you, you would've jumped him, too." Skeetah grimaces. "And the way he looked at Esch!"

"Rico fucked with Esch?" Randall, who has been pacing a ditch into the muddy yard as he argues, stops.

Skeetah snorts, glances at the window where I'm sitting, but the sun is too bright outside. He *can't* see me. His mouth twists like he has bitten into a peach seed, and he laughs once, a bitter, loud bark.

"You don't know shit, do you?" Skeetah readjusts his thumb over the hose so that the water shoots out in two hard sparkling streams. Where it hits China's side, it sounds solid. "You ain't got to go today. This ain't got nothing to do with you. Why don't you go shoot?"

Randall shakes his head, shoves his toe into dry dirt. The dust puffs and drifts in the still air. He looks toward the bathroom, and I sit back so that the tank of the toilet is cool and slippery through my T-shirt.

"I'm going," I hear him saying. "You made a promise. You said you would pay for camp if they lived," he says louder.

"All right!" Skeetah yells. "You kicking up dust, Randall!"

"You just like Daddy. Always crazy for something." I hear the side door off the kitchen scratch open and close as Randall leaves Skeetah to walk into the house.

The water stops. I lean so I can barely see out of the window. Skeetah is on his knees before China again, squirting the last of the soap on her coat, rubbing her whiter than white: she is the cold, cloudy heart in a cube of ice.

"Look at you, shining," Skeetah breathes into China's ear. "Cocaine white." He brushes her, his hand a blade. "Blinding."

The few dirt-scratched yards and thin-siding houses and trailers of Bois Sauvage seem a sorry match to the woods, like pitting a puppy against a full grown dog. Here, there are swimming holes that are fat puddles and some the size of swimming pools fed by skinny clear creeks, but the earth makes the holes black, and the trees make them as filthy with leaves as a dog is with fleas. There are clusters of magnolias that are so tall and green and glossy, they are impossible to climb, and the air around them always smells like peaches. There are oaks so big and old that their arms grow out black and thick as trunks, which rest on the ground. There are ponds that are filled with slime and tall yellow grasses, and at night, frogs turn them teeming, singing a burping chorus. There are clearings where deer feed, startle white, and kick away. There are turtles plowing through pine straw, mud, trying to avoid the pot. Marquise told us once that he went out into those woods with Bone and Javon after a hard rain to find some mushrooms they could take, and they came across a wolf, lean as a fox, dirty gray, who looked at them like they'd shot at him, and then disappeared.

The trail that leads into one of the deeper parts of the woods is up the road away from the house. China leads us, relaxed at the end of her chain; the leash is dull steel, the collar chrome. Skeetah stole it. He has reshaved his head, and he wears a hand towel around his neck like a scarf. Big Henry carries Junior on his shoulders, and Randall trails, a big stick in his hand, which Skeetah laughed at him for picking up when we were jumping the ditch, saying, *That ain't going to do nothing against these dogs.* Then he pointed at China and said, *But she will.* Randall carries the stick anyway. Marquise is probably already there with his cousin. Crows caw. I listen for the boys and the dogs somewhere out in these woods, but all I can hear is the pine trees shushing each other, the oak bristling, the magnolia leaves hard and wide so that they sound like paper plates clattering when the wind hits them, this wind snapping before Katrina somewhere out there in the Gulf, coming like the quiet voice of someone talking before they walk through the doorway of a room.

A cloud passes over the sun, and it is dark under the trees. It passes, and the gold melts through the leaves, falls on bark and floor: foil coins. Soon we reach a curtain of vines, which hang from the lowest branches to the needle-carpeted earth, and we crawl. Skeetah dusts China's breasts off, waves us on. We have been walking for a long time when I hear the first tiny bark.

"You tired?" Randall asks.

"No," I say. My stomach feels full of water, hurts with it, but I will not tell him that. I push aside a branch, let it go, but it still scratches my arm. Medea's journey took her to the water, which was the highway of the ancient world, where death was as close as the waves, the sun, the wind. Where death was as many as the fish waiting in the water, fanning fins, watching the surface, shadowing the bottom dark. China barks as if she is answering the dog.

The clearing is a wide oval bowl, which must be a dried-up pond that grows wide and deep when it rains; the bottom is matted with dry yellow reeds, and the trees grow in a circle around it. The boys and their dogs talk and smoke in clumps, pass blunts and cigarettes from one to another, ask *How old is yours* or *Where you got that collar* or *How many she done had?* There are around ten dogs here, around fifteen boys. I am the only girl. Marquise's little brother Agee is here, and he and Junior begin competing to see who can climb the fastest up a gray, low-limbed tree outside the circle of game dogs and game men. The dogs are brown and tan, black and white, striped brindle, red earth. None of them is white as China. She glows in the sun of the clearing, her ears up, her tail cocked. The dogs nap, pace, bark, strain against the leash, and lean out into the clearing where they will fight, trying to get into the sun, to feel it on their black wet noses. They will all match today, one dog against another. The boys have been drawn by gossip of the fight between Kilo and Boss to the clearing like the Argonauts were to Jason at the start of his adventure. They will throw their own dogs into the ring, each hoping for a good fight, a savage heart, a win, to return home from the woods, their own dangerous Aegean Sea, to be able to say, *My bitch did it* or *My-nigga got him.* Some of the boys are nervous; they put their hands in their pockets, take them out, swing their sweat rags in the air and swat at gnats. Some of the boys are confident: shoulders round and grinning. Big Henry wipes at his face with a sweat rag he's pulled out of his pocket, and Randall leans on his stick, frowning at the frolicking dogs. A hawk circles in the air above us, turns, vanishes.

Marquise is standing next to a boy who must be his cousin; they both are the color of pecans, both have their ears pierced with gold loops, and both are short, but the cousin is a little fatter. His T-shirt is so big it swallows him.

"What's up?" Marquise asks. "This my cousin Jerome."

"Cuz told me about y'all little problem." Jerome glances at Marquise, and then wipes his head with a rag, already wet, that he's pulled out of his pocket. "You ain't got to worry." He flicks his leash and his dog, Boss, gets up from where he has been lay-ing in the sun, walks to Jerome's side and sits. He is black all over with a white muzzle.

"You said he was big, cuz, but . . ." Marquise's whisper trails off to a laugh. "I didn't think you was talking this big."

Boss is huge. He is fat and tall, and his front legs are so bowed the front of him looks like a horseshoe. Where China's hair is silky, Boss's hair is coarse, so coarse that I can see the fight scars on him that have healed, black and fat as leeches. He lets his tongue hang out, smiles. His sides whoosh out and in as he pants, and he breathes so hard, he ripples Jerome's shirt.

"Where the other dog at?"

Marquise rises from petting his own dog, Lala, whose ears he has clipped and put earrings into, loops like his own, to nod across the clearing. Marquise never fights his dog, Lala. She is a soft tan color, and she is almost as clean as China. She lays in pine, cocking an eyebrow at us. Skeetah once told me that Marquise's dog sleeps in the bed with him, in the house, every night. Skeetah had shrugged and sort of smiled when he told me, but the way one side of his mouth had gone up while the other side of his mouth had gone down made me think that if Daddy weren't here, China would sleep at the foot of Skeetah's bed every night, too.

Across the clearing, Kilo is straining at a leash that Rico holds. He is sniffing at the ground, looking as if he is amazed, and then digging his paws into the dirt. It flies up and out between his back legs: he is tunneling through the dry grass and down through the bed of the pond. I wonder if there are frogs down there, dry and cool, hiding in the cracked mud. If they are trying to flatten themselves to hide from the sharp paw. Rico is half in the sun, half out, laughing toward Manny and some other older dark boy who has worn white shoes that look new to a dogfight in the woods. Rico's grill is bright, but Manny, his arms folded, is more gold than Rico's smile, and I hate him for it.

"I done fought Boss all the way from Baton Rouge to Pensacola," says Jerome. "He won more than he lost." Boss lays down in the pine straw again, snorts into it, so it flies up like feathers in front of his face. "He ready."

I edge in the shade next to Randall, who is stabbing his stick into the clay earth, again and again. Big Henry plucks his shirt away from his front, airs it out. He grins at me. Skeetah stands in the sun, the only boy in the yellow clearing who braves the light with the dogs. He ignores us, looks past us off into the woods, still as China at his side, who ignores us and looks off as well, standing, never sitting. I wonder if he has trained her to do this, to stand at his side, to not dirty even her haunches with sitting so that they gleam. China is white as the sand that will become a pearl, Skeetah black as an oyster, but they stand as one before these boys who do not know what it means to love a dog the way that Skeetah does.

The boys meet in the middle of the circle,

careful to keep their dogs at the edge; they hand their leashes to friends. They huddle to hammer the matches out.

"What the fuck you mean, you want Boss?"

"Yours is too big for mine."

"He a puppy, but he scrappy."

"She can take on any of them. She ain't weak."

"I say a two-fight limit."

"I say three."

"Who gives a fuck what you say?"

"I say two, too."

"Sugar got at least two in her."

"Homeboy got three."

"Ojacc can fight every one of them and whip all they asses."

A chorus of groans.

"Buddy Lee, too."

"Truck'll run all y'all over."

"Do you see Slim? Do you understand what he'd do to Kilo?"

"Ain't noboby for Kilo but Boss."

"Wizard want in on Kilo."

"I said Kilo ain't here for nobody but Boss."

"Y'all heard the man. Kilo ain't here for nobody except Boss."

In the middle of the dead circle, the boys snap like the air before a storm. Skeetah and China stand at the edge. The boys' arguing rises to an angry buzz, and the air that had been still before swoops and tunnels through the clearing, raising dust, making the boys close their eyes. Maybe Daddy is right; maybe Katrina is coming for us. Big Henry covers his nose with his rag. Did Medea bless the heroes before they set out on their journey? Did she stand on the deck of that ship like I stand in this clearing, womanly ripe, and weave spells for rain to cloak their departure, to cloak her betrayal? Had Jason told her he loved her? Manny holds Kilo's leash and stares at China. Skeetah and China do not move.

"Let's go," Marquise says.

Skeetah and China leave the circle, stand to the side of us, but a little away, a little closer, Skeet's shirt darkening wetly at the neck, down the middle of his back, China still except for her ears, which flick away gnats trying to land.

Skeetah fought China as soon as he figured she was full grown, at a year. There was always a clear winner to those fights with dogs owned by boys in Bois Sauvage, in St. Catherine. She has fought every one of these dogs. Except for two of her beginning fights, where China fought but still bled more than the other dog and had part of her ear sliced, she won by bearing down on the other dog, by grabbing his throat with her teeth, her face a fist. The other dog would yelp, and Skeet would call her off, and that is how everyone would know that China had won.

Now, no dogs sniff China. No dogs lope over to her and playfully snap, mouth her face or shoulder. She and Skeet stand apart, and when the first fight begins between the first two dogs, they are the only two that stand still. The fight is quick, messy. The dogs meet in the middle and tumble around the side of the pond bed, kicking up dirt and golden grass and sticks and blood. They twist and snarl and whine. The gray shrieks first, but it is the brown-and-white that falls, pulls away, wanting out of the harsh light, the burning bowl, the searing puffs of wind, the nail, the jerk, the tooth. The boys grab the dogs by the hind legs, pull them away from each other, cuss, let them go again. Junior is bouncing from foot to foot on his toes behind Big Henry, who wipes at his neck even though he is wiping so often there is no time for sweat to gather, to glaze. Randall, who had been flipping the stick over and over like a band major, has stopped, and he stares at the fight and holds the stick like a club. The gray is pulled away, yelping, while the brown-and-white one still strains against his boy's hands. Skeetah pets the watching China once, just a touch to the head, and she licks his finger. She never pulls away.

"Ojacc got him," the gray's boy says, admitting defeat. The brown-and-white's boy smiles, rubs his dog's head.

Marquise's dog, Lala, hops like a rabbit into the bowl, her gold bars flashing, and barks toward the brown-and-white dog as if she wants to congratulate him. Ojacc is still eager. He twists like a question mark, yanks one leg from his boy's hand, and bites. Lala skids to a stop, but the brown-and-white still sinks his teeth into her leg like a stapler. His boy pulls, and Marquise yanks Lala's leash with both hands. The brown-and-white lets go, growling.

"Hold!" his boy yells.

"Son of a bitch!" Marquise screams, and Lala limps to him, yelping. He kneels over her and she melts into him, true to her butter color. The dogs bark and rise up on their hind legs, pulling at their leashes, and the boys strain against them. China shifts on her feet and her breasts sway. Skeetah shakes his head, spits. The boys curl the leashes around their wrists, weave them up their arms. The dogs choke themselves to a standstill, laying their chins on their paws on the straw and grass. Marquise's dog will not stop whimpering, and when he puts his hand over her lips, slob runs through. After the next fight, Marquise lets her go and she sits with her back to his legs, facing the woods, and bows her head. Junior runs over to her, pets her head. By the time all the dogs but Kilo and Boss have fought, Lala is sitting with her bottom in Marquise's little brother's lap, her head on Junior's thigh, and she is licking his leg.

Rico and Kilo walk into the bowl. The other dogs and boys are breathing hard, bloody, wearing sweaty coats. Rico smiles as Kilo grins, stocky but tall where his master is short; his coat is red as the dirt under the pine needles, clean and dry as that. Rico winds the leash around his fist, winds Kilo in, pats him along the rough length of his side, looks up, and says, "We ready?"

Jerome leaves us. Boss waddles next to him. They stop a few feet away from Kilo and Rico. Boss flings his head up twice at Jerome, tapping the leash with his forehead, smiling, and Jerome squats next to him, slowly, whispering in his ear. Across the circle, Rico mouths something in Kilo's ear, but the wind blows again, and a cloud covers the sun, and their voices are lost in the whispering shuffle of the trees around us. And then the wind lags and catches again, and the cloud moves, and the clearing is a bright ball, and Jerome hollers "Ready!" and unhooks the leash from Boss as Rico backs away from Kilo. Boss and Kilo aren't tethered to anything or anyone and they are rolling across the bowl, furious at the other who stands in their eyesight, who has not lowered tail or head.

"Get him, son!" Jerome yells. He claps in exclamation marks, over and over. "Get him!"

They meet at the middle. They rise up on their hind legs at the same time, front legs meeting shoulder to shoulder like they are dancing. Boss's head, dull black, whips around first. His is the first bite. Kilo rears back and twists away. He snaps as he falls and sinks his teeth into Boss's neck.

"Shake him! Shake him!" Rico yells, leaning so far over that he looks like he is going to fall facedown in the circle.

Kilo ignores him. Kilo bites and lets go, snaps and bites again. His teeth flash white, flash red, flash again.

"Grab him, boy!" Rico yells.

Boss does not want to be grabbed. His

head is a knife, and he cuts a leaking gash on Kilo's shoulder. He sets Kilo to running red. He is slower than Kilo. But he is strong.

"Come on, son!" Jerome yells.

They both fall, separate. Kilo jumps up before Boss, growls, rushes back in. Boss lumbers to his feet and meets Kilo. They are teeth to teeth. They chew at each other's face, kissing. They growl into each other's throats.

"Come on, son!" Jerome yells.

But Boss thinks he has been called, that he should run to Jerome. He whirls and pours through the air, black as burnt oil, and jerks to a puddle in the dirt because Kilo has borne down on him, his teeth in Boss's back. Boss flings himself back at Kilo, his growl a great rip.

"Call him!" Jerome yells. The fight is no longer clean. Jerome has made a mistake.

"Kilo!" Rico shouts, and he grabs Kilo by his hind legs. "Kilo!" It is more a cough than a yell. Kilo lets go, tosses his head through a cloud of dust and hair and droplets of blood. Jerome grabs Boss by his front leg. Rico drags Kilo by his hind legs across the bowl, away from Boss. Both dogs are peppered in cuts. Rico's shirt is not so white anymore.

Jerome kneels, presses his rag into the

260

wound on Boss's back. It shows black through the rag, and when he wipes the gash, the blood runs clean. He presses again, waits until it is a trickle. Boss's white muzzle is streaked with red. Jerome nods at Rico.

"Again?" Jerome calls.

"Yeah," Rico says.

Junior lets Lala's head fall in the dirt.

"I'm going back to the tree," he says to Marquise's little brother. "You coming?" They leave Lala to sit up, looking confused. Big Henry stands with his arms crossed over his chest. Randall stares at Boss's back, his stick hanging at the side of his leg before he flips it up to rest on his shoulder, and he sighs.

Jerome slaps Boss on his haunch, and he is off across the clearing to meet Kilo. The two dogs blur into one. They have two heads, four legs, two tails. They are an ancient beast, fierce, all growling hunger, rising up out of the sea. Boss's head whips back, distinct for a blink, and he buries his teeth behind Kilo's shoulder.

"Shit," Randall breathes.

Kilo gurgles and bends himself almost in two, grabbing Boss's front leg.

"Shake him, son! Shake him!" Rico yells.

261

"Get him!" Jerome shouts.

They are boiling, red against black. Kilo is trying to shake blood loose. Boss growls and shakes his head again and again, giving back to Kilo what he is given. Neither rips; neither folds.

"They're even," Big Henry says.

Boss and Kilo's teeth are grinding into each other with each asking and answering jerk. They are sharpening the knives of their canines on a whetstone of flesh. Both hold. Neither will give.

"Call it," Skeetah says.

"Boss!" Jerome yells, and grabs Boss's back leg and drags.

"Kilo!" Rico grabs.

The dogs pull apart, are dragged away. Boss has many cuts, and his white muzzle has never been white, has always been red. Kilo's red shoulders look spread with redder yarn, a ratty maroon shawl, and his breathing is the loudest sound in the clearing, over the dying and rising wind. Daddy's hurricane is sending out feelers.

"Kilo got it," Rico says.

"Bullshit," says Jerome.

"What you talking about? He had him," says Manny.

"I don't know what you saw, but it sure wasn't Kilo winning," says Marquise.

"Everybody saw Kilo got him," says Rico's friend wearing the white shoes, which have turned yellow-brown.

"Everybody didn't see shit. It was even," says Big Henry, and suddenly everyone is talking at once. *Kilo had him. No, Boss had him. Nigga, you blind? No, you?* All the boys argue. The dogs around them bark and roll in the pine and lick their wounds and wag their tails. They raise their wet noses to the moving wind.

Rico rises from wiping Kilo, who bleeds and smiles. Rico clips Kilo's leash and leads his dog, who saunters with his head down, across the clearing to us. Rico is frowning at Skeetah, who still stands apart on the edge of the bowl, one finger a hair's width above China's head. She is so bright it is hard to look at her.

"So when I get my puppy?" Rico asks Skeetah.

"My dog ain't lose," says Jerome, clipping and standing.

"Ain't no clear winner," says Marquise.

"You hear everybody talking. It's a draw," Randall says, and he moves forward to stand next to Jerome, facing Rico. Rico sniffs and spits. I wish the wind would catch it, throw it back in his face or on his white, white shoes. Randall's stick is across his shoulders and behind his neck, and his arms hang over it like a scare-crow's. Big Henry shadows him, flanks Marquise. Manny starts walking across the clearing, the boy with the yellowed shoes behind him. They are all coming, all meeting in the middle. Like the dogs.

"I said" — Rico points his finger at Skeetah and China, who pants at his side — "where's my puppy?" He walks toward Skeet and the boys, who have moved into a loose cell around Rico and Jerome. Marquise is bouncing on his toes, curling his hands. If I were a boy, I would fight like Marquise, I think.

"No," says Jerome. "My dog didn't lose. Most it is is a draw."

"I gives a fuck what you say," says Rico, his finger now swinging to Jerome, his eyes on Skeetah. "And I want the white one."

"It's a draw. It's a tie." Randall blocks Rico, stands in front of Skeetah. He rolls his shoulders, grabs the stick in one hand, swings it wide and holds it like a baseball bat. Everyone is drawing together in a knot, tighter and tighter, black against the day. "You can't decide it."

"Yeah," Skeetah says. "We can." He unhooks the dull heavy chain from China's neck, smiles; she smiles with him.

How you going to fight her? Randall scream-whispered at Skeetah after Rico started laughing and led Kilo across the clearing to rub him down. *She's a mother!* The boys and their dogs spread around the circle of the clearing; the knot loosened, frayed. *And he's a father,* Skeetah said, motioning toward Kilo, *and what fucking difference does it make?* China nosed Skeetah's side. *Her titties,* Randall said. *Are for the puppies, and you don't have to worry about that,* Skeetah breathed. *The puppies,* Randall said, *what about the puppies? We all fight,* said Skeetah. *Everybody. Now leave me the fuck alone so I can talk to my dog,* he said.

"Randall?" Junior and Marquise's little brother have scampered down from their mimosa tree. "Skeetah going to fight China?"

"Go back to your tree," Randall says, "I mean it. Up."

"Go 'head," I tell Junior. "And don't come down til it's done."

Junior picks up a stick, throws it at Marquise's little brother, who wears a bright green shirt dusted with pink flowers from the tree and jean shorts with creases. *His*

265

mother did that, I think.

"Don't fall," I say.

"All right," Junior huffs, to let me know that I am getting on his nerves, and then they are running away.

Marquise is speaking loudly in the kind of voice that wants to be heard and saying that he thinks Rico is a bitch, his dog is a weak bitch, and hell naw Kilo didn't win. Big Henry is shaking his head, rubbing his forehead over and over with his sweat rag. Jerome is agreeing with Marquise, loudly. I can see why they are cousins. Boss is lounging again at Jerome's feet, bleeding faintly, tongue out, grinning again. Blood runs in his eye and he blinks. Kilo lolls on his back in the straw, curving into a C again and again. Randall is swinging his stick back and forth, again and again, like a golf club now, catching vines, ripping them down from their branches. He looks at me, his upper lip tight.

"Well?" Randall swings, and the stick flings up dirt and dry pine needles. "They'll die. *Fucking camp!*" he spits.

Across the circle, Manny is watching us. When the dogs were fighting, rolling like the spokes around the wheel of the clearing, gnashing and struggling muscle to muscle, tooth to tooth, it was easy to narrow my vision, to avoid Manny. Manny's eyebrows are together, his eyes are big; they almost look sorry. I tell myself I don't care and imagine myself tall as Medea, wearing purple and green robes, bones and gold for jewelry. Even though it feels awkward, I pull my shoulders back when I walk toward Skeetah, who is on the edge of the clearing in a cluster of ground palms, kneeling, whispering into China's ear, rubbing her so hard her skin slides in ripples with his hand. Skeetah smooths her, talks to her. Her fur looks silver in the shade. China is standing very still, staring across the clearing. Skeetah's tongue darts out of his mouth and a razor I did not know he had in his cheek flips out and over the tip of his tongue before he sucks it all back inside. He is reciting something, and he is saying it so fast that it sounds like he is singing it. *China White,* he breathes, *my China. Like bleach, China, hitting and turning them red and white, China. Like coca, China, so hard they breathe you up and they nose bleed, China. Make them runny, China, make insides outsides, China, make them think they snorted the razor, China. Leave them shaking, China, make them love you, China, make them need you, China, make them know even though they want to they can't live without you, China.*

267

My China, he mumbles: *make them know, make them know, make them know.*

When Skeetah faces Rico across the clearing, he has left China's chain on the ground and taken the chrome from her throat. She stands at his right leg, ears up, tail straight, and nothing moves on her. I cannot even tell if she is breathing. She is white, so white. She is the pure white heart of a flame. Kilo is all red, all muscle, a moving heart in the clearing. He barks high, once, and Rico unclips his leash and slaps him. Kilo runs.

"Go," Skeetah says.

China shoots across the clearing before Kilo can get to the middle, and she meets him with a searing growl. There are no snaps to legs or faces for her. There is only Kilo's neck. She rises with him, slings her head forth, and bites.

"Watch her, son!" Rico yells.

China grabs Kilo at the back of the neck again. She sinks her face into him. When she draws back, her jaws are shut, and she rips fur. She gasps like she is drawing a breath, and she dives in again with her teeth.

"Come on, Kilo!" Rico yells.

She would burrow into him with her head like a worm tunneling into red earth.

268

"Kilo!" Rico yells.

Kilo dives from the drive of her head. He latches onto China's leg. It is a weak move, easy, and I think that Rico has taught him this.

"Now shake her, boy!" Rico screams.

Kilo is shaking her. China is boring with her head again and again, turning what had been a shawl into a bright red scarf, but Rico is pulling at her leg, rippling from side to side; his muscles boiling so his fur is no longer earth, but water again, a red flood. He growls with each jerk, but the last one, as China swallows his ear and the side of his face with her sharp jaw and bites, slides into a squeak.

"Grab her!" yells Rico.

Skeetah refolds his arms, bows his head. China kisses the side of Kilo's face, a face-tonguing lover's kiss, mother to father, deeply.

"Fucking grab her!" Rico yells.

"China!" Skeetah calls, and China lets Kilo go even though he still gnaws at her foot. She looks back at Skeetah as if to say, *I am coming, love, I am here.*

"Kilo!" Rico yells. He grabs Kilo by the back legs and drags the dog toward him. Kilo smacks open his lips as if he has just eaten something he likes, and China's leg comes free. She is bounding toward Skee-tah, her smile red like smudged lipstick. The blood on her leg is a crimson garter.

"Fuck! He don't even have to drag her," Jerome says.

Rico wipes at Kilo's neck until the blood looks less like a scarf and more like a necklace. He studies his dog, who breathes so hard he sprays the ground with spit and blood, his nose to the earth. Manny kneels next to Rico, whispers. I know that whatever Manny is saying is showing the meanness in him, that he is Jason betraying Medea and asking for the hand of the daughter of the king of Corinth in marriage after Medea has killed her brother for him, betrayed her father. Manny's mouth moves and I read, *She ain't shit, ain't got no heart.* He looks at China when he murmurs, but it feels like he looks at me.

"You ready?" asks Skeetah. China stands next to him, heedless of the blood speckling her sides, her lips firmly sealed, her ribs bil-lowing and clenching. She stands evenly on the leg Kilo has chewed, which is red and gummy and raw above the joint.

Rico flashes a hand, quiets Manny. Manny stands, Rico with him. The boys have moved. They cluster behind Rico and be-hind Skeetah so that I have to move to the edge to see the dry pond bed, the red dashes where blood has fallen. The circle of boys that the dogs fought in all day has dissipated like fog.

"Fucking right," Rico says. He slaps Kilo's side. Kilo grunts to a stand, staggers to a run to the middle of the bowl. He is a creek becoming a river.

"Go!" Skeetah says. China raises her head to the sun and barks once, twice. It is a laugh. She digs her feet into the straw and jumps to a sprint.

"Grab her!" Rico yells.

Kilo eddies around China's shoulder. Swirls and bites. China bites back, returns the kiss, savagely.

"Grab her, son!" Rico yells.

They rise and clench each other with their arms, stand on their back legs. China kicks with her front feet, pushes away from Kilo's chest to unfurl like a whip to lash back around with her head, to bite and rip again, but when she leans back it is as if Kilo has just seen her breasts, white and full and heavy and warm, and he bows his head like a puppy to drink. But he doesn't drink. He bites. He swallows her breast.

"No," Skeetah says.

"Shake her," Rico calls.

Kilo is a whirlpool, spinning China, shaking her. She claws at him with her paws, her jaw wide, and tries to eat his eyes. But Kilo will not let go.

"Jump!" Skeetah yells. "Jump, China!"

It is what he tells her to do when he wants her to jump from trees. To leap. To fly. China bows into Kilo. She gathers herself, flexes like a muscle. She tongues Kilo's ear and bites and then leans back and pushes hard with her feet all at once. She rips. Her breast is bloody, torn. The nipple, missing.

"China!" Skeetah calls, and China lands on her front feet, already running toward him.

Kilo howls and falls backward away from China, his ear ragged.

"Come, Kilo!" Rico calls, and Kilo runs to Rico, dragging his ragged ear along the ground, butting Rico's leg and leaving a bloody print.

"I told you, Skeet," Randall says.

"Shut up," Skeetah says.

The gash is a red flame swallowing her breast.

"She can't fight," Randall says.

Skeetah is squeezing China's neck, murmuring in her ear. This time I cannot hear what he says. Skeetah is whispering so closely to China's ear I only catch half of his lips behind the red-veined white of her ear. Her breast drips blood. China licks Skeetah's cheek.

Rico stands, already smiling.

"Maybe I don't want the white one," Rico says. "Maybe I want the colored one that got more Kilo in it." He laughs.

Skeetah stands, and China, stout and white, looks up at him.

"She fights," Skeetah says.

Randall pulls the stick from his shoulders, swings it around to his front.

"She's already fucked up enough," Randall says.

"Cuz, if she lost, she lost," Big Henry says, slowly, as if he is tasting the words.

"She didn't lose," Skeetah breathes.

Rico laughs.

Skeetah shrugs and touches the tip of China's nose with his finger.

"She's mine, and she fights."

Kilo grimaces.

"Let's give this nigga what he want," Rico says to Kilo.

There is sweat and blood running red and gray down China's ribs.

"Go ahead, Kilo."

Kilo runs.

"Go, China! Go!" Skeetah screams, and China hurtles forward, her bloody breast streaming fluid, leaving a trail in the brush.

They meet. They rise. They embrace. They bite, neck to neck. They rip growls from each other, and the wind punches into the clearing and carries the growls away.

Kilo grabs China's shoulder again, jerks his neck to make her shake.

Skeetah's fists are curled tight, and his whole body seems to bristle.

"Make 'em know!" Skeetah calls, barely louder than speaking.

China hears.

"Make them know."

She is fire. China flings her head back into the air as if eating oxygen, gaining strength, and burns back down to Kilo and takes his neck in her teeth. She bears down, curling to him, a loving flame, and licks. She flips over and is on top of him, even though he still has her shoulder. He roils beneath her. She chews. Fire evaporates water.

Make them know make them know make them know they can't live without you, Skeetah says. China hears.

Hello, father, she says, tonguing Kilo. *I don't have milk for you.* China blazes. Kilo snaps at her breast again, but she shoulders him away. *But I do have this.* Her jaw is a mousetrap snapped shut around the mouse of Kilo's neck.

When Kilo screams, it is loud and high, as if the wind whistles when it slides past China's teeth.

Skeetah smiles.

Skeetah calls, "Come, China!"

China spins, takes away part of Kilo's throat.

China comes.

"Hold! Hold!" Rico screams, sweaty, his face twisted sour. He drags Kilo across the dusty bottom of the pond. Manny kneels, takes in me, Skeetah, and China in one glance, and looks like he hates us all. I wish it wouldn't hurt, but it does.

Kilo keens.

There are pink mimosa flowers drifting and falling on the breeze. Marquise's brother has left Junior; he has scampered out of the tree to hide his face in Jerome's leg while his pink-dusted shoulders shudder. Junior squats in the mimosa still, his hands white on the branches, jerking as if he would break the wood. His eyes are wide, glued to the screaming Kilo. Junior shakes a beat to Kilo's keening, and it is a song.

THE NINTH DAY:
HURRICANE ECLIPSE

The sound of someone throwing up in the bathroom wakes me. In my half sleep, I see myself in the bathroom, hunched over the toilet, one hand on the back of the bowl, vomiting. But then the retching becomes louder, sounds like my tongue is curling up and out of my throat, and I realize I am not throwing up. I have never been so loud; have never made that sound. The bathroom disappears and I wake to the half-light of dawn, the ceiling, Junior asleep in his twin bed with his sheets and pillow kicked to the floor, and our door cracked.

It's Daddy on the floor of the bathroom. Daddy with one hand on the back of the bowl, one knee on the floor. Daddy looking like he's about to dive into the toilet, lose his tongue.

"Daddy?"

"Get Randall," he breathes, and then his

276

back curves and he sounds like he's being ripped.

The hallway is still dark. Randall is in his bed, Skeetah isn't. After the match yesterday, he washed China under the lightbulb outside the back door. He rubbed her down and then sat on the back steps and dabbed antibiotic ointment from a dirty crumpled tube into her where Kilo had torn her and made the flesh show. Her leg and shoulder and her ripped breast looked like meat, and Skeetah took the same worn-out Ace bandage he'd wrapped his side with and cut it in thirds. He wrapped her leg, her neck and shoulder, her stomach, and pinned. She stood, eyes slits, panting easily, letting him patch her up. Every few minutes, she would wag her tail, and he would rub her somewhere it wasn't red: her feet, her back, her tail. He must have slept in the shed with her. I have to shove Randall twice before he wakes up, his eyes rolling white, his arms up to guard his face.

"What?" he says. "What's going on?"

"It's Daddy. He in the bathroom throwing up."

Randall looks at me like he can't see me. "What?"

"Daddy. In the bathroom. He's sick."

Randall nods at me, blinks. He's waking.

"Said he needed you."

By the time we get to the end of the hallway, Randall is bouncing, shaking the sleep off his arms and legs. Daddy has laid his head on the toilet, his face turned to us, his eyes closed, his arms hanging knuckle down on the peeling tile so that they look like sapling pine trees.

"I'm sick," Daddy moans. "Can't stop."

"Come on, Daddy."

"No." Daddy tries to push Randall away from him as Randall bends over, grabbing Daddy under his arms, but Daddy is weak, and his hands fall away like dry branches. "Got to stay by the toilet."

"I'ma put a garbage can next to your bed." Randall tugs Daddy up, gets his chest in the air, but Daddy's legs drag, and Daddy hangs there limp as sheets on a clothesline before they've been stretched and pinned. When the grandparents were still living, Mama washed all the sheets for both houses at once, and there was so much bedding that Daddy had to hang extra lines. Mama would walk through and hang them bunched first before spreading them. The sheets were so thin we could almost see through them. They made cloudy rooms, and we played hide-and-seek in them. In the winter, they made our faces wet and achingly cold, but in the summer, it was so hot the sheets didn't stay wet long, but we smashed our faces into them anyway, trying to find the hidden cool. Mama yelled at us for dirtying them once when we left muddy prints on them; afterward, we let our hands hover over them, shoved our noses into them to see if we could see the other person running down the next billowing hallway. Now, washing and hanging clothes is me and Randall's job: I don't even think Skeetah knows how to work the washing machine.

"Grab his legs," Randall says, so I bend and lift. Daddy is heavier than he looks. His eyes are closed and he is wheezing into his bicep; his breath gargles in his throat. "Come on."

I have to back down the dark hallway, so we shuffle slowly. After Mama died, Daddy taught Randall and me how to use the washing machine. It was our job to wash the sheets, to hang them up. At first we only washed them when Daddy told us to, and later we washed them when they'd get so dirty we'd wake up often in the middle of the night, itching, scratching a shin, an ankle. This is how we hung the sheets in the beginning, when we were both too short to put them over the line: the wet sheet sagging in the middle, us counting and lifting and flinging the damp cotton at the same time hoping it would catch. Daddy's ankles feel smooth as oranges. I don't expect them to be so smooth.

"One, two, three," Randall says, and we are lifting and rolling Daddy onto the bed like our sheets. For one moment, Randall is half his size, thin as a stretched belt, his knees big as softballs, all bone and skin, and we are children again, and Mama has just died and we are hanging her sheets. My eyes sting. Daddy leaves a wet trail across the pillowcase. He moans and holds his bad hand.

There are more beer cans on the nightstand, half empty. They shake when Randall kneels next to the bed, looking for Daddy's medicine, which is on the floor.

"Your hand hurt?" Randall asks. Daddy rolls on his side, facing us, and I go to the bathroom and come back with the garbage can and put it under his nose next to the bed. There are candy wrappers and wadded-up toilet paper at the bottom of the can, but it is mostly empty. Randall turns on Daddy's bedside lamp, reads the bottles to see which is his pain medicine. He is big and dark and every inch of him is pebbled with muscle, and sometimes I wonder if

Daddy is amazed at how this tall machine of a boy came out of him and Mama. Sometimes I wonder if he's amazed at Randall. And then I see Manny, almost as bright as China in the clearing, and wonder what will come from him and me: something gold and broad like him, black and small like me, or something more than either of us. Daddy came to one of Randall's games, once, and stood by the gym doors the entire time, nodding to himself with his baseball cap in his hand, frowning at the court and half watching the game. He left before half-time.

"Daddy, it say here you wasn't supposed to drink alcohol with these antibiotics. Or with these pain pills."

Daddy shakes his head and lays still.

"Beer ain't nothing," he croaks into the pillow. "Just like a cold drink."

"It's probably why you throwing up."

"I can't lay here." Daddy's good hand is shaking. "Got to get the house ready."

"Esch, get some water." Randall grabs a can, crushes it in one hand with his long fingers, which closes like a spider. "And take these with you."

I load the beer cans into my shirt. Daddy mumbles. When I come back with the water, Randall is handing Daddy his pills, and

Daddy is at least up on an elbow, even if the side of his head is smashed into the headboard. He gulps down all the water and the pills as if taking it down fast will stop it from coming back up later.

"The hurricane," Daddy says.

"You tell us what to do," Randall says, and then asks me to get Daddy two pieces of bread for his stomach and put them on the table.

The breeze has become a wind today, its gusts stronger, harder than yesterday in the woods and clearing. With my fingers I find a flashlight in the metal storage box on the back of Daddy's pickup truck along with a hammer and a drill. The nails are are all along the bottom of the box, like feathers and hay in a chicken coop. *The windows first,* Daddy had said. *You have to cover all the windows.* Picking the nails out is slow; I prick my finger on one, suck it, but there isn't any blood, just the pain. I wonder if China's ruined nipple will feel like this in her puppy's mouth when it heals: hard, healed over hurt.

Skeetah walks out of the door of the shed and slides the tin slab he has been using as a door back in place. He turns on the water at the faucet, bends and drinks, lets it run over his head. When he comes over to me, the water is streaming in beads down his neck, down and over his collarbone like Kilo's red shawl.

"What y'all in Daddy's truck for?"

"He sick," I say.

Randall is leaning half in and half out of the truck, tuning the radio to the black radio station. His legs are so long that they rest flat-footed on the hard packed dirt below the passenger door. He yells into the windshield so Skeetah can hear him. "He wants us to get the house ready for the hurricane."

"He say to do the boards first," I tell Skeet. He is shirtless, and his belt is looped so tight around his shorts that the waistband hangs from it like a shower curtain, and the leather cuts into his skin. They are the shorts from the day before. I was right; he slept in the shed with China.

"I can't," Skeetah says. "I need to wash China again, treat her cuts. Make sure they don't start looking ugly."

"That's going to take what? Fifteen, thirty minutes?" Randall is leaning out of the truck now, the music curling back up behind him, tiny and metal-sounding because Daddy's truck doesn't have any bass. The song tinkles to an end, and the DJ, a woman, speaks smoothly, her voice calm and almost

283

as deep as a man's.

"Hurricane Katrina is now a category three hurricane. It is scheduled to make landfall in Buras-Triumph, Louisiana, sometime Monday morning. The NHC has issued a hurricane watch for southeastern Louisiana and the Mississippi and Alabama coasts. We at JZ94.5 will keep you updated about the status of the storm throughout —" Randall switches off the radio. Skeetah works his mouth, looks down at the ground. His eyebrows, so dark and even they look drawn on, meet and form a hook. Daddy's do that. Mine are so light you can barely see them.

"I need to go to the store for some supplies. Wraps and stuff," Skeetah says.

"You can pick up some more canned goods when you go." Randall rolls his eyes.

"I ain't got no money for that."

"Well, then how you was going to get —" Randall stops mid-sentence. "Shit. I'll get some money from Daddy's wallet. Get the cheapest. Anything in a can. We ain't going to be able to cook nothing."

"I know that," Skeetah says.

"I shouldn't even have asked." Randall rubs his head. "Don't get caught."

"I don't."

"How are you going?"

"I already called Big Henry."

"Hurry up and get back." Randall turns on the radio station again. The rapper sounds like a squirrel. Randall starts fidgeting with the knob, but leans out again. "We need your help!"

"Yeah," Skeetah says. He wipes the water shawl away, and it smears to a tie running down the middle of his ribs. The air is so hot and close that even with the wind, the water will not evaporate. "Keep an eye on China," he says, and the sudden wind takes him into the house.

"Junior?"

I need him to pick the nails out of the bin. His small spider fingers can do it better than mine. He is not in his bed, but his sheets and pillow are still on the floor. I pick them up, put them on the mattress. The curtain at our window flutters. I turn the fan off.

"Junior."

He isn't in the bathroom. Whoever used it last left the toilet seat up, as usual. The door to Skeetah and Randall's room is closed; I can hear Skeetah shuffling around inside. There is a hole in the bottom middle of their door from where Skeetah got mad once and kicked in a dent; Daddy came up behind him and kicked him hard for that one, and then tried to slap him in the face.

"Junior in there?"

"Naw." The walls are so thin it sounds like Skeetah is standing next to me. It was because of China that Skeet had kicked the wall: once China got fat enough and her breasts big enough for Daddy to notice that she was pregnant, Daddy told Skeet he didn't want the Pit overrun by dogs. He was drunk when he said it, and he didn't say it again after that night, after Skeet had blocked his hand when Daddy tried to slap him and said, *Don't hit me in the face,* like he would take it anywhere else but there.

"Junior?"

He is standing next to Daddy's bed, his small, narrow back to me, his bald head bent. One arm hangs at his side, and the other he holds in front of him like he's in an Easter egg race, balancing a boiled egg on a spoon. But there is no spoon here, only his pointer finger, which he holds steady in front of Daddy's sleeping nose, nearly brushing Daddy's scraggly mustache, the naked chicken skin above Daddy's lip. I have never seen Junior so still.

"What are you doing?"

Junior jumps. He turns and whips his finger behind his back. There are bruises under his eyes, so he looks like a little brown

286

nervous man. I grab the finger and pull him out of the room, shut the door.

"Esch," Junior whispers. He looks at the floor like he is looking through it, down to his hollows in the dirt under the house.

"What was that?" I ask. I squeeze, and there is only skin over bone. His finger is still pointed. He moans and tries to pull away, but I hold.

"He wasn't breathing."

"What do you mean, he wasn't breathing?"

I drag him down the hallway, and he curls and drops and digs in with his feet, but I get him to our room. I kneel in front of him.

"What were you doing?"

Junior is looking at my throat, my hand, anywhere but my face. I yank, and he looks at my face.

"He looked like he was asleep but then he looked like he wasn't breathing so I wanted to feel him breathe. Let me go!"

"Don't go in there when he's sleep no more." I shake Junior's arm again. "He's sick."

"I know," Junior mewls. "I know he sick." Junior closes his hand and pulls suddenly, and his hand slides between mine like wet rope and is out. "I know about his hand and the beer and his medicine." He bounces. "I saw it when he smashed it. I found it!" Gets louder. "I see things!"

"Found what?"

"His ring!"

"Junior!"

"Here!" Junior yells. I can't see his baby teeth, small and yellow like candy, only his throat, wet and pink, and he is an infant again, his mouth always open, always trying to find the nipple so that he'd grab our fingers, the blanket, his bib, the paws of his lost dogs, and suck them. He is the baby Junior and then he isn't; he is a miniature Skeetah, and the hand he hadn't been using to check Daddy's breathing digs into his pockets and whips something out, something small and maroon, the size of a quarter, and throws it across the room. "It wasn't no good to him noway!" He is breathing like he's been running, and then he is skittering down the hallway like a spider. I almost catch him at the steps.

"Randall!" I yell, "get Junior!"

Randall jackknifes out of the truck, and he is a long black line streaking around the corner of the house where Junior has gone, and then I hear him banging underneath the house. Junior is laid so flat I cannot see him.

"Junior," Randall yells, "get from under there!"

Junior is silent.

"You going to make me come under there and get you!" Randall says from between clenched teeth, and he must be crawling because Junior has popped up on my side of the house and is trying to run, his eyes white and rolling like a rabbit's, but I have him, and he is kicking, kicking, and I'm surprised he doesn't have fur.

"What did he do?" Randall walks around the corner, the front of him red with dirt.

"He had Daddy's wedding ring."

"He what?" Randall is frowning.

"He had Daddy's wedding ring. He found it on the finger and took it off. It was in his pocket." Each word makes Randall's face slide and break until it looks like a broken glass with all the lines in it, and I know it's because he can't believe what I'm saying.

"Boy, what the hell is wrong with you?" Randall yells. He yanks Junior from me, and his other hand comes down hard on Junior's skinny bottom. "What is wrong with you?" Randall yells, and his voice is higher. He hits again. "Junior!"

Junior runs in circles from Randall's hand, so they spin, but Randall is faster and stronger, and his hand comes down again and again.

"That's so. Nasty. You. Could've. Got. A disease!" Randall slaps twice, and his hand is as stiff as a board. "Why did you do it?"

"She gave it to him!" Junior wails. His voice is a siren. "And it wasn't no good for him no more!" He sobs. "I wanted it!" He wails. "Her!"

Skeetah laughs when we tell him what Junior did.

"He's dead wild."

"He's bad."

"Did y'all at least find it? He going to be up in there trying to stash it somewhere."

"I did," I say. It was on my bed, and I'd picked it up with a handful of toilet paper and washed it off in the sink. The gold was dull and old, an almost silvery pale, and nothing about it looked like it had ever touched Mama's skin. "It was covered in blood." I'd thrown up after I cleaned it.

Junior is hiccupping, bent over double into the top of the toolbox on the back of Daddy's truck, picking out nails. His sobbing hiccups echo up and out of the metal, loudly. He drops the nails he finds on the truck bed, and they ping.

"What'd you do with it?" asks Skeetah.

"I put it in my top drawer," I say.

clusters. They look like tadpole sacs, huddled together, sticking to each other for company: cloudy at the heart. When Junior and I brought them in, they were dusty, opaque. I rinse a dishrag for Junior and one for me, and we sit on the floor in the kitchen and we scrub. This is a hurricane eclipse, the wood over the windows, the inside of the house so dark that the white of Junior's shirt is the brightest thing. We sit in the square of light left by the open door, and we wipe the rags pink. This is what we will drink. This is what we will use to cook. Randall is trying to fill the holes in the wood, but he can't. There isn't enough wood. Light cuts through the house, slinky and thin as electricity lines from the chinks of exposed glass. Daddy gets up out of bed, cussing and banging into things, and stumbles to the bathroom. He throws up. He yells for water, and I make Junior bring it. When I pee, I take the flashlight I found in Daddy's toolbox to see that Daddy's missed the toilet, and that there is throw-up on the bathroom floor. I clean it up with the rags we wiped the jugs with; when we take the rags outside to rinse them under the hose instead of in the sink full of dishes, they run yellow and red.

■ ■ ■

Fill my gas tank.

Junior sits in the middle, his legs dangling, black and skinny. Randall drives. I let my hand fall out of the passenger window, let the wind pick it up, bear down on it, take it as if it is holding it. Both windows are down because Daddy has no air-conditioning, and my legs stick to the rugs that Mama laid over the seat when we were small and the upholstery would get so hot in the summer it would feel like it was melting our skin. *It's too hot for them kids,* she'd said, and she'd beaten the rugs until they were clean, and then she'd washed them, and then she'd tucked them over the seats. Before Randall sat in the driver's seat, I could see that Daddy had worn his side thin. The rest of the fabric feels almost as thick as when Mama put it in. I remember it had itched the first time I rode in the truck cab with them, but I hadn't complained. Back then we'd all fit in the cab, and there was no seat belt law. Now we ride up and through the country toward the interstate, where the closest gas station is. The pines whistle and whip at the side of the road, the fitful wind making them dance. The strip of sky ahead and over the pines is overcast, gray, and then the sun will shine through it in fits, burn through like fire through wax paper. At the gas station, Randall doesn't even let Junior get out so he can go in the store and find something to beg for; I go inside and pay with cash, and Randall pumps. The AC is so cold and the fluorescent lights so bright that it makes it hard for me to breathe; I feel hot, my body sodden as a dripping sponge, my breasts and stomach full of boiling water, my limbs burning. Randall fills the tank, and on the way back he opens up the truck on the back road, presses the gas. We tear down the asphalt, past the trees, and the engine howls; we beat the sky and the wind. Junior bares his teeth and grins.

Cook whatever's in the 'frigerator.

There are six eggs in the refrigerator. A few cups of cold rice. Three pieces of bologna. An empty cardboard box from the gas station that holds chicken bones sucked dry. A half gallon of milk. Ketchup and mayonnaise. The stove is gas, so when Randall lights the burners, the kitchen glows orange and shadows climb the walls. The day tries to light the open doorway and fails. Junior sits in that dim light of the door, his chin on his knees, hugging his legs. He draws designs in the dirt on the floor. He is mad because Randall told him that no, he couldn't watch TV. That he was still in trouble. Randall fries the eggs with the bacon grease Daddy keeps in the old Community Coffee tin on the counter; he dumps in the rice and creole seasoning. I fry the bologna slices, and China must smell them because she starts barking, loud, begging barks. On four plates, we divide the eggs and rice, the bologna sliced in half, saving a little for Skeetah. Junior and Randall drink the milk. I bring Daddy his plate, but he is asleep, so I set it on his dresser and leave him there, dozing in the cave of his room. It is dark, but still he sleeps with his bad arm over his eyes.

Park my truck in the clearing by the pit.

The only real clearing on the Pit is by the pit. They had to cut trees so they'd have room to maneuver the dump trucks, to open the earth. Randall drives Daddy's truck around the house, skirts the trees, the mirrors barely clearing on each side. The chickens scatter before the truck, clucking in complaint, the wind picking them up so they fly in clumsy leaps. Randall parks next to the makeshift grill we cooked the squirrel on; there are tiny lumps of black char stuck to the metal, and red ants stream over it, a living line. While we are rolling up the windows of the truck and locking the tool-box, Junior kneels next to the grill. By the time we are done, Randall shakes his head at Junior, tells him *come on;* Junior's finger is in the middle of the ants, and they have diffused to a puddle over his hand. They are all curving, all stinging, all burying their bites in his skin. Junior has a prideful look on his face, says, *Look how long I can do it.* When Randall grabs him by his arm and I brush the ants away, Junior's skin is puffy, white and red, bumps swelling under the skin.

What is wrong with you, Junior? Randall asks.

Get the cheapest you can get, Randall had said, so when Skeetah and Big Henry begin unloading the trunk, I expect cardboard boxes cut in half full of tomato soup. Skeetah pulls out a big bag of dog food, hoists it up over his shoulder, and carries it to the shed. Then he pulls out another fifty-pound bag of dog food and dumps it next to the first, where they sit like lumpy twins. China is barking, high-pitched, from the shed. She is hungry.

"All right!" Skeetah yells, and she stops

mid-bark, swallows it. He slides the tin shed door over, and she walks out calmly, brushes him with her head, noses his pants, licks his hand. He squats and rubs her.

Randall and Junior and I have been sitting in the yard for the past hour or so, jobs done; the house is too dark, too hot. It is a closed fist. Junior had been playing with an old extension cord, using it like a rope. He'd kept tying it to trees and twirling the cord like a jump rope. The tree was his partner, but he had no one to jump in the middle. Finally Randall untied the cord and I walked over and grabbed the other end. While the sky was darkening, the sun shining more fitfully through the clouds, we turned the cord for Junior and he jumped in the dust.

Randall walks to the car first. There are two boxes shoved in the corner of the trunk, the tops open and folded apart. In one, there are around fifteen cans of peas, green writing on silver, and a few of potted meat. And in the second box, there are two dozen bags of Top Ramen. Randall grabs the box with the peas and meat in it, and I grab the box with the ramen. Randall holds his box with one arm, his muscles knotting, and shrugs at Skeetah, raises his hand like he is throwing a ball in the air toward a goal raised too high.

"Why did you get all these peas?"

"It's all they had."

"And only three potted meats?"

"They was wiped out. Last things on the shelves."

"I told you not to get nothing that need to be cooked. What we going to do with a box full of Top Ramen?"

"We going to eat it." Skeetah looks up from China. He is checking her breasts, peeling back the tan wrap to see the scabs that line the red watery wounds. China licks his forearm.

"What we going to cook Ramen with? You know the electricity go out in a thunderstorm; what you think it's going to do in a hurricane?"

"We got the grill in the woods. We can cook them over a fire."

"The wood is going to be *wet*."

"It ain't even going to be that big of a deal. Probably turn and miss us."

"No, Skeet. We been listening to the radio all day. It's a category three and it's coming right for us. Got two sacks of dog food! How long you think these peas going to last us?"

"We got other stuff in the house!" I hate peas. My stomach, which has lately been pulling at me, driving me to eat at all hours of the day to feed the baby, burns. "Barely enough for five people!" I say, my voice harder than I have ever heard it.

Skeetah unwraps China's breast, and it hangs free, already bruised and wilted from disuse; it is a dark mark on her, marring what was once so white, so pristine. The scar makes what remains even more beautiful. Skeetah looks at China like he would dive into her if he could and drown.

"You ever tasted dog food?" Skeetah asks.

Randall's box jerks, and he looks as if he wants to throw it.

Big Henry closes the trunk, holds up his big hands palms out, like he would calm us.

"Man, we got a little extra. Me and Mama got cases of cold drinks and canned goods at the beginning of the summer, and we been eating from her garden since, trying to save them. Sure Marquise got some extra, since his mama been hollering about him eating too much since they trying to make sure they got enough to eat just in case, too. Skeetah, you ain't got to eat dog food."

"It's salty. Taste like pecans. And if worse comes to worst, we can eat like China." Skeetah rubs China from her shoulders to her neck, up along her razor jaw, and holds her face, which goes wrinkly with the skin smashed forward. It looks like he is pulling her to him for a kiss. She squints. I want to kick her. Randall shoulders his box, grabs the ramen box from me, and turns to walk into the house. Junior is tying his cord around an old lawn mower now, pulling at it like he's playing tug-of-war. The sun shines, blazes like fire, funnels down in the gaps between the trees, and lights up Skeetah and China so that they glow, each kneeling before the other, eyes together. Skeetah has already forgotten the conversation, and China never heard it.

"We ain't no dogs," Randall says. "And you ain't either." He walks between the thumb and pointer finger of the house, it clenches, and he is gone. The day goes cloudy, and stays.

THE TENTH DAY:
IN THE ENDLESS EYE

I ate skeet's eggs and bologna. He was out in the shed with China, cleaning her. I ate them all. I cleaned the plate with my tongue, licked the plate clean. I could've eaten the plate. Randall glanced at me once and then went to pulling all the cans out of the cabinets. We sat at the kitchen table and divided and stacked and counted: twenty-four cans of peas, five cans of potted meat, one can of tomato paste, six cans of soup, four cans of sardines, one can of corn, five cans of tuna fish, one box of saltine crackers, some cornflakes we could eat without milk. The rice, sugar, flour, and cornmeal were useless. There were thirty-five Top Ramen noodle packs.

"Shit!" Randall yelled and threw the can of tomato paste he was holding across the room. Outside, the wind pushed between the buildings.

■ ■ ■ ■

After breakfast, I hear them talking while I'm in the bathroom. The rooster is crowing outside, and China answers him, barking. They are in Daddy's room. When I pee and lean over to grab the toilet paper, my belly pushes into the tops of my thighs, insistent. I ignore it, ease open the door, and creep down the hallway so I can listen to Randall and Daddy through the open door.

"I know," Randall says. "But we still don't have enough."

"Y'all eat them dry anyway."

"Junior eat them dry. Nobody else do."

Daddy breathes hard so I can hear it catching on mucus in his throat, and then he coughs it out.

"I got enough money in case it's an emergency after the storm. Never know what will happen."

"But what about —"

"It's just a few hundred, son," Daddy wheezes. He has only ever called Randall that and has only done so a few times. "I made sure we had enough can goods to last us a few days. No more, no less."

"I don't think it's enough."

"FEMA and Red Cross always come

through with food. We got that much. If it's not too bad, might still have gas."

"Everybody still growing, Daddy. Esch, Junior, me. Even Skeet. We all hungry."

"We make do with what we got." Daddy coughs. "Always have. And will." He clears his throat, spits. "Your mama —" he says, and stops. "Y'all found my wedding ring?"

"Yeah. Junior did," Randall said. "I'll go get it."

And then there is just the sound of the box fan blowing hard and steady from Daddy's dresser, moving the hot air a few feet before dying in the hot box of his room. I follow him into me and Junior's room, root through my drawer, find the ring, sit it in the middle of his sweaty hand so he can return it to Daddy, who will slip it into his pants pocket, his shirt pocket, on a chain around his neck, anywhere that it will still touch his skin since he has lost the finger for it.

Only Daddy can stand being inside the house, dark and close. All of us, as soon as we can, are outside. There is a blue-gray sheet over the sky, and there is no sun, and the day is only better than the house because there is a pushy wind blowing, the kind that drags at my clothes and shows my body for what it is. The light comes from everywhere and nowhere. The chickens are sitting in a low tree, on some old fence posts, on an old washing machine, on the dump truck and the bonfire wood of their collapsed chicken coop. They huddle, and it is as if they can't bear to be on the ground, in the blowing dirt. I sit on the steps, Junior beside me, his wet skin to mine, Randall on the gas tank with his ball, throwing it up and catching it before the sulky wind can take it away.

Skeetah is building a pile of things outside of the shed. I would say that he is cleaning the shed out, but I cannot, since he is not taking out any of the tools, the oil drums, the broken lawnmowers and bike frames and pots for plants. His pile is all for China: dog food, chains, leashes, blankets, her food bowls. He washes out her bowls with his hands and sits them on the step next to Junior and me, where they sweat small puddles. He carries her blanket to the clothesline and hangs it, and then he bends in two, crouching through the junk in the yard for something.

"What he doing?" Junior asks.

I shrug.

Skeetah straightens up with a large stick in his hand, a branch knocked loose by a rainstorm, and begins beating the blanket. Dirt showers down, fitful as cold rain. Some of it floats a little longer than it should, a slow cloud, and I realize that some of China is in the blanket, that her hair is coming away. It makes me think of cereal in milk, of Rice Krispies in sugar.

"We need more food," I say.

Randall catches his ball, hugs it to his stomach.

"Any ideas?"

I suck my lips. Feel like chewing something.

"Not yet," I say.

Randall frowns. Junior lays his head on my shoulder.

"I'm tired," he says.

I want to say, *It's too hot for you to be hanging on me,* but I look at his baseball knees, his head, which seems too big and heavy for his stringy neck, and instead I say, "Do you want some noodles?"

"Yeah."

Skeetah is frowning, beating the blanket clean. China starts from her crouch where she has been sitting next to the bucket, running from the first dig of her toes into the dirt. She runs up to the pilings that were the chicken coop and leaps, grinning, barking. She is trying to lick their feathers. The chickens bear down, huddle. China flies past, turns to the fence posts, jumps there,

306

almost meeting them with her head. They squawk and hop, alight again on the wood. She ignores the dozen in the tree and races for the washing machine. She flies and lands on it, and the chickens roosting there scatter.

"Skeet!" I yell.

"China," Skeet calls and hits the blanket again.

I go into the dark house to cook Junior's noodles, and Daddy sleeps so hard and is so quiet that it feels like I am alone there.

"We should look for eggs," says Randall. He says this while Junior is sitting on the steps, his face buried in the bowl, slurping at the soupy water left after he has sucked the ramen in long wormy strings over his chin and into his lips. He hates when I break the noodles before I boil them in the pot.

"They need to be in the refrigerator."

"We can boil them. They'll keep for days."

Junior is drinking the last of the soup, still hunched over the bowl. I wish I'd made myself some; my tongue turns loose at the idea of the salt. Junior's back is a young turtle's shell, so thin it would snap if stepped on.

Skeetah is piling the folded blanket on top of the food bags along with the leashes and

China's practice tires and the syringes and the medicine he stole from the farmer. Junior sticks his finger into the bowl, wipes it along the bottom to get the seasoning, and licks it. He bangs into the kitchen, throws the bowl into the sink, and bangs back out. He runs over to Randall, the soles of his feet flashing yellow, the color of China's eyes.

"You should put some shoes on," I say.

"You coming, Skeet?" he asks as Randall slides from the gas tank, upright, already squinting into the woods, the dust, the wind.

"I'll catch up. Gotta exercise China. She going to be cooped up, and she ain't going to like it."

Randall shakes his head and walks around the washing machine, the lawn mower, the old broken RV like he is finding his way through a maze. The chickens cluck at him, ruffle and settle their feathers against the pushing air as he passes. I am hungry.

"We could use more eyes," I say. "Mama taught you how to do it, too, and you know Junior don't know how to spot them yet."

"In a minute." Skeetah shrugs. China, at his knee, lets her head fall to the side, tongue out, as if it is the first time she's ever seen me. Her ears fold over like napkins.

I sigh, don't even know if he can hear it over the wind, and follow Randall into the detritus of the yard to hunt. The wind pushes against me so hard that I imagine it is the wind Medea called up after she slew her brother, to push the boat so quickly that the wake was a bloody froth; I barely have the energy to walk, to push back. On mornings like this when I am hungry, the nausea is always worse. There is the sound of China's scrambling against Skeetah, of the tin shed shaking, of him laughing and China barking, but I leave them to it behind me and keep my eyes on the ground.

The chickens have made their own plans for the storm; they have packed their eggs away, hidden them well. As Randall and Junior and I spread out underneath the oaks and the pines, hunting, Randall crouches down to Junior, and he tells him how Mama taught us to find eggs. *Look but don't look,* she said. *They'll find you. You gotta wander and they'll come.* She'd leaned over like Randall, her strong hand soft on the back of my neck, steadying me like a dog. *They're usually brown and have some feathers stuck to them,* she'd say, pointing. *The eggs look that way because of the mama. Whatever color the mama is, that's what color the egg is.* Her lips were pink, and when she leaned over like that I could smell baby powder drifting from the front of her dress, see the mole-marked skin of her chest, the soft fall of her breasts down into her bra. *Like me and you,* she said. *Like me and you. See?* She smiled at me, and her eyelashes met her eyelashes like a Venus flytrap. Her thick arm would rub against mine, and I would follow her pointing, and there would be a whole treasure of eggs, nestled one against the other: cream and white and brown and dark brown and speckled so that they almost looked black. The hens would lurk, murmuring. *The cock, he always running off being a bully,* she said. *But the mama, the mama always here. See?*

The pines shrug in a sky that covers like a wet T-shirt. Below, Randall fills Junior's shirt with eggs that they gather from the most difficult places, places that only Junior, with his pin fingers, can reach: in the elbows of the dump truck's engine, between the bottom of an old stinking refrigerator and the earth, wedged into the coils of a mattress chewed bare by animals. I search and find nothing.

The eggs in the front of Junior's shirt are warm; they pull the front of the neck down to a V, and where his collarbones meet, it looks like two marbles against the skin. I set the eggs in the black pebbled pot that Mama used to cook gumbo in, count them as they roll and settle. Randall holds the sides of Junior's shirt because Junior seems to be bending to the roll of the eggs. Twenty-four. There are twenty-four eggs to boil, to save, to eat. They are something.

When Manny appears, there is no sun to reach out its hand, to stroke him like a dog, to make him blaze and shine. He does not burn, but still there is something about him that glows, like a fire that is dying and the heat lives in the ashes, plain. I see him first because I am sitting on the steps. Junior's and Randall's backs are to him as they place the eggs in the pot. When Manny sees me looking at him, he catches on the secret mid-walk, like it's a untied shoestring, and his eyes go wide, whiter in his face. But he keeps walking, becoming larger and more real in the gloom and wind and shaking green of the day until his footsteps are louder than the insects, which quiet one by one as if he is the coming storm. *Where do they go?* I think, and he is looking at Randall's back, not my eyes, and I hate him, and I wonder if I will ever stop loving him.

"Cuz," he says.

Randall almost drops the twenty-fourth

egg he holds.

"Shit," Randall says and turns.

"Sorry." Manny's shoulders. I loved his shoulders and his neck most of all. I want to open my mouth on his neck just once. He is the lightest thing in the clearing. I want to have him blazing over me again, just once. But he looks at Randall, and he half grins. It is only then that I can see the scar on his face, the skin pulling wrong. He has not come here for me. "We talk?"

Randall bends, places the last egg in the pot, puts the pot in my arms, and talks to Manny but looks at me. "Yeah," he says. "Can you start these?" They walk outside together, stop at the foot of the back steps.

I stand with the pot. The eggs wobble against one another, sound like rocks at the bottom of a dry creek, rolling from a foot.

"Junior, go play," Randall calls through the door. Junior shoots away, freed from his chores. He is all bald head and blurred arms and legs. I run water into the pot in the sink until it covers the eggs.

"Skeetah ain't here?"

"Think he somewhere off in the woods running China."

"She's a beast."

"Yeah."

I sprinkle salt into the water, but there is

312

more rice than salt in the shaker.

"Coach called you about the game?"

"Said they was paying for Bodean to go to camp."

"I didn't know."

I light the stove with a match and set it to boil. I stand a few feet away from the door in the dark of the kitchen so they can't see me, and I squint through the screen.

"I'm sorry," Manny says.

"Well." Randall sighs.

"I don't know what happened."

"My best friend got into a fight with my brother is what happened."

"I had other shit on my mind. Wasn't nothing against Skeet."

"He don't think that. He think you made him poison his dog."

"I wouldn't do no bullshit like that. You know me."

Randall has nothing in his hands. Manny fans his face like he's waving away gnats.

"He also think you dogging my sister."

"Randall, come on, man."

"What you want?"

"We like family."

Manny shoves his hands into his pockets and bends in like he's curling for a blow, as if he's ashamed to say what he's said.

"Rico your family. I ain't blood."

"Like blood."

"That's the problem." Randall shakes his head like a horse trying to fling off reins. "I'm the only one."

"That ain't true."

"Yeah it is."

"I done watched Junior grow up with all of y'all. That's real."

"What about Esch and Skeet?"

"Them, too."

"No," Randall says. "It's not the same." Bubbles of air, tiny as those that rise up out of the mouths of fish in water, rise from the bottom of the pot, gather in the middle. Vapor mists from the center. "I got shit to do. I'll see you later."

Randall walks into the kitchen and I look up from the pot like I haven't been standing on my tiptoes in the faint blue light of the burner's fire, like I haven't been listening.

"It's going to take forever to boil. Leave it," Randall says. He doesn't look at me when he says it, tall and straight. He stalks past, closes the door to his room. I hear it shut, and I am out the screen door, running, still on my tiptoes, feet barely touching the ground. There he is, there, receding under the trees, a setting sun. I jump the ditch to the road.

"Wait!" I call. My voice is higher than I

have ever heard it.

Manny stops, turning, and his face is a magnolia flower tossing in the wind, his eyes the bright yellow heart. Now I see it, now I don't.

"What?" he says when I catch up to him. "Randall wanted something?"

Manny's eyes slide past me to the ditch, to the road, up to the sky the color of a scoured pan.

"No," I say. "Me."

"I gotta go." He turns, shows me the back of his head, his hair, his shoulders. Now I see it, now I don't.

"I'm pregnant."

He stops in profile. His nose is like a knife. "And?"

His hair grows so fast it's already starting to curl. Sweat beads at his hairline.

"It's yours."

"What?"

"Yours."

Manny shakes his head. The knife cuts. The sweat rolls down his scar, is flung out onto the rotten asphalt.

"I ain't got nothing here," he says. Manny blinks at me when he says it. Looks at me head-on, for the second time ever. "Nothing."

Nothing. For some reason I see Skeetah

when I blink, Skeetah kneeling next to China, always kneeling, always stroking and loving and knowing her. Skeetah's face when he stood across from Rico, when he told China, *Make them know.*

I am on him like China.

I fought Skeetah and Randall for play when we were younger. Once I punched Skeet in the stomach when we were wrestling and my arms felt like noodles, like he had no muscle to hit and I had no muscle to hit him with. I kicked Randall in the chest when he was picking with me and knocked the wind out of him. Once I fought a girl in the middle school locker room for laughing at my budding breasts; she sneered that I needed to tell my mama that I needed a training bra. My mama was four years dead then. That girl plucked my shirt where a bra strap would be and pushed me, and I turned back on her and swung blind, trying to smash her face in, kicking at her legs, elbowing her, beating with my whole body. She was twice my size, but I surprised her before she was able to push me off. I fell over the bench and the lockers cut a gash in my arm, but I left that girl with a knot rising purple on her head and a lip pink and tender as a pickled pig's lips in a jar. She always says hello to me when she sees me in

316

the hallway, three years after the fact. I am fast.

I am slapping him, over and over, my hands a flurry, a black blur. His face is hot and stinging as boiling water.

"Hey! Hey!" Manny yells. He blocks what he can with his elbows and forearms, but still I snake through. I slap so hard my hands hurt.

"I love you!"

"Esch!" The skin on his throat is red, his scar white.

"I loved you!"

I hit his Adam's apple with the V where my thumb and pointer finger cross. He chokes.

"I loved you!" This is Medea wielding the knife. This is Medea cutting. I rake my fingernails across his face, leave pink scratches that turn red, fill with blood.

"Stupid bitch! What is wrong with you?"

"You!"

Manny grabs me under my armpits, picks me up off the ground, and throws. I fly backward. My toes land first, skimming the road, then my heels thud, but I am moving too fast to stop and I hit the ground with my butt. I try to catch myself with my stinging hands and then they sting more. I've scraped the skin off.

"How you come to me saying something's mines when you fuck everybody who come to the Pit?"

"You the only one I been with!" I rush him again.

"You better go to Big Henry with that bullshit!" Manny twists and shoves me away from him again, but I take the neck of his T-shirt with me when I go.

"I know!" I say. "I know it's yours!"

"No it ain't."

"I'ma tell Randall."

"You think they don't know you a slut?" He spits this and it is red; I have drawn blood.

Manny shakes his head and snorts, skipping backward away from me, and then he is running down the narrowing road, being swallowed by the rustling brush, and I am shaking like the leaves, like the green around me, bent in the first fingering rush of the coming winds.

"You are!" I yell.

Tomorrow, I think, *everything will be washed clean.* What I carry in my stomach is relentless; like each unbearable day, it will dawn. I watch Manny getting smaller and smaller, and my ribs break like dry summer wood, and burn and burn and burn.

"The baby will tell," I scream. "It'll tell!"

318

But the wind grabs my voice up and snatches it out and over the pines, and drops it there to die.

Randall finds me sitting in the ditch. My legs are over the side, and the blackberry vines are scratching them and there are ants crawling on my toes, but I don't care. Tears run down my face like water and I cover my face with my shirt but it is too hot and I can't make it go away. I can never make it stop never nothing. When Jason betrayed Medea to exile so he could marry another woman, she killed his bride, the bride's father, and last her own children, and then flew away into the wind on dragons. She shrieked; Jason heard.

"What's wrong?"

"Nothing." I tell him this through the cotton.

"We going to the white people's house."

"Who?"

"You and me."

"For what?"

"We need supplies." Randall says, and the day quiets for a moment, and I can hear the breath going in and out of him. "Did he say something to you?"

"No." I wipe my face, let the shirt slide away and down. My eyes feel swollen and

warm as ripe grapes. "He ain't say nothing."

"I need your help, Esch." I have never
seen one part of Randall soften when he's
awake, not the long line of his arms, his legs
like steel posts, his face, always changing
and making and saving and shooting things.
But now, just for a breath, his face goes soft,
and he looks like the baby pictures Mama
took of him, pictures of a Randall I'd never
seen before. "Please, Esch."

I bend over and scrub my face dry with
my shirt, but the tears still come.

"I can't," I sob.

"Please," Randall whispers.

"Why?" I breathe.

"I need you."

I scrub, wipe like I could wipe the love of
Manny, the hate of Manny, Manny, away.
And then I get up because it is the only
thing I can do. I step out of the ditch and
brush the ants off because it is the only
thing I can do. I follow Randall around the
house because it is the only thing I can do;
if this is strength, if this is weakness, this is
what I do. I hiccup, but tears still run down
my face. After Mama died, Daddy said,
*What are you crying for? Stop crying. Crying
ain't going to change anything.* We never
stopped crying. We just did it quieter. We

320

hid it. I learned how to cry so that almost no tears leaked out of my eyes, so that I swallowed the hot salty water of them and felt them running down my throat. This was the only thing that we could do. I swallow and squint through the tears, and I run.

The start of my run through the woods with Randall is easier; where me and Skeet sprinted, hand in hand, Randall and I jog. I don't breathe hard at the beginning, and I force myself to ask questions, to speak through the other pain.

"Where's Junior?"

"Running around somewhere in here."

"Skeet?"

"Him, too."

There are no chattering squirrels, no haunted rabbits, no wading turtles in the woods. I don't know where they have gone, but there are none here. When I look up into the sky, the gray of it shaking as I run, I see birds in great flocks that would darken the sun if we could see it through the thickening clouds. They are all flying away, all flying north. The flocks break and dip and soar, and they are Randall's hand on a basketball, Skeet's on a leash, my legs in a chase. I watch them until they vanish past the trees, and then there is only us, the woods, the leaves rattling underfoot. Vines catch my arms, my head; we tear through until we break out into the clearing before the fence, the field, the barn, the house, and I drop to my knees, and Randall leans back as if he would fall, both of us breathing hard, looking wet and newly born.

There are no cows, no egrets. Randall leaps over the fence without using his hands, jumps high as a deer, but I crawl through on my stomach, my belly feeling like a bowl sloshing with water. I swallow most of it now, and my face is wet with mostly sweat. We pick our way across the field, kicking at cow droppings and mushrooms. The grass seems denser, thicker. There is no blue truck, no white man and woman, no chasing dog. The windows of the house and the barn have been boarded over with thick pieces of plywood, but when I put my ear to the board over the window that Skeetah broke while Randall holds me up, one arm around the soft push of my abdomen and his other arm like a set under my butt, I can hear the cows, big and stupid, shuffling in the barn, letting out little low-ing complaints, knocking the walls as if they are looking for escape. I wipe my eyes.

"The house," Randall says.

Randall lets me down slow. The wood is rough under my hands. When I look at the boards in front of me, I see one dark splash like paint, one maroon tear from where Skeetah fell out of the window; it's his blood. I wonder if the old limping man smiled when he saw it, felt some kind of joy at the fact that the boy was hurt, or if the limping white man just shook his head as he boarded it over, the anger making the hammer fly bad, bend the nails crooked so that they curve like commas.

The boards of the house are more even, more secure. They are not a patch-up of boards of different sizes like our house; there is no glass left peeking through cracks, only plywood closed smooth and tight as eyelids.

"Here." Randall tries to slide his finger between the board and the wall, but only his fingernail fits. "You try," he says, but my fingers will not go in either. I don't even think Junior's could. "We should've brought a crowbar."

I shake my head.

"Fuck!" Randall yells. He punches the plywood and it dints, dimples in the middle, and there is the sound of breaking wood and breaking glass. When he pulls his fist back, he's split the skin, smashed it, and he leaves blood on the board. He holds his hand. His face looks like how I imagine the glass behind the board looks; hard and lined, each piece sliding away from the other where they split, black in the cracks. His eyes look wet. "Shit." The blood pools in the valleys between his knuckles, rolls to waterfall between his fingers. He looks at me. "I couldn't do it even if I did have a crowbar."

"You ain't Skeet," I say. The taste of my tears is like raw oysters.

"We have to, Esch."

"It's too thick."

"We have to try."

Randall knees his chest like he is putting on pants and then he kicks his heel hard into the center of the plywood where he dented it. The glass behind it shatters. He kicks again and the wood splits; it sounds like a shot. Randall stops, and we both look around, scared, but there is no old man swinging a gun like an axe, no pink-dressed woman, just the cows lowing in the barn in the dark, the wind rustling past the trees, the air so wet and hot it could be rain.

"One more time," Randall says, and then he kicks again, all of his muscle straining against the hot day, the sealed gingerbread house, and the board cracks in two but will not fall because of the nails, and Randall is crouching on the ground, clutching his bad knee.

"The wrong knee," he says, and blows on his kneecap like he's scraped it bloody and he is trying to blow away the pain and grit, like Mama did to our scrapes when we were younger. If the scrapes were on the front of our knees, she would put our dirty feet in the middle of her chest to clean the wounds, and we could feel her heart beating, strong as the thud of the ground when we walked, through our soles. "Look inside."

I put my eye to the slit and there is darkness and the gauzy blow of curtains. Under the darkness, there is the empty smell of potpourri and Pine-Sol. Two fingers can fit through the crack, nothing more.

"There's nothing there. It smells clean. Probably took everything when they evacuated."

Randall rubs the skin around and below his knee.

"She looked like the type of woman that wouldn't leave nothing to spoil."

Randall laughs, but it is dry and scrapes past his throat like brown leaves scratched along the ground by wind.

"Come on," Randall says.

Randall clutches his hand to his chest when he walks, hopping on his bad knee. I stop at the edge of the clearing and look back at the barn, the cows safe inside it. I can see them brushing against one another in the rank hay dark, their wet noses turned up toward the ceiling, wondering where the blue has gone, the bitter green grass, their bird familiars. How they'd crave the touch of a wing.

On the walk back, it is weird to see Randall walking without swinging his long loose arms. The wood is a sleeping animal: still empty. It is all wrong. I hear the rustling before Randall does, and I have to reach out to stop him, since he has been watching his bad knee.

"Look."

It is China. She drops something rust-colored and then shoves her nose in it from side to side like a screwdriver. Then she points with her head and dives into what she has dropped, rolling in it; she moves like smoke, the pink pads of her feet waving in the air. Her eyes are squeezed shut and she wears a wide, gum-bearing leer. Her fur is turning red.

"What is that?" Randall asks.

China must hear because she stops her squirming mid-roll and springs up, water frozen to ice, her lips sealed, her tail out. She sees us, looks down at her prize, and then raises her nose to the simmering sky and barks, once. Then she runs away.

It is a dead chicken, opened raw and still warm. I imagine that it looks like the inside of my throat, pink with salt and blood.

"That's ours," I say, but Randall is silent as he starts walk-hopping toward the Pit and the house.

"What are you doing?"

Randall says it like he's been at the park all day, running himself darker and straighter on the court, running himself until all he becomes is muscle and breath. He is tired, and he stands in the doorway of his room, the hall light on overhead, staring. It was a long walk. I shuffle down the hall, alcohol in hand, a wet paper towel for his fist, which he holds close enough to his face to suck. Junior sucked his knuckles until he was two, then he stopped.

Skeet is sitting on his bed, and China has her forelegs on his lap, her nose up; when her neck moves, she is graceful as the spider lilies that grow out on the bayou, bending out over the water. She is licking Skeetah's chin. There are pink smears from the chicken on her jaw. Skeetah is smiling, the kind of shy smile I haven't seen on his face since he used to steal packets of Kool-Aid when we were younger and suck the bitter powder, his teeth electric blue or blood red. The puppies sigh and whine in their bucket, which is in the corner of their room along with the fifty pound bags of dog food, the leashes, the half-shredded tires, China's blanket.

"I'm bringing her inside for the storm." Skeetah doesn't look up.

"Fuck no," Randall says.

"I ain't leaving them in the shed."

"Why not?"

"It ain't strong enough is why not."

"Ain't nothing wrong with it."

"It's too flimsy for them."

"This is a house, Skeetah. For humans. Not for dogs."

Skeet looks up. The shy smile, gone. He stops China's licking by muzzling her with both hands, and she is as still as any of the wrecks in the yard. The scabbed-over wounds on her make her look as rusted as they are.

"I'm not leaving them out there."

Randall's face shatters then, and all that's left is an open window.

"I'm telling Daddy."

"Fucking tell him then." Skeetah is all teeth. He lets go of China and stands, and she slides off of him, lands squarely, follows Skeet out of the room. All three of them stand in the door of Daddy's room as Randall yanks it open and goes in.

"Daddy." No sound. "Daddy!"

Daddy lays on his side with his back to us like he's just fallen from something tall, a tree or a fence, and has shattered bone. He rolls over to face us, drags himself up on an elbow.

"What?" This sounds ripped from him, as if he is speaking around the pain. "What do you want?"

"Skeet trying to bring the dogs inside for the storm."

"Inside?" Daddy's eyes shine in the dark like an armadillo's. "Inside what?"

"Inside the house."

"No," Daddy says. He lays back on his pillows, rolls toward his hand.

"No," says Skeetah. He elbows past Randall, stands in front of him. China weaves through at his thigh, sits, her tongue out, looking almost like a normal dog. "I'm not leaving them out there."

"No?" Daddy faces him, lurches up on an elbow. "What you mean, no? I said they couldn't stay and they can't!" He would be shouting if he was better, but he stops for breath between every other word, and what comes out is in wheezes.

"If they go, I go," Skeetah says.

"What?" Daddy breathes.

"If they go out in the shed, I go in the shed." Skeetah steps farther into Daddy's black room, and he is a blankness in the dark, his voice coming from no face, no head. China glows like white sand on a moonlit river beach.

"You ain't going out in no shed" — Daddy coughs, his throat dry — "with no dog."

"Yes, I am." The darkness moves. "And if Randall try to stop me, we going to fight. All of us."

"Don't make me get up." Daddy swings his legs over the side of the bed, pushes up with his good hand, but his feet get tangled up in the sheets, and he tries to untangle them with his bad hand, and then yanks it back up and wobbles, high from the pain medicine. He lists like he's drunk.

Skeetah moves to leave Daddy's room and comes into the light from the lighbulb in the hallway like a swimmer surfacing from a dark swimming hole: Manny swimming up from the bottom of the black hole, eating light, splashing out, being born.

"Everything deserve to live," Skeetah says. "And her and the puppies going to live."

"Skeet," Randall says, and Skeet and China stop in their walk, all three of them meeting in the doorway, China's ears flat on her head, tail up, still and tense as Skee-tah.

"What?" Skeetah barks. They are on either side of a crooked mirror, one short, the other tall, both muscle and tendon, tension, wounded knuckles, hands curling.

"I ain't sleeping in the room with her." Randall reaches. His good hand grabs.

"Stop!" Daddy's voice is hard, loud. He slumps like it was all he had in him to breathe it out. "No. No fighting."

I have to lean to hear him. He sways, punches his good arm in the mattress to hold himself up.

"It's a category five," Daddy says. "Woman on the news say it's a category five."

"Oh," I say, but it is more a breath than a word. Daddy has faced a category 5, but we're too young to remember the last category 5 hurricane that hit the coast: Camille, almost forty years ago. But Mama told us stories about that one.

"She stay in the room, Skeet. If I see her once out, I'm kicking her out in the middle of the storm, you hear? Randall, make do."

Daddy's arm buckles.

"I need some soup, Esch."

Skeetah folds his arms, cocks his head at Randall like a dog. Randall shakes his.

"We usually sleep in the living room

anyway, Randall," I say, whispering, remembering how tender he was when he found me in the ditch.

"Esch," Daddy breathes. He lays back on his side, facing the door.

"Yeah, Daddy," Randall says. "I'll get it." He brushes by, stiff-armed, and leaves me and Skeetah standing in the hallway. The gas hisses on in the kitchen.

"Everything need a chance, Esch," Skeet says, and he and China turn into his doorway. China sprawls on the floor, ears pointed to the ceiling again. Her tail thumps, and she smiles. The skin on either side of her scabbed breast pulls tight. Skeetah takes the puppies out one by one, cupping their round bellies, and lays them on the floor, where their noses start twitching and they begin jerking toward China. She looks at them like she looked at the chickens earlier. She licks. "Everything," Skeetah says and looks through me.

THE ELEVENTH DAY: KATRINA

When mama first explained to me what a hurricane was, I thought that all the animals ran away, that they fled the storms before they came, that they put their noses to the wind days before and knew. That maybe they stuck their tongues out, pink and warm, to taste, to make sure. That the deer looked at their companions and leapt. That the foxes chattered to themselves, rolled their shoulders, and started off. And maybe the bigger animals do. But now I think that other animals, like the squirrels and the rabbits, don't do that at all. Maybe the small don't run. Maybe the small pause on their branches, the pine-lined earth, nose up, catch that coming storm air that would smell like salt to them, like salt and clean burning fire, and they prepare like us. The squirrels pack feathers, pack pine straw, pack shed fur and acorns from the oaks in the bowels of their trees, line them so that they are buried deep in the trunks, so safe they can hardly hear the storm cracking around them. The rabbits stand in profile, shank to shank, smell that storm smell that hits them all at once like a loud sound, and they tunnel down through the red clay and the sand, down until the earth turns black and cold, down past all the roots, until they have dug great halls so deep that they sit right above the underground reservoirs we tap into with our wells, and during the hurricane, they hear water lapping above and below while they sit safe in the hand of the earth.

Last night, we laid sleeping pallets in the living room, whose windows we'd lined with mismatched wood. Randall and I, side by side, on the floor, and Junior on the couch. We brought our own limp pillows, our flat and fitted sheets, and our old electric blankets short-circuited cold long ago. We piled them to create mattresses so flimsy we could feel the nubby carpet on the floor underneath us when we sat. We washed all the dishes. We filled the bathtub, the kitchen and the bathroom sinks to the brims with water that we could use for washing and flushing the toilet. We ate a few of the boiled eggs, and Randall cooked noodles for all of us. We balanced the hot bowls in our laps and watched TV. We took turns picking shows. Randall watched a home improvement show where a newlywed couple converted a room in their house from an office into a mint-green nursery. I chose a documentary on cheetahs. Junior picked last, and once there were cartoons on the screen, even after Junior fell asleep, we let them turn us bright colors in the dark. Daddy stayed in his room, but he left the door open. Skeetah stayed in his room with China and the puppies, but that door was closed.

Before I fell asleep, in the flickering light from the television and one dusty lamp, I read. In ancient Greece, for all her heroes, for Medea and her mutilated brother and her devastated father, water meant death. In the bathroom on the toilet, I heard the clanking of metal against metal outside, some broken machine tilting like a sinking headstone against another, and I knew it was the wind pushing a heavy rain.

On the day before a hurricane hits, the phone rings. When Mama was living, she picked it up; it is a phone call from the state government that goes out to everyone in the area who will be hit by a storm. Randall has answered it since we lost Mama; he lets it play at least once each summer. Skeetah answered once and hung up before the recording could get beyond the *hello*. Junior never has picked it up, and neither has Daddy. I picked it up for the first time yesterday. A man's voice speaks; he sounds like a computer, like he has an iron throat. I cannot remember exactly what he says, but I remember it in general. *Mandatory evacuation. Hurricane making landfall tomorrow. If you choose to stay in your home and have not evacuated by this time, we are not responsible. You have been warned.* And *these could be the consequences of your actions.* There is a list. And I do not know if he says this, but this is what it feels like: *You can die.*

This is when the hurricane becomes real.

The first hurricane that I remember happened when I was nine, and of the two or three we get every year, it was the worst I've ever been in. Mama let me kneel next to the chair she'd dragged next to the window. Even then, our boards were mismatched, and there were gaps we could peer out of, track the progress of the storm in the dark. The battery-operated radio told us nothing practical, but the yard did: the trees bending until almost breaking, arcing like fishing line, empty oil drums rattling across the

336

yard, the water running in clear streams, carving canyons. Her stomach was big with Junior, and I laid a hand on it and watched. Junior was a surprise, a happy accident; she'd had me and Skeetah and Randall a year apart each, and then nothing else for nine years. I kneeled next to her and put my ear to her stomach and heard the watery swish of Junior inside her, as outside the wind pulled, branch by root, until it uprooted a tree ten feet from the house. Mama watched with her eye to the slit formed by the board over the window. She rocked from side to side like the baby in her would not let her sit still. She stroked my hair.

That storm, Elaine, had been a category 3. Katrina, as the newscaster said late last night after we settled in the living room, echoing Daddy, has reached a category 5.

During Elaine, Randall and Daddy had slept. Skeetah had sat on the other side of Mama, opposite me, and she'd told us about the big storm when she was little, the legend: Camille. She said Mother Lizbeth and Papa Joseph's roof was ripped off the house. She said the smell afterward was what she remembered most clearly, a smell like garbage set to rot, seething with maggots in the hot sun. She said the newly dead and the old dead littered the beaches, the

337

streets, the woods. She said Papa Joseph found a skeleton in the yard, gleaming, washed clean of flesh and clothing, but she said it still stank like a bad tooth in the mouth. She said that Papa Joseph never took the remains down to the church, but carried it in an oyster sack out into the woods; she thought he buried the bones there. She said she and Mother Lizbeth walked miles for water from an artesian well. She said she got sick, and most everybody did, because even then the water wasn't clean, and she had dreamed that she could never get away from water because she couldn't stop shitting it or pissing it or throwing it up. She said there would never be another like Camille, and if there was, she didn't want to see it.

I fell asleep after everyone else did last night, and now I wake before everyone. Daddy snores so loudly I can hear him from his room. Randall sleeps with his face turned to the sofa Junior is asleep on, his back to me, curved like he hides something. Junior has one arm off the sofa, one leg, and his cover hangs from him. The TV is dead. The house is quiet in a way it never is, its electric hum silent; in our sleep, the arriving storm has put a strangling hand over the house. We've lost power. Through the crack in the living room window, the morning is dark gray and opaque as dirty dishwater. The rain clatters on the rusted tin roof. And the wind, which yesterday only made itself known by sight, sighs and says, *Hello.* I lay here in the dark, pull my thin sheet up to my neck, stare at the ceiling, and do not answer.

Mama had talked back to Elaine. Talked over the storm. Pulled us in in the midst of it, kept us safe. This secret that is no longer a secret in my body: Will I keep it safe? If I could speak to this storm, spell it harmless like Medea, would this baby, the size of my fingernail, my pinkie fingernail, maybe, hear? Would speaking make it remember me once it is born, make it know me? Would it look at me with Manny's face, with his golden skin, with my hair? Would it reach out with its fingers, pink, and grasp?

The sun will not show. It must be out there, over the furious hurricane beating itself against the coastline like China at the tin door of the shed when she wants to get out and Skeet will not let her. But here on the Pit, we are caught in the hour where the sun is hidden beyond the trees but hasn't escaped over the horizon, when it is coming and going, when light comes from everywhere and nowhere, when everything is gray.

I lie awake and cannot see anything but that baby, the baby I have formed whole in my head, a black Athena, who reaches for me. Who gives me that name as if it is mine: *Mama.* I swallow salt. That voice, ringing in my head, is drowned out by a train letting out one long, high blast. And then it disappears, and there is only the sound of the wind like a snake big enough to swallow the world sliding against mountains. And then the wind like a train, again, and the house creaks. I curl into a ball.

"Did you hear that?"

It is Skeetah; I can barely see him. He is only a wash of greater darkness that moves in the dark opening of the hallway.

"Yeah," I say. My voice sounds like I have a cold, all the mucus from my crying lodged in my nose. *A train,* Mama said. *Camille came, and the wind sounded like trains.* When Mama told me this, I put my nose in her knee. I'd heard trains before when we went swimming on the oyster shell beach, and the train that ran through the middle of St. Catherine would sound loudly in the distance. I could not imagine wind sounding like that. But now I hear, and I can.

"Where's the lamp?"

"On the table," I squeaked. Skeetah walked toward the table, bumping into things in the half-light, and fumbled the kerosene lantern to light.

"Come on," Skeetah says, and I follow him to the back of the house, to his and Randall's room, which seems smaller than it is, and close and hot and red in the light of a smaller kerosene lamp that Skeet must have found in the shed. He shuts the door behind us after eyeing Daddy's open door. The wind shrieks. Trees reach out their arms and beat their limbs against the house. Skeet sits on his bed next to China, who sprawls and lifts her head to look at me lazily, and who licks her nose and mouth in one swipe. I climb onto Randall's bed, hug my knees. The puppies' bucket is quiet.

"You scared?"

"No," Skeetah says. He rubs a hand from the nape of China's neck over her shoulder, her torso, her thigh. She lets her head roll back and licks again.

"I am," I say. "I never heard the wind sound like that."

"We ain't even on the bay. We back far enough up in the trees to be all right. All these Batistes been living up here all these years through all these hurricanes and they been all right. I'm telling you."

"Remember when Mama told us that the wind sounded like that when Camille hit?" I squeeze tighter. "Elaine wasn't nothing like this."

"Yeah, I remember." Skeetah rubs his fingers under China's chin, and it is like he is coaxing something from her because she leans toward him and grins, tries to kiss him. "I can remember her saying it." He stops rubbing China, leans forward to put his elbows on his knees, rubs his hands together, looks away. "But I can't remember her voice," he says. "I know the exact words she said, can see us sitting there by her lap, but all I can hear is my voice saying it, not hers."

I want to say that I know her voice. I want to open my mouth and have her voice slide out of me like an impression, to speak Mama alive for him as I hear her. But I can't.

"At least we got the memory," I say. "Junior don't have nothing."

"You remember the last thing she said to you?"

When Mama was birthing Junior, she put her chin down into her chest. She panted and moaned. The ends of her moans squeaked, sounded like bad brakes grinding when a car stops. She never screamed, though. Skeetah and Randall and I were sneaking, standing on an old air-conditioning unit outside her and Daddy's window, and after she pushed Junior out, once he started crying, she let her head fall to the side, her eyes like mirrors, and she was looking at us, and I thought she would yell at us to get down out of the window, to stop being nosy. But she didn't. She saw us. She blinked slow. The skin above her nose cracked and she bit her lip. She shook her head then, raised her chin to the ceiling like an animal on the slaughter stump, like I've seen Daddy and Papa Joseph hold pigs before the knife, and closed her eyes. She started crying then, her hands holding her belly below her deflated stomach, soft as a punctured kickball. I had never seen her cry. But she hadn't said anything, even after Daddy called some of their friends, Tilda and Mr. Joe, to the house to watch us, even after he carried her and Junior out to the truck and she slumped against the window, watching us as Daddy drove away. Shaking her head. Maybe that meant *no*. Or *Don't worry — I'm coming back*. Or *I'm sorry*. Or *Don't do it. Don't become the woman in this bed, Esch*, she could have been saying. But I have.

"No," I say. "I don't remember."

"I do," Skeetah says, and he props his chin on his fists. "She told us she loved us when she got into the truck. And then she told us to be good. To look after each other."

"I don't remember that." I think Skeetah is imagining it.

"She did." Skeetah sits up, leans back in the bed again, and lays a still hand on China's neck. She sighs. "You look like her. You know that?"

"No."

"You do. You not as big as her, but in the face. Something about your lips and eyes. The older you get the more you do."

I don't know what to say, so I half grimace, and I shake my head. *But Mama, Mama always here. See?* I miss her so badly I have to swallow salt, imagine it running like lemon juice into the fresh cut that is my chest, feel it sting.

"Did you hear that?"

"What?" I sound stuffed again. Leaves slap the roof in great bunches. The rain is heavy, endless, hits the roof in quick crashing waves. At least the wind doesn't sound like a train again.

"That," Skeetah says, his head to one side, his ear cocked toward the window. His eyes gleam in the light of the lamp. He stands up, and China stands up with him, ears straight, tail pointed, tongue gone. Somewhere out in the storm, a dog is barking.

"Yeah," I say, and then all three of us are at the window, peering out of the light edge left by the boards. We hear the dog but can't see it; what we do see is the pines, the thin trees bending with the storm, bending almost to breaking. Even the oaks are losing leaves and branches in the gray light, the beating rain. The dog barks loudly, fast as a drum, and something about the way the bark rises at the end reminds me of Mama's moans, of those bowing pines, of a body that can no longer hold itself together, of something on the verge of breaking. The high notes are little rips. It circles the house, its bark near and far. Is it one of Junior's mutts, his mangy family member, seeking shelter, the cool bottom of a house and a knobby-kneed boy and no rain?

"We can't." Skeetah leans toward the window as if he could push his way through the glass and board and save that invisible dog, who for him, I know, must be China. She drops from where she has been standing on her hind legs with her paws pressed against the wall and leans into Skeetah's side, head-butts his thigh, her smooth white head and floppy ears as soft as the swaddling blankets that Daddy brought Junior home in after he returned from the hospital and Mama didn't. *This your little brother. Claude Adam Batiste the second. Call him Junior.* And then, *Your mama didn't make it.* The searching dog barks one last time before the rain and wind tighten like a choke collar and silence him. China growls in answer, but swallows it when Skeetah kneels before her, takes her face in his hands, and smoothes her ears back so that her eyes are slits and she grins and her skin pulls tight and her head could be a naked skull.

China squeals and jumps up into a bark, skitters back and forth across Skeetah's bed, over his knees; this is what makes me look up from my crouch on Randall's bed, from my stomach, from me trying to burrow into myself, to safety. China looks to the ceiling, her teeth gleaming in the dark, ripping barks.

"China, what's . . . ?" Skeetah reaches out to grab her, to stop her from curling and running, and there is a loud, deafening boom. When it comes, China leaps from Skeetah's bed and rushes to the door as if she would rip the wood to splinters with her teeth. Skeetah yanks the door open, and Randall is running into Daddy's room with a lantern, Junior clinging to his waist while the wind yells outside and the house shudders. There was no need for the lamp; there is a hole in the ceiling in Daddy's room, the trunk and branches of a tree tossing in the opening. It is a large bush growing wrong. China barks, her nose to the wind.

"Daddy!" Randall runs forward into the wind and rain streaming through the gaping hole, the gray day fisting through it. Daddy is on his knees in front of the dresser, pushing an envelope down his pants. He stands and sees us.

"Go on!" Daddy says. He waves at us, the bandage on his wounded hand flashing light. He is slack and then tight like a clothesline catching in the wind, and he shoves us out of the ruined room and into the hallway, pulling the door shut behind him. Junior will not let go of Randall.

"We'll stay in the living room." Daddy says this as he slumps over on the sofa, pushing his head back into the cushion like Mama pushed hers back into the pillow, baring his neck. He's blinking too much.

"Your hand," Randall says.

"It's fine," says Daddy. "We going to stay here until the storm's over."

"When you think?" Skeetah asks.

"A few hours."

347

China squeals and barks again.

"She knew," I say.

"Knew what?" Daddy's face is wet, and I don't know whether it is water or sweat.

"Nothing," Skeetah says.

"About the tree," I say at the same time. Skeetah rubs China's neck, and she gives a swallowed growl and sits, lays her head along Skeetah's thigh and up his hip, her nose to him.

"She didn't know nothing," Skeetah says, and then he and China step as one, a new animal, toward the light opening of the hallway where the wind whistles in a thin sheet under Daddy's door. They are going back to Skeetah and Randall's room.

"Come in the living room, Skeet," Daddy says. He rolls his eyes, closes them. Bares his teeth. "Please."

I pick my blankets up, wrap them around me, and sit where I had lain. Skeetah walks back in with China, sets the bucket and China's food and leashes and toys in the corner of the living room farthest away from Daddy, next to the TV. Skeetah lays his blanket against the corner, makes a chair, and China drapes herself across his lap, long and white, and lays her head along her paw and begins licking the pink pads of her feet. Skeetah rubs her, sets his small kerosene lamp down, and in the half-dark, China gleams butter yellow with the flame.

"Junior," Randall says, "I know you ain't pee yourself."

Junior leans over, touches the ground beneath his butt, his face in his thighs.

"I didn't do that."

"Then why it's all wet over here?"

We have been sitting in the living room, terrified and bored. I'm trying to read by the oil lamp, but the sound of the words are not coming together over the sound of the wind and the rain relentlessly bearing down on the house; they are fragments. Jason has remarried, and Medea is wailing. *An exile, oh God, oh God, alone.* And then: *By death, oh, by death, shall the conflict be decided. Life's little day ended.* I shut the book, don't even mark my place, and sit on it. I am cold. Skeetah and China look like they've fallen asleep, his hand on her flank and her breastbone on his knee, but when Randall says this, their eyes open to slits at the same time. The half deck of UNO cards that Randall had been attempting to teach Junior how to play stick to the floor around Junior's legs. I shrug out of my covers; the thin stream of air that whispers from under Daddy's door brushes past me like a boy in a

349

school hallway, insistent and brusque, and *Why are my shorts wet? Is it gone? Am I bleeding? Shouldn't I be cramping?* I stand. The floor underneath me is dark.

China rolls to her feet, her teeth out, and Skeetah grabs her by her scruff as she lunges. He holds her still. He stands, looking calmly about the room.

"It's water. It's coming in the house," Skeetah says.

"Ain't no water coming in the house. Wood just getting a little damp from the rain," Daddy says.

"It's coming up through the floor," says Skeetah.

"Ain't nowhere for it to come from." Daddy waves at the room, waves like he's stopping one of us from giving him something he doesn't want: his antibiotics, a letter from a teacher, a school fundraising brochure.

"Look," Randall says, and he walks over to the window facing the street and bends like an old man, peering out. "Lot of trees on the road."

"But you don't see no water," Daddy says.

"No."

Skeetah and China walk past Junior, who stands where Randall left him in front of the sofa. Junior is picking up each foot, setting it down; he looks at the bottoms as if he cannot believe that he has feet and that they are wet. He pulls his shorts away from him, but they stick anyway. Skeetah peers out of the window, with China next to him.

"There," Skeetah says. Randall and I run to the window at Skeetah's side, but Junior is there first, and we are all over each other, our feet wet, the carpet a soaked sponge where we stand, Daddy looking at the window like it isn't boarded up, like he can see through it.

There is a lake growing in the yard. It moves under the broken trees like a creeping animal, a wide-nosed snake. Its head disappears under the house where we stand, its tail wider and wider, like it has eaten something greater than itself, and that great tail stretches out behind it into the woods, toward the Pit. China barks. The wind ripples the water and it is coming for us.

There is water over my toes.

"The Pit," Randall sighs.

Daddy gets up then, walks slowly over to the window, each bone bent the wrong way in each joint. Randall moves so Daddy can see out of the crack.

"No," Daddy says.

I shift, and the water licks my ankles. It is cold, cold as a first summer swim. China barks, and when she jumps down from the window and bounces, there is a splash.

"Daddy?" Randall says. He puts his arm over Junior, who, cringing with his eyes wide, hugs Randall's leg. But for once, Randall's arm doesn't look like metal, like ribbon, like stone; it bends at the elbow, soft, without muscle, and looks nothing but human.

"Daddy!" Junior squeals, but he buries his face in Randall's hip, and Randall's hip eats the end of the word. Junior rises an inch or so; he must be on his toes. The water is up to the middle of my calf.

"Look," I say.

There is something long and dark blue between the trees. It is a boat. Someone has come to save us. But then I squint and the wind lags clear for one second, and it is not a boat, and no one has come to save us. It is Daddy's truck. The water has picked it up, pushed it from the Pit. The snake has come to eat and play.

"Your truck," Skeetah says.

Daddy begins to laugh.

The snake has swallowed the whole yard and is opening its jaw under the house.

"Open the attic," Daddy says.

The water is lapping the backs of my knees.

"It's stuck," Randall says. He is pulling at the string that hangs from the door of the attic, which is in the ceiling of the hallway.

"Move," says Skeetah.

The water is tonguing its way up my thighs. Skeetah hands me the puppies' bucket.

"Hurry," Randall says.

The three puppies squeal little yips that sound like whispered barks. These are their first words.

"Pull down," Daddy says. He frowns, holds his hand up like he is pulling the cord.

The water slides past my crotch, and I jump.

"All right!" Skeet yells. He pulls himself up on the cord, like he is swinging from a swing rope in a tree, and the attic door groans downward.

"Up!" Randall says, and he is shoving Junior up the ladder into the attic. China is swimming next to Skeetah, her head bobbing like a buoy.

"Go!" Skeetah says, and he pushes me toward the ladder. I float on the water, my toes dragging on the hallway carpet. He grabs my back and steadies me as I slog into the attic with the bucket.

"Esch!" Junior says.

"I'm here." Junior's eyes are white in the dark. The wind beats the roof, and it creaks. Randall is next, then Daddy, and last, Skeetah and China. I cup the bucket with my knees, sit on a pile of boxes, fish out a broken ornament that is digging into my thigh. Christmas decorations. Randall is sitting on an old chain saw, Junior cowering next to him. Daddy takes out the package he put in his pants after the tree fell into his room. It is a clear plastic bag. He opens the packet, pulls out pictures. Just before Skeetah pulls shut the attic door, seals us in darkness, Daddy makes as if he would touch one of the pictures, hesitant, as lightly as if he is dislodging an eyelash, but his glistening finger stops short, and he wraps the pictures again and puts them in his pants. *Mama.*

The attic door moans shut.

The roof is thin; we can hear every fumbling rush of the wind, every torrent of rain. And it is so dark that we cannot see each other, but we hear China barking, and her bark sounds like a fat dog's, so deep, like dense cloth ripping.

"Quiet, China!" Skeetah says, and China shuts her jaw so quickly and so hard, I can hear the click of her teeth shuttering together. I put my face down in the bucket; the puppies do not hear. They mewl still. I feel them with my hand, still downy, their coats just now turning to silk, and they squirm at my touch. The white, the brindle, the black and white. They lick for milk.

"The house," Randall says, and his voice is steady, calm, but I can hardly contain the panic I feel when the house tilts, slowly as an unmoored boat.

"It's the water," Skeetah says. "It's the water."

"Shit!" Daddy yells, and then we are all bracing in the dark as the house tilts again.

"Water," I say.

"It never came back here." Daddy breathes. "The damn creek."

"Daddy," I say, and I'm surprised at how clear my voice is, how solid, how sure, like a hand that can be held in the dark. "Water's in the attic."

The water is faster this time; it wraps liquid fingers around my toes, my ankles, begins creeping up my calves. This is a fast seduction. The wind howls.

"There was a family . . . ," Randall says.

"We know," Daddy says. Fourteen of them drowned in Camille. In their attic. The house lifts up off of its bricks again, and rocks.

"We're not drowning in this fucking attic," Skeet says, and I hear a banging, again and again. I look up and debris falls in my eyes. He is beating at the inside of the roof. He is making a way.

"Move," Randall says. "Junior, go by Esch." And I feel Junior's little pin fingers on my wrists, and he bangs into something, and he is a monkey on top of the bucket, locked to my lap. "I got it."

Randall is swinging something in the dark, and when it crashes into the roof, it makes a dent, a chink of light. He bashes the wood, grunts. Whatever he swings is making a hole. He swings it again, and the wood opens to a small hole no bigger than my finger, and I see that he is swinging the chain saw, hitting the roof with the blunt end.

"Any gas" — Randall bashes — "in here?"

"Can't remember," Daddy yells. The storm speaks through the hole, funnels wind and rain through. We squint toward it. The water is over my crotch. The house lists.

Randall cranks once, twice. He pulls the cord back a third time and it catches, and the saw buzzes to life. He shoves it through the finger-wide opening, cuts a jagged line, draws it back out, cuts another jagged line, a parenthesis, before it chugs to a stop. He tries to crank it again, but it will not start. He swings it instead, an awkward hammer, and the wood cracks, bends outward. He swings again, and the closed eyelid he drew with the cutting saw, with the blows, flutters, and the roof opens. The storm screams, *I have been waiting for you.* Light floods the flooded attic, close as a coffin. Randall grabs Junior, who swings around and clings to his back, his small hands tight as clothespins, and Randall climbs out and into the hungry maw of the storm.

It is terrible. It is the flailing wind that lashes like an extension cord used as a beating belt. It is the rain, which stings like stones, which drives into our eyes and bids them shut. It is the water, swirling and gathering and spreading on all sides, brown with an undercurrent of red to it, the clay of the Pit like a cut that won't stop leaking. It is the remains of the yard, the refrigerators and lawn mowers and the RV and mattresses, floating like a fleet. It is trees and branches breaking, popping like Black Cat firecrackers in an endless crackle of explosions, over and over and again and again. It is us huddling together on the roof, me with the wire of the bucket handle looped over my shoulder, shaking against the plastic. It is everywhere. Daddy kneels behind us, tries to gather all of us to him. Skeetah hugs China, and she howls. Daddy's truck careens slowly in the yard.

Skeetah is hunched over, picking at his jeans. He takes off his pants, tries to hold them still in front of him; the legs whip in the wind. He shoves China's back legs into the crotch, and then he flings one pant leg over his shoulder, and the other he tucks under his underarm.

"Tie it!" Skeetah yells.

I tie it in a knot. My fingers are stiff and numb. I pull the wet fabric as hard as I can, test it. China's head and legs are smashed to his chest, pinned under the fabric. She is his baby in a sling, and she is shaking.

"Look!" Skeet says and points. I follow his finger to the hollow carcass of Mother Lizbeth and Papa Joseph's house. The top half and the eaves of the house are above water. "It's on a hill!" Skeetah screams.

"How are we going to get there?" Randall yells.

"The tree!" Skeetah is inching down the roof to a spreading oak tree that touches our house and stretches to MaMa's house. It rises like a jungle gym over the seething

358

water. "We're going to climb the tree!"

"No!" Daddy yells. "We're going to stay here!"

"What if the water keeps coming?" Randall asks. "Better for us to take that chance than stay here and drown!"

Junior's teeth are sealed together, his lips peeled back. His eyes are blasted open. As Randall picks his way down the roof toward the branch, Junior looks back. Randall braces an arm across his chest, holds Junior's arm.

"Just like the first time we swam in the pit, Junior! Hold on!" Randall crouches at the edge of the roof with Skeetah, both of them hunched like birds, feathers ruffled against the bad wind, both of them holding their bundles closely. Skeetah leaps.

He catches the closest ricocheting branch, lands half in and half out of the water. China yelps and begins to struggle, but Skeetah grips her harder with one arm and pulls himself down the branch until it bows to the water. And then he leaps again, for the next whipping branch. He jumps and grabs. I reshoulder my bucket, pick my way toward the edge. The wind flattens me down to the roof. Randall leaps, lands on the same close branch with his stomach, his arms iron again, binding Junior to him. Both Skeetah and Randall scramble along the half-naked branches of the oak with one arm and both legs, using the limbs to pull themselves and their burdens until they reach water, when they kick their feet, scoot back up the branch, and leap for the next whipping limb. Randall stops, braces himself on the branch, looks back.

"Come on!" he yells.

I grip the tin with my toes, my fingers, crouched on my haunches at the edge of the roof. Readjust the bucket. My heart is a wounded bird, beating its wings against the cage of my ribs. I don't think I can breathe.

"Jump," Daddy says.

I lean out and leap.

The hurricane enfolds me in its hand. I glide. I land on the thickest branch, the wood gouging me, the bucket clanging, unable to breathe, my eyes tearing up. I scramble at the wood, pull myself along the branch, my feet in and out of the water, the steel handle to the bucket digging into my shoulder, my living burden already so heavy. The bare bones of Mother Lizbeth's house are so far away; I do not know if I can carry it that far. I inch to the end of the branch where it plunges beneath the water to join the trunk of the tree, and I dig in with my hands and feet. Clutch. Jump. Catch the next branch, where Randall is waiting. The branches we are grasping and grabbing shudder, twist in the water and air. The little branches whip like clotheslines come unpinned. It is an animal, alive, struggling against the water, trying to shove us off its back.

I look back to see Daddy hurtling through the air. He hits the branch so hard with his torso that his body jackknifes and his face is almost in the water. He is shocked still; he's knocked the wind out of himself. He looks up at us, blinks. Whispers it, but we cannot hear it, only see it. *Go.*

Skeetah has worked his way to the middle of the tree, which buds out of the water, and he is swimming and thrusting from branch to branch. We follow him through the whipping branches, the undulating water. Through plastic bags that skim the surface of the flood like birds. Through the clothesline that knots the branches like fishing net. Through our clothes, swept from the flooded house. Through the plywood, ripped from the windows, pried away by the teeth of the storm. Through the rain that comes down in curtains, sluicing against Daddy's lazily spinning truck, the detritus, until we cluster at the end of the farthest-reaching branch, the one closest to the

361

grandparents' house. We clutch each other and the swaying branches. China is pawing at Skeetah's breast, snapping her head back and forth. She is jerking away from him, and he clutches her with one white-tipped hand. The bucket feels like it's tearing the skin on my shoulder, feels like I'm carrying three grown dogs instead of three puppies. Where barely the top of the tree had been visible at our house, the branches here are clearly above the flood. The water here comes up to the middle of the closest window: the house must have been built on a small hill, and we never noticed it.

"I'ma swim, break the window. Y'all come in," Skeetah says.

"Hurry," Randall says.

"Esch, you come with me!" Skeetah says.

"This ain't the time!" Daddy yells.

"This ain't about the puppies!" Skeetah squints at me.

"She too small!" Daddy hollers. He grabs my free elbow with his good hand. Grips.

"She's pregnant." Skeetah points.

Daddy's face shuts, and he pushes.

Daddy saw it, that second before he pushed me. My big T-shirt and my shorts fitting me like a second skin, sodden with water. Where I used to be all sharp elbows and thighs straight as pines and a stomach like a paved road, my wet clothes show the difference. Daddy saw the curve of a waist, the telltale push of a stomach outward. Daddy saw fruit. I'm flailing backward with the bucket, the squeaking puppies. And in that second after he pushes me, Daddy is reaching out with his good hand, his bad hand hooked to the branch he crouches on, his eyes open and hurt and sorry as I haven't seen him since he handed Junior over to me and Randall, said, *Your mama* — and I kick, grasping at the air, but the hurricane slaps me, and I land in the water on my back, the puppies flying out of the bucket, their eyes open for the first time to slits and, I swear, judging me as they hit.

"Esch!" Randall yells, and Junior tightens his legs like a looping shoestring across Randall's waist. Randall grips Junior's shins, those legs thin as rulers. Randall can't jump in. "Swim!" he screams.

I kick my legs and palm water, but I can barely keep my head above it. It is a fanged pink open mouth, and it is swallowing me.

"Fuck!" Skeetah yells. He looks down at China, who is thrusting up and against his sling.

"Esch!" Junior screams, and the water is dragging me sideways, away from the window, out into the yard, toward the gullet of the Pit. I snatch at the puppy closest to me, the brindle, which is limp in my hand, and shove it down my shirt. The white and the black-and-white have disappeared.

"Fuck!" Skeetah screams. He grabs China's head, whispers something to her as she scrabbles against him. Her teeth show and she jerks backward away from him. She writhes. Her torso is out of the sling he has made. Skeetah grabs China by the head and pulls and her body comes out and she is scrambling. She flies clear of him, twists in the air to splash belly first in the water. She is already swimming, fighting. Skeetah jumps.

The water swallows, and I scream. My head goes under and I am tasting it, fresh and cold and salt somehow, the way tears taste in the rain. *The babies,* I think. I kick extra hard, like I am running a race, and my head bobs above the water but the hand of the hurricane pushes it down, down again. *Who will deliver me?* And the hurricane says *sssssssshhhhhhhh.* It shushes me through the water, with a voice muffled and deep, but then I feel a real hand, a human hand, cold and hard as barbed wire on my leg, pulling me back, and then I am being pushed up and out of the water, held by

364

Skeet, who is barely treading, barely keeping me and him afloat. China is a white head, spinning away in the relentless water, barking, and Skeetah is looking from her to me, screaming, *Hurry up! Hurry up!* at Randall, who is breaking what was left of the glass and wood of the window with his hands, his shoulders, his elbows, and diving through, while Junior clings to him close as a shell, and Skeetah is pushing me through the window, his hand a leash loop wrapped too tightly around my arm, his other hand treading, and he is calling, *China, come China,* but she is nowhere, and Daddy is swimming and sinking and jerking toward us, his bad hand flashing, and he is through the window and we are all struggling, grabbing at walls, at broken cabinets, at wood, until Randall stretches his way up to the open ceiling and hauls himself and Junior into the half-eaten attic, where the hurricane fingers the gaping roof, and Skeet pushes me up and through while Randall almost breaks my wrist with his grip as he hauls me up, and then Skeetah kicks off of something buried under the flood and is up and through the opening, and Daddy is on his back in the water below, treading with one hand and two feet, and Randall is hollering, *Help him!* and Skeet is laying next to the hole in the attic floor, looking at us, his face sick, twisted, and he is reaching a hand down to Daddy, hoisting him up, and the puppy must be dead in my shirt because it is not moving and I pull it out as I cough and cough up the water and the hurricane and the pit and I can't stop and Skeetah is braced, looking out the ravaged roof calling China, watching her cut through the swirling water straight as a water moccasin into the whipping, fallen woods in the distance, and Junior is rocking back and forth, squatting on the balls of his feet, his hands over his eyes because he does not want to see anymore; he is wailing *NoNoNoNoNoNoN-oNoNoNoNO.*

THE TWELFTH DAY: ALIVE

We sat in the open attic until the wind quieted from jet fighter planes to coughing puffs. We sat in the open attic until the sky brightened from a sick orange to a clean white gray. We sat in the open attic until the water, which had milled like a boiling soup beneath us, receded inch by inch, back into the woods. We sat in the open attic until the rain eased to drips. We sat in the open attic until we got cold, and the light wind that blew chilled us. We huddled together in Mother Lizbeth's attic and tried to rub heat from each other, but couldn't. We were a pile of wet, cold branches, human debris in the middle of all of the rest of it.

I scooted past Daddy, whose eyes were closed as he mumbled against his maimed hand and his good hand, which were folded like he was praying, past Randall, who still held Junior, who still had his hands over his eyes, to Skeetah. He crouched where the attic's roof was mostly gone, near the front of the long, low half room, and leaned out the gaping absence. He looked like he wanted to jump. I touched him in the middle of his shoulder blades. His skin was warm, hot as if he'd been running, as if the day was blazing bright. He jerked but didn't look back at me as he scanned the boiling water, the trees popping and flying, the old washing machine spinning like a bumper car around the yard, the wind ripping the land away. The wood under me felt wet and spongy, like it wanted to give. I put my legs to either side of his thighs, scooted up behind him, slid my arms under his armpits, and rested my face on his shoulder.

"I failed her," he said.

He blinked hard.

"No you didn't." I spoke into his neck.

"Yes," he said. His voice sounded like a rake being dragged over rocks.

"You didn't fail us," I said.

He shook his head, and his cheek brushed my forehead. The muscles under his jaw were jumping. He started to shake. I hugged him tighter, held him the way I'd embraced those boys I'd fucked because it was easier to let them get what they wanted instead of denying them, instead of making them see me. My arms had never been so strong.

I squeezed. With my whole body, I squeezed. I could hold him together, but he jerked so hard it felt like he was trying to shake himself apart, separate at the knuckles, pop loose his ribs, dislocate his shoulders, and dislodge his knees: shudder into nothing, a pile of skin and bone and limp muscle. No Skeet.

"It's going to be all right," I said.

The hurricane laughed. A tree, plucked from its branches, hopped across the yard and landed against Daddy's truck with a crunch, stopped short like it had won a game of hopscotch without stepping out of the lines. The sky was so close I felt like I could reach up and bury my arm in it.

Skeetah squinted into the storm, so I looked with him, searching for anything white, anything in the direction that China had whirled away, swimming furiously, barking. Plastic bags, a broken dryer, an old refrigerator. We could see nothing that held heat like China, nothing fighting. The hurricane gusted and peeled back a corner of our house, flung tin with a clatter into the air.

"It ain't steady now," I said. "It's easing up." I could see the living room, a messy doll's house. The trees cracked in protest around us. Skeetah hummed.

"China," he said.

The tractor, which had been buried under the water, peeked its head out, the top of its hood appearing from under the water.

"When it gets to the middle of the tires, I'm going," Skeetah said.

I said nothing, just hooked my fingers together, like I could've kept him there in a living chain.

When the first slice of rubber appeared over the rolling water, Skeetah started. He was a school of fish in my arms. The wind gusted and the trees clattered. There was a whirling sound in the sky, a whistle that was descending and rising, circling. The hurricane groaned, and it was like hearing a million Daddys moan and push back their chairs after eating plates full of fish fried whole, white bread for the bones, beer. The iron at the center of the tire peeked through, and it was an eye opening. Skeetah shrugged out of my embrace all at once: a school of fish exploding around a rock.

"Where you going?" I asked.

Skeetah was already past me, past Randall, in front of Daddy.

"Skeet?" Randall asked. Junior buried his face in Randall's muddy shirt.

Skeetah was at the hole we'd climbed through. The glass in the window had cut his face, his thighs, his chest, and his skin was running red. Then I looked at my arms, Randall, Junior, Daddy; we were all bleeding, all gashed.

"Boy," Daddy said.

"I got to find her," Skeetah said.

"The storm ain't over." Daddy rolled to his side, lifted his knees, and settled again as if he was trying to get more comfortable, find purchase to stand up, but none of us could with the bones of the ceiling folding so low.

Skeetah turned in his crouch. All that jumping, stilled. He was one animal again, or at least he thought he would soon be.

"She's waiting for me," he said, and jumped down through the ceiling, splashing in the water below.

"Skeet!" Randall yelled.

I looked out of our ragged window, the ripped roof, and saw him wade out into the yard, the water at his waist, his head up, his shoulders back, his arms raised, and his hands extended palms down inches over the water, as if he could calm it.

"Be careful," Daddy breathed, and I watched my brother walk almost naked out into the departing storm. He headed toward the Pit, the water swirling around him, the broken tops of the trees, the debris rising

371

like a labyrinth up out of the water. He paused, turned his head, and looked back at us. I waved through the ruined window. The air was getting cold. He turned and vanished around a tree growing sideways, into the maw of the maze. He left a thin wake.

When the water left, the front part of Daddy's truck was sitting on top of the smashed gas tank. The lower half was on the ground. All the water that had been in the car was out, and it left a muddy slime on the windows. The yard was one big puddle that we waded, so icy at our ankles, the first cold water we'd felt since the March rains, to the back door of the house, which was blasted open. The screen door was gone. The inside of the house was wet and muddy as Daddy's truck. The food we'd gotten had been washed from the shelves, and we hunted for it like we did for eggs, finding some silver cans of peas. We found Top Ramen, still sealed, in the sofa. We put them in our shirts. My hands were pink with Skeetah's blood from hugging him earlier. I washed them in a puddle in the living room.

"We can't stay here. We need shelter." Randall grimaced. "Your hand, and the water . . ." Randall trailed off. "Who knows what the water had in it."

Daddy shook his head, his lips weak as a baby's. He looked dazed. He stared at his truck, the ruined house, the yard invisible under the trees and the storm's deposits.

"Where," he said, and it was a statement with no answer.

"By Big Henry," Randall said.

Junior was on Randall's back, his eyes finally uncovered and open. He looked drunk.

"What about Skeet?" I asked.

"He'll find us," Randall said. "Daddy?" He raised an arm to Daddy, flicked his head toward the road.

"Yeah." Daddy cleared his throat.

"We can fix it," Randall said.

Daddy looked down at the ground, shrugged. He glanced at me and shame flittered across his face like a spider, sideways, fast, and then he looked past the house to the road and started walking slowly, uneven, limping. There was a gash in the back of his leg, bleeding through his pants.

We picked our way around the fallen, ripped trees, to the road. We were barefoot, and the asphalt was warm. We hadn't had time to find our shoes before the hand of the flood pushed into the living room. The storm had plucked the trees like grass and scattered them. We knew where the road

373

was by the feel of the stones wearing through the blacktop under our feet; the trees I had known, the oaks in the bend, the stand of pines on the long stretch, the magnolia at the four-way, were all broken, all crumbled. The sound of water running in the ditches like rapids escorted us down the road, into the heart of Bois Sauvage.

The first house we saw was Javon's, the shingles of his roof scraped off, the top bald; the house was dark and looked empty until we saw someone who must have been Javon, light as Manny, standing in front of the pile of wood that must have been the carport, lighting a lighter: a flicker of warmth in the cold air left by the storm. At the next nearest house, when the neighborhood started to cluster more closely together, we saw what others had suffered: every house had faced the hurricane, and every house had lost. Franco and his mother and father stood out in the yard looking at each other and the smashed landscape around them, dazed. Half of their roof was gone. Christophe and Joshua's porch was missing, and part of their roof. A tree had smashed into Mudda Ma'am and Tilda's house. And just as the houses clustered, there were people in the street, barefoot, half naked, walking around felled trees, crumpled trampolines, talking with each other, shaking their heads, repeating one word over and over again: *alive alive alive alive.* Big Henry and Marquise were standing in front of Big Henry's house, which was missing a piece of its roof, like all the others, and was encircled by six of the trees that had stood in the yard but that now fenced the house in like a green gate.

"It's a miracle," Big Henry said. "All the trees fell away from the house."

"We was just about to walk up there and see about y'all," Marquise said.

Big Henry nodded, swung the machete he had in his hand, the blade dark and sharp.

"In case we had to cut through to get to y'all," Marquise explained.

"Where's Skeet?" Big Henry asked.

"Looking," Randall said, hoisting Junior farther up on his back.

"For what?" Marquise asked.

"The water took China," I said.

"Water?" Big Henry asked, his voice high at the end, almost cracking.

"From the creek that feeds the pit." Randall said. "The house flooded through. We had to swim to the old house, wait out the storm in the attic."

I wanted to say: *We almost drowned. We*

had to bust out of the attic. We lost the puppies and China.

"We need a place to stay," I said.

"It's just me and my mama," Big Henry said. "Plenty of room. Come on." He flicked the machete blade, threw it to Marquise, who caught the handle and almost dropped it.

"You all right, Mr. Claude?" Big Henry asked Daddy.

Every line of Daddy's face, his shoulders, his neck, his collarbone, the ends of his arms, seemed to be caught in a net dragging the ground.

"Yeah," Daddy said. "I just need to sit for a while. My hand." He stopped short. Big Henry nodded, placed one of those big careful hands on Daddy's back, and escorted us through the milling crowd, the crumbled trees, the power lines tangled like abandoned fishing line, to his home. He looked at me over his shoulder, and the glance was so soft, so tentative and tender, I wanted to finish my story. I wanted to say, *I'm pregnant.* But I didn't.

Amongst the older women in hair curlers and oversized T-shirts and slippers, the girls in sweatpants and tank tops, the boys riding their bikes, the men gathered in clusters pointing at each other and at the sky, I saw

Manny. He was sitting in the back of a white and silver pickup truck parked half in, half out of the road, surrounded by the tops of ripped trees. He was staring across the crowd at us, and from that far away, he was all muscled shoulders and golden skin and black, black eyes. There were wide smears of mud all across his legs, his chest. He raised one forearm in a short, stiff wave. Randall hunched over next to me, eyeing Daddy's and Big Henry's backs.

"Is it him?" he whispered.

I nodded, looked down at the ground.

"I knew you had a crush on him, but —" Randall cleared his throat. "I didn't think he'd do anything about it."

"I wanted to," I said.

"I'm going to beat the shit out of him," Randall said, the words whistling out of him.

A girl separated herself from the crowd, sat down next to Manny on the truck, laid her head on his shoulder. Shaliyah. Manny sat there stiffly beside her, still looking at me, at Randall, waiting for a wave, a nod, anything. I slid my fingers into the crook of Randall's elbow, and Junior's leg rubbed the back of my hand. His skin, and Randall's skin, was warm; I walked so that Randall was my shield, my warm cover, my brother.

"No, Randall," I said. "You don't need to.

I already did."

Randall snorted, but he didn't let Junior go, and he squeezed his forearm to his waist, folding my arm into his, pulling me with him. We walked to Big Henry's front door together.

Big Henry's mother, Ms. Bernadine, is half Big Henry's size, with wide hips and thin shoulders, and now I know where he gets his careful hands. She settled Daddy on the sofa in the dark, hot house, unwrapped and cleaned and rewrapped his hand in the light from the open door and the open windows. Her hands were small and quick as hummingbirds, and just as light. She made potted meat sandwiches, and when one of her brothers brought over a small generator, she hooked the refrigerator up to it from an extension cord along with a small fan, and this she put in the window in the living room, and pointed it at Daddy's face, which was gray and twisted.

Marquise had run up to the house to find Skeetah and took his dog along: Lala gleamed like melted butter, untouched by the havoc of the hurricane. He said when he got to the house, Skeetah heard his dog barking and came out of the woods. Skeetah was wearing wet, muddy shorts he'd salvaged from the wreckage, but he was still barefoot. When Marquise tried to get him to come down to Big Henry's house, he'd asked for Marquise's lighter, said he'd camp out at the house because he was waiting for China to come back. Marquise had argued with him, but Skeetah ignored him, so Marquise left. When Marquise told us the story, he chewed the inside of his cheek, looked ashamed that he hadn't been able to drag Skeetah down into Bois. "He's stubborn," Randall said. "You can't make him do nothing he don't want to do."

That night, when people with working trucks and chains were clearing the streets of trees and burning wet, smoking bonfires, we slept on thin pallets on Big Henry's living room floor, and his mother whispered to Big Henry in the kitchen: "Ain't they one more?"

"Yeah," he said. "He's looking for his dog."

"As long as they need," she said. "At least they alive."

"Yeah," Big Henry said, and I knew he was looking at us, Junior under my armpit, sweating and twitching in his sleep, Daddy still as a stone on the sofa, Randall laying facedown, his head buried in his folded arms, almost diagonal in the small living room. One or two sodden bugs whirred

379

outside, and I wondered where Skeetah was, saw him sitting before a fire, his head cocked to the night, which had turned hot after the cold air left by the storm passed. Waiting.

Big Henry and his uncle Solly, the one who brought the generator and who is tall and skinny and has blurry home-done tattoos up and down his forearms, are talking in the doorway. The sun has burned away the last of the clouds of the storm's wake. It arcs through the door, slides past Big Henry, and burns my face.

"That bridge is washed out."

"The old one over the bayou? The first or second one?"

"The little third."

"What about the bridge on the east side?"

"That one's okay. Road's full of water, they say. But you can drive through it."

"What it look like?"

Solly clears his throat. Spits.

"It's bad." He clears his throat again. "Real bad." Solly shrugs. "Where your mama say I need to put that tarp again?"

Big Henry leads him outside to show him the bad spot on the roof. He is barefoot, and his feet look white and tender as a baby's.

"Esch." Daddy's voice from the sofa sounds like he has a Brillo pad lodged in his throat. I turn my head just so I can see his face out of the corner of my eye. This is the way you approach a bristling, unfamiliar dog.

Daddy makes a low humming noise. He sits up, folds his useless hand and his good one over his stomach. Looks at the dead TV.

"What Skeetah said. Is it true?"

I look at the carpet, fuzzy and maroon, that grows fluffy at the edge of the sofa he lays on; no one has ever stepped on it there. I nod, an inch's slide of my head, into the pillow.

Daddy makes a clicking noise in this throat. Clears it and swallows.

"I shouldn't have pushed you," he says.

He rubs his good hand over his face like a cat cleaning its jaw and nose. His nose and cheeks are greasy and shine in the dark. I am quiet, feel every inhale and exhale like an explosion.

"It . . . happened," Daddy breathes and stops.

I am blinking quickly, a feeling like boiled water splashed over my chest, soaking up my face.

"I'm sorry," Daddy says.

I want to say, *Yes*. Or *I know*. Or *I'm sorry, too*. But I squeak, small as a mouse in the room. Wonder where the baby will sleep, wonder if it will lay curled up in the bed with me. If I will teach Junior to give it a bottle, the way Daddy taught us. He is old enough now.

"How long has it been?" Daddy asks.

"I don't know." My voice is so high it sounds like someone else is talking, like I could turn my face and see another girl there, lying on the floor between her brothers, answering these question.

"When we can, we need to find out."

"Yes," I say, facing him, seeing him folding in on himself, soft where he had been hard, the rigid line of him broken. His helpless hand. Junior will feed the baby, sit on the bed with pillows on both sides to support his arms. He will sit still long enough for that.

"Make sure everything's okay."

I nod.

"So nothing will go wrong."

Daddy is rubbing his pocket with his good hand. I hear the crinkle of plastic. For a moment, Mama is there next to him on the sofa, her arm laid across his lap while she palms his knee, which is how she sat with him when they watched TV together. I

382

wonder if that is phantom pain, and if Daddy will feel his missing fingers the way we feel Mama, present in the absence. But it is still terrible when Daddy looks up at me again, past my left shoulder to the opening door, and she isn't there.

If it is a girl, I will name her after my mother: Rose. Rose Temple Batiste.

"You want to go to St. Catherine?" Big Henry is talking as he walks through the screen door; his pink feet nudge Randall's head on accident, and Big Henry jumps back and rattles the door frame. Randall looks up sleepily. I palm Junior's head and rub.

"What?"

"I got gas. We can ride. See what it's looking like."

Randall is waking up slowly. He stretches, talks through his yawn.

"We get back, we'll go up to the house and try to find some more food. We know y'all ain't got it to spare."

"We can go get Skeet," I add.

Daddy is shaking his head. The side of his short afro is smashed flat.

"Skeetah ain't going to come," Daddy says. He is gripping the wrist under his bad hand, rubbing at the skin like he could peel it off. The wire that had seemed to line his bones before the accident, before the hurricane, that made him so tall when he stood next to Mama, has softened to string. "I need something for this."

If it is a boy, I will name it after Skeetah. *Jason.* Jason Aldon Batiste.

"We'll find something," Big Henry says. I shake Junior awake. Outside, the sky is blue, clear of clouds.

The bayou formed by the meeting of the river and the bay is as calm as it would be on any summer day, and it is hard to tell the hurricane has been here except for where the wind dragged the water across the road and left it there. The bayou is where we had thought the water would come from, the reason we thought we were safe, but Katrina surprised everyone with her uncompromising strength, her forcefulness, the way she lingered; she made things happen that had never happened before. Now, all the people from St. Catherine's that had family in Bois Sauvage and had sheltered there during the storm for fear of what the hurricane would do to the towns on the beach, follow each other in a long line across the drowned bayou to their homes. Big Henry stays close to the car in front of him; the road has disappeared in patches, and it is only the bent bayou grass rimming the sunken asphalt that gives us any idea that we are not driving into the water, that Big Henry won't set the car spinning like Daddy's, set us to sink. The water parts and flutters like a fish's fin away from the tires, and then closes again, muddy. I wonder what the storm has stirred up from the bottom of the bay, and what it has dragged in and left in the warm, mud-dark water.

"Where are the trees?" Junior asks.

In Bois, some stand still: a few young saplings, hardy oak trees low enough to the ground to avoid the worst of the storm, but stripped of all their leaves and half their branches, as naked as if it is the dead of winter. Here in St. Catherine, they have been mown down, and there is too much sky. In Bois, the houses stand, and are ripped and torn in some places, like Skeetah and Rico after the fight, some of them leaning tipsily, like ours, half drowned. Here, there is too much sky. Something turns in my chest, spreads, and drops; it leaves nothing.

The first main road we get to in St. Catherine, the one that runs through the length of the town on the north side so that it is farthest away from the beach, is washed over with mud. The houses that were here are gone, or they have been flipped over on their heads, or they've slid sideways to bump into their neighbors, ripped from their foundations. The high school has been flooded, and the elementary school is smashed flat as a pancake; the power lines that still stand across the street have a four-wheeler hanging from the wire. A parking lot where the owners used to keep eighteen-wheeler truck beds is empty: eight of them are now upside down across the street from the lot, looking like Legos, tossed messily, smashing the trees. What used to be a trailer park looks like a stack of fallen dominoes, and there is one trailer on top of another trailer on top of another trailer, stacked like blocks. And everywhere there are people, looking half drowned; an old white man and an old black man camping out under a tarp spread under a lone sapling; a family of Vietnamese with sheets shaped into a tent over the iron towing bar used for mobile homes, plywood set under the draping to make a floor; teenage girls and women foraging in the parking lot and hollow shell of a gas station, hunting the wreckage for something to eat, something to save. People stand in clusters at what used to be intersections, the street signs vanished, all they own in a plastic bag at their feet, waiting for someone to pick them up. No one is coming.

"What?" Big Henry says, as if someone has asked him a question.

An older woman sits at the corner of one of the smaller roads that we turn down to get to the main road that runs closer to the beach. She has a towel draped over her head, and the plastic and metal chair she sits in leans to the left. She waves her hand, and we slow down.

"Can't pass down there. Can't pass no-where near down there."

"Yes, ma'am," Big Henry says.

"Y'all got any food?" she asks. She is missing her teeth on the side, and she is that in-between color where I can't tell if she is white or light-skinned black, but I can tell that she is old, the lines of her face rippling outward like her nose, her eyes, and lips were stones dropped in still water.

"Yes," I say, and I fish out one of the Top Ramen packets we brought with us, pass it to Big Henry in the front seat, who passes it out the window to her. She grabs it, peers at it, and then starts laughing. Her grin is mostly gums. Her T-shirt has a blue and pink teddy bear on it, and it used to be white.

"Well, all right." She laughs. "All right."

Big Henry drives as far as he can, which is only around a hundred feet, before he stops the car, pulls it as far to the side of the road as he can without driving into the ditch, and parks. Mud has splattered up the side of the car, patterned it like lace. Junior is scrambling onto Randall's back again, and Randall loops and knots his arms under Junior's legs. Junior's cheek brushes against Randall's: I haven't seen him set Junior down since the hurricane. There is a house sitting in the middle of the road, facing us, like it guards the secrets we will find farther in. We pick our way around it.

There are more houses in the street. One house, square and even as a box, two stories, has been knocked off of its foundation and spun to the side. Another house has landed on another house, wood on brick, and settled. The foundations, cinder blocks, rise up out of the earth, stop a few feet in the air, slim and expectant, robbed of their houses. A woman in a baseball cap picks through the rubble of a spun house; her son, who looks around Junior's age, squats in the dirt near the street and stares, face puckered, as we pass. A man in a yellow T-shirt pokes around his house's foundation with a stick. We pass what used to be the elementary school, the gym where Randall, a few days ago, played for and lost his chance at going to basketball camp and being recognized by a college scout for his talent, for being Randall, where Manny learned who I was and disowned me, where Skeetah fought for me, and there is nothing but mangled wood and steel in a great pile, and suddenly there is a great split between now and then, and I wonder where the world where that day happened has gone, because we are not in it.

"Shit," Randall breathes. He grips Junior's leg harder, and Junior whimpers but says nothing. "It's all gone," he says.

We stand in our small group, staring at the mess, and then I step away, and we leave, but Randall is the last to start walking, and he glances back again and again at the gym that was there but isn't. Power lines stretch across the mud-clogged road like great lazy snakes; we hop over them. With all the trees gone, it is easy to see that we are approaching the train tracks, the same train tracks that carried the trains we heard blowing raucously when we were younger, swimming in the same oyster-lined bay that came in and swallowed Bois, swallowed the back of St. Catherine, and vomited it out in pieces. A house sits in the middle of the track. It is yellow, and its windows have been blasted open by the storm, but its curtains remain. They flutter weakly. We climb around it, look east and west along the track, and see many houses lining it: it is a steel necklace with wooden beads.

Beyond the track, there are no beads. No houses stand here. There are only great piles of wood. Sometimes they are all the same color, and that's how we know a house stood here, stood there. There are no foragers here, picking through the rubble. What could be salvaged? What hasn't been buried or swept back out to sea? The stumps of the trees are raw and ragged, and the plywood from the houses is raw and ragged, and everything has been ripped in half. Closer to the beach, so close I can glimpse it if I squint and look toward the horizon, are oak trees. Some that stood in the park stand still; others have been ripped from the earth, their naked crowns facing the ocean. Those that remain look dead. Narrow streets where dentists' offices were, where restaurants that served catfish and hush puppies were, where veterinarians' offices were, where small dim bookstores and the kinds of antiques stores that I would never dream of walking into for fear of breaking something have been savaged; all the storm left are boards and siding stacked like pancakes flung on plates of concrete slabs.

We reach the end of the road. Here the hurricane has ripped even the road that rimmed the beach away in chunks so there are red clay and oyster shell cliffs. The gas station, the yacht club, and all the old white-columned homes that faced the beach, that made us feel small and dirty and poorer than ever when we came here with Daddy, piled in his truck, for gas or chips or bait on our swimming days, are gone. Not ravaged, not rubble, but completely gone. The hurricane has left a few steel beams, which stick up like stray hairs, from concrete foundations. There are rivers running down the highway that lines the beach. Past that, on the beach, there is a sofa. A man with white hair and an open button-down shirt is sitting on the arm of the sofa, and he is holding his head or he is rubbing his eyes or he is smoothing his hair or he is crying, and a dog, orange and large in the sun, is sniffing around him in circles, and then it is running and it is barking excitedly at what it has found. A closed black casket. It sniffs, raises its leg, and pees.

"Ain't nothing left," Big Henry says.

It is quieter than I have ever heard it in St. Catherine. There is only wind and the flat blue-gray water, which is so tame there

391

isn't even the loud swish and draw of waves. Big Henry's voice carries, and the dog looks up toward us and goes back to sniffing his treasure.

"Come on," Randall says.

Big Henry and I follow him. Junior bobs up and down on Randall's back, as gently as if he were sitting in a boat on calm water. We tiptoe on the edge of the ravaged road. I am scared more of it will slide. We climb over half of an oak tree, a car empty as a naked sardine can, what is left of a neon grocery store sign.

"Over here," Randall says and leads us down one of the side streets, away from the quiet, open expanse of the sea. "Here."

He jumps up on the concrete slab behind what used to be a bank but is now only the safe, large as an elevator, in the middle of a foundation, and bends to look down in the folds of the concrete.

"Look."

"The liquor store," Big Henry says.

"For Daddy," Randall says, and then we are all on our knees, balancing on the haphazard slabs that rock when we walk, peering under boards, finding glass shards from wine bottles, vodka, gin, gleaming red, dark blue, purple in the shadows. I find a bottle of Mad Dog, lime green, unbroken.

Randall finds an orange one. Big Henry finds a red one, and a small bottle of gin. Junior points and Randall unwedges a big gallon jug of vodka. Big Henry slides two bottles of Mad Dog in his shorts pockets, and I slip the bottle of gin and the orange Mad Dog in Randall's pants, and he hooks his thumb through his belt loops to hold his pants up. Big Henry grabs the vodka jug. I squat down to look in the hot concrete crevasses again, to find another treasure that I can take back for Skeet, something that will help me tell him the story of what we found, but there is nothing here but broken bottles, smashed signs, splintered wood, so much garbage.

Big Henry squats next to me. Randall is pointing down the street, pointing something out to Junior, where the library was that he visited with his school once, maybe.

"I heard what you said. When you was talking to your daddy."

I will have to tell Skeetah as clearly as I can, and he will have to close his eyes and for one second not think of China and listen as I tell him the story of Katrina and what she did to the coast.

"Who the daddy?" Big Henry asks. There is no blazing fire to his eyes, no cold burning ice like Manny's. Only warmth, like the sun on the best fall days when the few leaves that will turn are starting and the air is clear and cloudless.

"It don't have a daddy," I say. I palm a piece of glass, marbled blue and white, blunt at the edges, grab another that is red and a pink brick stone. I slip all three into my pockets. Like Skeetah told me the story of the last thing that Mama said to us, I will tell him this. *This was a liquor bottle,* I will say. *And this, this was a window. This, a building.*

"You wrong," Big Henry says. He looks away when he says it, out to the gray Gulf. There is a car out there in the shallows of the water. The top gleams red. "This baby got a daddy, Esch." He reaches out his big soft hand, soft as the bottom of his feet probably, and helps me stand. "This baby got plenty daddies."

I smile with a tightening of my cheek. My eyes feel wet. I swallow salt.

"Don't forget you always got me," Big Henry says.

I hold the stones so tight in my fist in my pocket that they hurt. I wish I could tell Big Henry this: *I wish you were there when the water came, you with your big hands, your legs like tree trunks sunk in the earth.* I lead the way over the ruined ground to Randall and Junior, who watch us approaching.

I will tie the glass and stone with string, hang the shards above my bed, so that they will flash in the dark and tell the story of Katrina, the mother that swept into the Gulf and slaughtered. Her chariot was a storm so great and black the Greeks would say it was harnessed to dragons. She was the murderous mother who cut us to the bone but left us alive, left us naked and bewildered as wrinkled newborn babies, as blind puppies, as sun-starved newly hatched baby snakes. She left us a dark Gulf and salt-burned land. She left us to learn to crawl. She left us to salvage. Katrina is the mother we will remember until the next mother with large, merciless hands, committed to blood, comes.

Skeetah's made a clearing in what used to be the yard but is now a tangle of tree branches and wood and car and wire and garbage. Our house looks like it has been painted in mud, slathered dark. It looks tilted wrong by the water. The night wind feels cool only because it is less hot than the day. Ms. Bernadine gave us a big cup of water each for a bath; a shower was wetting the rag in the water, soaping it, stripping in Big Henry's warm tiled blue bathroom that smelled faintly like rotten eggs, soaping my whole body, and then rinsing off with the water from the cup. It was heaven. She unwrapped and washed Daddy's hand, leaned in close, said, *It's a little red.* Daddy had replied, already slurring, *We'll deal with it.* Dinner was sardines and Vienna sausages, canned corn, dry ramen we ate like crackers, grape and red soda; even after I sucked the last of the sugary hot bite of the soda down, licked the last fish oil from the sardines from my fingernails, I was still hungry. We drove up to the house and had to park the car almost on top of the trees that had been dragged out of the street and left at the side of the road near the ditch.

Skeetah must have found an axe, or maybe he used his bare hands to break the wood; he sits in the middle of the downed trees, his fire big, higher than the fire we barbecued on, so big that the flames leap past the top of his head, burnish him black and gleaming like the glass I found earlier. He sits on an overturned bucket in the circle of mud and dirt that he has made, his elbows on his knees, his eyes intent on the fire. He wears a pair of jean shorts and tennis shoes, and next to him is a rubber tire, a chain that is the same, dark cloudy gray of the hurricane clouds on top of that. China's things. He has found China's things.

"We brought you some food," I say. He looks up, unsurprised, like he has been expecting us. The whites of his eyes are very white, and he seems more still than I have ever seen him before, as still as if there is some hard stone inside of him, at his center: a concrete foundation left still.

"Thank you," he says. "Your shoes." Skeetah motions to another, smaller pile I had not noticed. A muddy pile of shoes that looks exactly like the kind of pile the puppy China made. "I found them."

We sift through the pile. Skeetah peels open the top of one of the Vienna sausage cans, unties the bag of saltines, makes a small sandwich, and begins eating. He chews very slowly. Crumbs gather at the corner of his lips, and he licks them away.

"You should come down with us," Randall says, jamming his foot into his shoe. Junior slides down Randall's side, a small black shadow. I throw him his shoes. Randall sits in the dirt, and Junior settles in his lap. Randall lets his chin sit on Junior's bald, sweating egghead.

"We got plenty of room," Big Henry says. He inhales his cigarello, and the tip lights red. "You could sleep in my room."

"We're worried about you." I say it because they won't.

Skeetah smiles around the food, shakes his head. He picks up the cream soda we brought him, his favorite, opens it, and takes a sip.

"I'm not going nowhere," he says. He eats another cracker sandwich. The meat smells rich in the dark; the crackers smell like nothing. All of it smells like it is burning because of the smoky fire, which is unbearably hot. I sit next to Skeetah but scoot backward to feel leaves still green and fat on the fallen trees tickle my back. "She's somewhere out there, and she's coming back."

"You didn't see St. Catherine," Randall says. "Look like somebody dropped a bomb. Like war."

"Bois ain't St. Catherine." Skeetah frowns for a moment, a dark line like a slash between his eyes, his lips and nose like a puzzle with the pieces fit together wrong, and then his face is smooth and polished again. "She can swim."

"You can come back up here during the day," Big Henry suggests.

"No."

"If she come back, Skeet, ain't like she going to leave again," I say.

"Ain't no *if*." Skeetah rubs his head from

his neck to the crown like his skin is a T-shirt he could pull off and over his skull. Like he could pull who he is off and become something else. Like he could shed his human shape, in the dark, be hatched a great gleaming pit, black to China's white, and run off into what is left of the woods, follow the line of the creek, and find China sniffing at the bole of an oak tree filled with quivering squirrels, or sniffing at the earth, at the rabbits between the waters. "Not *if*. When."

When he looks back up at me, he is still again: sand seared to rock.

"She's going to come back to me," he says. "Watch."

We will sit with him here, in the strange, insect-silent dark. We will sit until we are sleepy, and then we will remain until our legs hurt, until Junior falls asleep in Randall's arms, his weak neck lolling off Randall's elbow. Randall will watch Junior and Big Henry will watch me and I will watch Skeetah, and Skeetah will watch none of us. He will watch the dark, the ruined houses, the muddy appliances, the tops of the trees that surround us whose leaves are dying for lack of roots. He will feed the fire so it will blaze bright as a lighthouse. He will listen for the beat of her tail, the padding of her feet in mud. He will look into the future and see her emerge into the circle of his fire, beaten dirty by the hurricane so she doesn't gleam anymore, so she is the color of his teeth, of the white of his eyes, of the bone bounded by his blood, dull but alive, alive, alive, and when he sees her, his face will break and run water, and it will wear away, like water does, the heart of stone left by her leaving.

China. She will return, standing tall and straight, the milk burned out of her. She will look down on the circle of light we have made in the Pit, and she will know that I have kept watch, that I have fought. China will bark and call me sister. In the star-suffocated sky, there is a great waiting silence.

She will know that I am a mother.

ACKNOWLEDGMENTS

I'd like to thank my editor, Kathy Belden, and all the folks at Bloomsbury for championing my novel. I'd like to thank my agent, Jennifer Lyons, who believed from the first word. My time as a Stegner Fellow at Stanford University gave me time to write and revise this manuscript, and I'm deeply grateful to the English and creative writing departments at Stanford for that. During my time at Stanford, Elizabeth Tallent and Tobias Wolff were insightful readers and mentors. I couldn't have written this novel without valuable feedback and encouragement from the truly amazing writers in my Stegner workshop: Sarah Frisch, Justin St. Germain, Stephanie Soileau, Jim Gavin, Vanessa Hutchinson, Ammi Keller, Harriet Clark, Will Boast, and Rob Ehle. In addition, many other writers have provided me with essential encouragement, friendship, and feedback: Mike McGriff, J. M. Tyree,

Molly Antopol, Skip Horack, Shimon Tanaka, Jeremy Chamberlain, Peter Ho Davies, and Elizabeth Ames Staudt. In DeLisle, thanks to Mark Dedeaux, the Miller family, Sarah Hatcher, Jillian Dedeaux, Aldon Dedeaux, Judy Ann Dedeaux, Dorothy Smith, and everyone in my extended family who always gave me a place to return to and be loved. Finally, I'd like to thank my immediate family: Joshua for being my heart, Nerissa and Charine for being my sister-fighters, De'Sean for being my Buddy, Kalani for being my lion, Jerry for encouraging me as an artist, and Norine for performing miracles every day and making a way out of no way.

ABOUT THE AUTHOR

Jesmyn Ward grew up in DeLisle, Mississippi. She received her MFA from the University of Michigan, where she won five of the school's esteemed Hopwood Awards for essays, drama, and fiction. Ward was the recipient of a Stegner Fellowship at Stanford and is currently the John and Renée Grisham Visiting Writer in Residence at the University of Mississippi. Her debut novel, *Where the Line Bleeds,* was an *Essence* Magazine Book Club selection, a Black Caucus of the ALA Honor Award recipient, and a finalist for both the VCU Cabell First Novelist Award and the Hurston/Wright Legacy Award.

The employees of Thorndike Press hope you have enjoyed this Large Print book. All our Thorndike, Wheeler, and Kennebec Large Print titles are designed for easy reading, and all our books are made to last. Other Thorndike Press Large Print books are available at your library, through selected bookstores, or directly from us.

For information about titles, please call:
(800) 223-1244

or visit our Web site at:
http://gale.cengage.com/thorndike

To share your comments, please write:
Publisher
Thorndike Press
10 Water St., Suite 310
Waterville, ME 04901